W9-AKN-728

ONLY SUMMER

Rachel Cullen

Copyright © 2018 by Rachel Cullen

All rights reserved.

ISBN-13: 978-1725540552

To my sister, Sarah – thank you for being my first reader, and for telling me to keep writing

This is a work of fiction. Names, characters, places and incidents are of the author's imagination or, if real, are used fictitiously.

Prologue – Sabrina

"You have to speak up, I can't hear you," Danielle requests.

"Sorry, I can't talk much louder. There are other people in here," I complain, trying to hold the phone closer to my face – not an easy task with my massive iPhone 7 Plus. This situation calls for my old Motorola Razr flip-phone, hands down the best phone ever made.

"Where are you?" Danielle asks.

"I'm in the ladies' room at Eleven Madison Park," I whisper, attempting to keep my voice down inside a bathroom stall in one of the most expensive restaurants in Manhattan.

"Wow! Aren't you fancy? I ate Abby's leftover chicken nuggets and broccoli for dinner. Why are you calling me if you are supposed to be at dinner? Isn't there $500 worth of food waiting for you in the dining room?" she questions.

"I think Peter is going to propose," I blurt out.

"Oh my God!" Danielle screams into the phone, loud enough that I have to hold my gigantic device away from my ear, and possibly so loud that the other women in the bathroom can hear.

"I don't know what to do," I say quietly, playing with the intricate beading on my skirt while I wait for her response.

"You hang up the phone. You go back out to your table, and you say "Yes" when Peter asks you to marry him," Danielle says definitively.

"You make it sound so easy. I just don't know if I can do it," I moan, not caring anymore if the other ladies' room occupants hear my apprehension.

"Breen, listen to me. I have known you forever, and you have never been happier than you are with Peter. You have been together for over two years and it's like you're an entirely different person now."

"Hey, that's pretty harsh," I challenge.

"Sorry, that's not what I meant. You know I love you, and I've always loved you. But I've never seen you like this – you finally found someone to love. Instead of just finding random guys to sleep with, it's like you're completely comfortable with yourself. And you've talked about marrying Peter, I've heard you!" Danielle accuses.

"I know, but that was hypothetical. This is real. As in forever!" I exclaim.

"How do you even know he's going to propose tonight? At this point, you've been gone so long, maybe he's left the restaurant!" Danielle teases.

"First of all, we're eating *here*. Who comes here for dinner, not on an expense account, unless there is some huge occasion?" I counter.

"As I said before, I had chicken nuggets for dinner, so clearly *I* don't. But when Jim and I were married, we went there for dinner a few times, just because he liked it – and because he was pretentious and a horrible person; oh wait, I don't think those things are related, sorry, I got off track," Danielle laughs.

"That's another thing, you're telling me to get engaged, but you're not quite the poster girl for marriage, are you?" I remind her.

"That's because Jim was the wrong guy. He was a terrible mistake, but that doesn't mean marriage is bad. And I am getting married again, so you can't use that argument," she says triumphantly.

"We're about to have dessert, I think that's when he's going to do it. What should I do?" I ask again.

"I told you what I think you should do. But whatever you decide, please, please, do not break Peter's heart. He is a good guy and he doesn't deserve it. Remember, you're not *that* Sabrina anymore, you aren't scared of commitment, you have been living with him for two years and things are great – just let yourself be happy," Danielle advises.

"Okay, thanks for listening," I say, wishing I could make that promise.

Chapter 1 – Heather

I don't know why everyone has this attitude that school is over and summer has already begun. There are still three weeks left, and I need every minute of that time.

I know the girls think I'm boring now, or maybe mean; actually I don't even know what they think of me anymore. But I know for sure they don't think I'm "fun," like some of their friends' moms. The ones who let them play hooky so they can go into the City and have a "girls' day" or the moms who don't care if they dye their hair or have sleepovers on weeknights. It's not that I don't *want* to be that mom. Well, it's mostly that I don't want to be that mom, but it's also that I don't know *how* to be that mom.

Even though I've left the kitchen, I know the to-do list is lying in the middle of the marble island, mocking me. For every one thing I cross off the list, there are three more added to the bottom. I know I shouldn't complain, since most of the things on the list are there to help us get ready to spend two months on Cape Cod (I feel guilty even having an internal monologue of complaints), but this year's trip to the Cape is different from previous vacations for so many reasons.

Instead of my dreaded to-do list, I could make a list of all of the things that are different about this summer's "vacation" than last summer's vacation:

1. Last summer we went for two weeks, this summer we are going for two months.
2. Last summer Kevin came with us the whole time, and this year he is going to *try* to come out on weekends.
3. Last summer we rented the same house we always rent in Chatham near all of our friends, this summer we are renting a house in Brewster near where I used to go as a child, and where we know no one.
4. Last year I had two boobs, this year I only have one.

I crumple the list up and throw it in the trashcan next to my desk, partly because I don't want anyone to find it, and partly because there's only so much self-pity I can tolerate.

***

"Mom, where *are* you?" Brooke calls impatiently. Because she is eleven-years old, the world revolves around her, so she obviously can't bother to spend time looking for me.

"I'm in my office," I call out, trying not to sound as tired as I feel.

"Hi sweetie," I say as Brooke walks in and takes a seat on the arm of the Baker sofa. I take a deep breath to prevent myself from telling her not to sit there, since I know that will only result in an eye-roll and her immediate departure. My mother never tolerated this kind of behavior when I was her age (*she* was always the boss, which is clearly not the case here), but I try to remind myself that things were different then, and there are a lot of things about how I was raised that I wouldn't want to replicate from my childhood.

"How was your day?" I ask.

"It was okay, I guess. I can't *wait* for summer," Brooke complains, sliding backward from her perch on the sofa's arm, so she can lie down and drape her legs over the back. She takes up more than two-thirds of the couch, which seems impossible at her age, but given my unfortunate height of 5'10" and her father's 6'4" frame, it isn't surprising that Brooke is already 5'3" at the end of sixth grade. It seems like only yesterday that she was pulling herself up on this exact couch and cruising back and forth from one end to the other, occasionally falling on her little diaper-cushioned bottom and giggling like it was all a big game. Now she is practically a woman, not quite; but she looks a lot older than eleven (*almost* twelve, as she keeps reminding me). We share the same dirty blonde hair, but hers is streaked with spectacular highlights that will only get better with the summer months. She has also lost all of her "baby fat" over the last year; all of a sudden there are cheekbones and hipbones that were never there before.

"Only a few weeks left," I remind her, in my most cheerful voice.

"But I have to take exams before then," she whines.

I try not to laugh, since I know that will not be appreciated, but it's hard for me to get worked up over sixth grade final exams after going through college and graduate school, but I know it's all a matter of perspective. I'm sure I thought middle school tests were a big deal when I was *in* middle school.

"At least you only have one week of *classes* left," I say, trying to be helpful.

"Ugh," Brooke says, burying her face in a throw pillow.

"I wanted to talk to you about something before Caitlin comes home from school," I say, glancing at my watch and noting that we only have about ten minutes before this happens.

"What?" Brooke says suspiciously.

"You know that we're going to be on the Cape for two months this summer, and Dad isn't going to be there the whole time," I tell her.

"Yeah, I know. And we have to go to that tiny town where you used to go when you were little and I don't know anyone and don't have any friends. I know all this already, and it sucks. I can't even remember why I'm excited for summer," Brooke protests.

"Right, okay. Since Dad isn't going to be there the whole time, I was thinking of getting someone to come with us to help me out, and just hang out with you guys sometimes," I say, relieved that I've told her this much.

"A babysitter?!?!" Brooke screams, getting to her feet, her face contorting into an ugly scowl.

"Don't think of it as a babysitter. But you're not old enough to be at the beach all day by yourself, and Caitlin certainly isn't. And you can't drive, right?" I offer, trying to make a joke.

"You have *got* to be kidding me! This is going to be the worst summer ever!" Brooke shouts, as she stomps out of my office.

Well, that could have been worse, I tell myself, although I'm not sure how much worse it could have been. I'm sure she'll be fine once we get there, but this won't help her mood over the next few weeks, as we get ready. At least Caitlin will be excited; she still loves babysitters.

I slowly pull myself up from my desk, hating how tired and old my body feels. I want to be at the front door to meet Caitlin when she gets dropped off, so she doesn't have to come search for me. Although, even if she did, she would be happy when she found me, and full of stories about her day at school – I'm reminded of the differences between seven and eleven year old girls with every interaction I have with my daughters.

***

"No phones at the table," Kevin says sternly, looking directly at Brooke.

"Ugh," Brooke groans, exaggerating every movement placing her phone in her back pocket.

"That's not what I meant, and you know it," Kevin says, maintaining eye contact with our oldest daughter.

Brooke opens her mouth to complain, but then wisely decides to close it and marches into the unlit dining room to place her phone on the table, before returning back to her seat.

"Better?" Brooke asks with a snide tone, as she settles herself on the oak bench next to her sister and across from Kevin at the farmhouse table in the center of the kitchen.

I look at Kevin to see if he's going to call her on her tone, but he seems placated by the phone's removal. The smile is back on his face, giving him an almost boyish look, which is getter harder for him to achieve as he approaches his forty-fifth birthday this year. But, as men seem to do, he just gets more handsome as he ages. He's grown into his salt and pepper hair, keeping it in the same crew cut he's had since college. He even looks good in reading glasses, which he got last year and has been wearing more and more at the office and late at night at the computer; I hate that it hides his blue eyes, but luckily he doesn't have to wear them all the time. Now he's sitting here in his post-work uniform of polo shirt and khaki shorts, and he looks like he walked off the pages of a J. Crew catalog even though he's been up since 5:30 this morning and put in an hour at the gym and eleven hours at the office.

"Yes, better," he answers. "See, now we can have a nice family dinner," Kevin says cheerfully.

"Pizza's not a family dinner, it's fast food, right?" Caitlin asks, repeating something she's heard me say many times.

"We're eating as a family, so it's a family dinner," Kevin counters. "And your mom was busy today, so she didn't have time to make dinner. There's nothing wrong with pizza. I think it's delicious," Kevin says, taking a big bite for emphasis.

I wonder if Kevin really thinks I was busy today, or if he just wants the girls to think I was too busy to cook and not too tired again. If only I were too busy too cook, what a blessing that would be.

"Did you *go* to work today?" Brooke asks me, in an accusatory tone, her anger from our earlier conversation still visible.

"You know I'm still on extended leave, I'm not going to go back until after this summer," I remind her, "at the earliest," I add.

"Sorry, Dad just said you were *so* busy, I thought he meant you went back to work," she challenges.

"Everything your mother does is work," Kevin says, defending me.

"So, are you girls getting excited for Cape Cod?" Kevin asks, trying to change the subject.

"Yes!" Caitlin shouts happily, her excitement palpable.

"Not really," Brooke says.

"Are you kidding? You love the Cape?" Kevin asks.

"No. I love Chatham, and our old house, and all of my friends there," she answers.

"You've never really been to Brewster, you're going to love it. And you'll make new friends. This house is right on the beach, remember we used to have to drive from the old house," Kevin adds, trying to be helpful.

"If you're so excited, why aren't you coming?" Brooke asks him.

"I am coming. I'll be there on weekends, and at the end of August. And you know that I can't take the entire summer off from work. Someone has to pay for the elaborate lifestyle you lead," Kevin says, trying to diffuse the tension. He has more patience for her than I do, but he also only has to deal with her in short intervals. I wonder what would happen if he were here all the time – would he still be so tolerant?

"And Mom is getting us a babysitter!" Brooke spits, finally getting to the issue that's been bothering her all afternoon.

"A babysitter? All summer? Really? Is she going to live with us?" Caitlin asks, excited at the possibility.

"What's wrong with that?" Kevin asks matter-of-factly.

"I'm too old for a babysitter," Brooke says.

"You're eleven," I tell her, feeling a need to add to the conversation.

"Almost twelve," Brooke reminds us.

"Look, I know it isn't ideal, but your mom is going to need a little bit of help this summer and you'll probably have a lot of fun with the babysitter if you give her a chance," Kevin offers.

"What's her name? When can we meet her?" Caitlin asks.

"I need to figure that out," I tell the girls, realizing that "find babysitter" on my to-do list cannot be put off any longer.

Chapter 2 – Megan

Finally, the bell rings! I knew if I stared at the clock for long enough it would have to move all the way to 3:15 and release me from Mr. Stilson's endless lecture on chemical bonds. Does he actually think anyone is listening on the last day of class? I mean I know we still have to take exams, but this is my last official day of classes for junior year – only one week left of grueling tests and then I'm a senior!

"Are you ready?" Jessica asks, interrupting my daydream. She is standing over my desk, packed up and clearly ready to get the hell out of school.

"Yes, let me get my stuff, I'll be there in just a minute. Who else is coming?" I ask.

"I think Georgia is coming, but not sure about anyone else. Hurry up, Megan," Jess urges.

"Sorry," I apologize, as I quickly put the remaining binders in my backpack. Even though classes are done and it is a beautiful June day, I still have a long weekend ahead of me buried in textbooks, and I don't want to forget anything.

"Where should we go?" I ask Jessica, as I heft my enormous backpack onto my back and follow her into the hall. As anxious as I am for the year to be over, I can already tell I will miss this place over the summer and be in a hurry to get back here in the fall – hard to believe that I've only been a Dalton student for two years, but I feel so at home here. Girls like Jessica and Georgia have been at Dalton since kindergarten, so they literally have grown up here, but I think I love it even more, since I know how lucky I am to be here.

"What about that cafe we went to last weekend?" Jessica suggests, as we approach Georgia in the hall.

"Perfect!" Georgia says, giving each of us a double-cheek air-kiss as a greeting and smoothing out invisible wrinkles in her tiny black t-shirt and white jean shorts.

"But it's all the way over on the West Side," I point out.

"It's not that far from your apartment, we can just go there after," Georgia says helpfully.

"We definitely don't want to do that. It's so cramped – with my little sister and Gloria there, we won't have anywhere to hang out," I remind them. "We should go somewhere around here, and then we can go back to one of your places?" I suggest.

"I don't care where we go, I just want to get out of *here*," Georgia says, motioning to the hallway around us.

"We can go back to my place," Jess offers. "No one's home. I don't even know if my parents are in town this weekend," Jess adds.

"Sounds good to me," Georgia says, slinging her Louis Vuitton bag, bulging with books, over her shoulder.

"Great!" I say happily. I feel a little guilty that I didn't want to have the girls at my apartment, but Abby's stuff is always all over the place and her nanny, Gloria, is great, but she always hovers over us asking questions about school and boys. But at Jessica's, it's nothing like that – she has almost the same amount of room that we used to have in our house in Rye, but in an apartment in Manhattan, AND she always has it all to herself!

We walk mostly in silence for the nine or ten blocks to Jessica's apartment on 93rd and 5th Avenue; although the only reason we aren't talking to each other is because we are all staring at our phones, furiously texting away. Georgia took her phone out first (presumably to text her boyfriend Ian), then Jess took hers out, and I didn't want to look dumb walking next to them with nothing to do, so I pulled mine out of my backpack and sent Ryan a quick text, although since he's at work I knew he wouldn't respond. Then I sent Danielle a text letting her know where I was going, but she's also at work, so she didn't respond either. Now I'm looking at Instagram and trying to look busy.

Jess puts down her phone as we walk into the spacious lobby of her 5th Avenue building and I follow her lead, since I wasn't doing anything anyway.

"Hello, Miss Wyatt. Hello ladies," the doorman says to Jess as we cross the vast marble lobby toward the elevator.

"Hi Bobby," Jessica says happily, as she presses the elevator call button.

"Hi," Georgia and I echo, as we enter the elevator, the door closing quickly behind us.

Although I've been here dozens of times, it still surprises me a little bit each time when the elevator door opens on the eighteenth floor and there are only two apartment doors in the hallway. Jess casually opens the door to her apartment and we enter a foyer that looks like a museum, but Jess throws her bag on the French-looking chaise as she walks in, as if it's the mudroom, and tosses her keys and phone on the antique center hall table with the elaborate floral display, and invites us to do the same.

Before the divorce, when I used to live in Rye, we lived in a huge house with a ton of rooms that were decorated by a fancy designer. But our house didn't look anything like this; it looked like people might actually *live* there. Jess's apartment is ridiculously ornate, it reminds me of the tour I took at Versailles. Okay, maybe it's not quite that fancy, but there's a lot of gold and tapestries on the walls and really heavy, old furniture that I'm scared to sit on. Truly the craziest thing about this apartment is the view. There are at least six rooms that have floor-to-ceiling windows with views overlooking Central Park. Jess has never lived anywhere else, so she doesn't seem to realize how awesome it is, but it's pretty amazing. I tried to tell her once, but she looked at me like I was crazy, so now I just appreciate it quietly.

"Do you guys want a drink?" Jess asks.

"I thought you'd never ask!" Georgia says, making her way over to the full size mahogany wet bar in the living room.

"Help yourself," Jess says. "Megan, what do you want?"

"I'll have whatever you're having," I reply. "But I can only have one. I have to go home later and I think I'm supposed to babysit Abby tonight," I tell them.

"Oh that sucks," Jess says, while filling up three tall glasses more than half way with vodka.

"It's not that bad. Maybe Ryan will come over," I suggest, even though I haven't heard from him yet today.

"Are you sure Ryan doesn't have a friend for me?" Jess whines, as she hands me a glass of Sprite and vodka that will get me totally wasted if I drink even half of it.

"I'll ask him again," I promise her. "But he says all the guys he knows either already have girlfriends or are total losers," I tell her. I leave out the part about Ryan saying Jess is too spoiled to inflict on most of his friends. I think that's a bit harsh considering some of the trust-fund kids Ryan knows at Columbia, but as much as I love her, Jess can come off as a bit overindulged if you don't know her very well.

"What are we talking about?" Georgia asks, carefully maneuvering her tiny body onto the couch while holding her drink in one hand and texting Ian with the other. Georgia has the body of a supermodel, if supermodels could be five feet tall. I don't think she even weighs ninety pounds, although her boobs are so big, that the weight of those alone might push her over the top. Sometimes I can't help staring at her, because it's crazy that she's got the hourglass figure of Lily Aldridge, but she's basically the same size as a sixth grader. And of course her boyfriend is over a foot taller than she is. It's so weird to watch them together, it's like she's a doll when she sits on his lap – I can't even imagine them having sex (okay, that's a lie, I've totally thought about it, because it's just *so* weird, and then I feel gross for thinking about it!)

"We're talking about how you and Megan have taken the only two guys in all of Manhattan, and how I'll be single forever," Jess complains, taking a huge gulp of her drink.

"Maybe you'll meet someone this summer?" I suggest, taking a sip of my drink and wishing it tasted a lot more like Sprite.

"In Costa Rica?" Jess questions critically.

"There will be lots of other people there on the trip. Maybe there will be some hot guys doing volunteer work too," I offer.

"I bet all the hot guys already did their volunteer projects, or at least did *some* community service and didn't wait until the summer before senior year," Jess laments, feeling sorry for herself.

"Yup, because that's what hot guys are known for," Georgia adds, finally putting down her phone and joining the conversation.

"You'll still have all of August in Southampton," I remind her.

"But there's no one there," Jess says, dramatically, tipping back her glass to finish off her drink.

"Seriously? There's *no one* in Southampton?" I challenge.

"Of course there are people there. But I know all of them. It's the same guys who have been going there forever. I've known them since I was two. It's like they're all my brothers, but I would never actually *date* any of them," she says and shudders.

"And not all of us are lucky enough to go on vacation with our boyfriends for the entire summer," Jess says, shooting Georgia a look that I think is supposed to be funny, but it comes off a little mean.

"It's not a *vacation*," Georgia protests. "Ian and I both happen to be interning in D.C. this summer, for different programs."

"And then?" Jess asks.

"Then our families are going to Italy together for three weeks," she says sheepishly.

"Ha!" Jess says, but she's smiling.

"It's not my fault that my dad and Ian's dad are best friends. It's actually kind of annoying most of the time. But sometimes it works out," Georgia says.

"Do you want another drink? I need a refill," Jess says, hopping up from the couch; clearly done talking about her romantic woes.

"I'm good for now," I reply, taking another small sip from my drink, trying to make a dent in it, so Jess doesn't give me any shit.

"I'm almost done, I'll take another," Georgia says, slurring slightly.

I can't believe Georgia finished her drink; she's going to be trashed! And Jess's parents may be away, but I'm sure Georgia's mom and dad will be home tonight – that should be interesting.

"Hey Megan, did you figure out what you're doing this summer?" Georgia asks.

"Not yet," I say sadly.

"Oh. Sorry," Georgia says, unsure how to respond.

"I don't get it. How can you have *no* plans?" Jess asks, bewildered.

I know that I've explained this to both of them before, but sometimes they just don't get how unique my parental situation is – sometimes it's hard for me to really understand it, let alone explain it to anyone else. My parents got divorced about four years ago, and then my dad almost immediately married a much younger lawyer who worked for him (Danielle). When I first met her, I couldn't stand her, but that was only because I didn't give her a chance. When she got pregnant and my dad cheated on her and wanted nothing to do with another baby, she moved out and divorced him. That was about the time that I realized I really liked Danielle and my dad was the problem. Shortly after my half-sister Abby was born, my dad showed his true colors by sleeping with our 19-year old au pair and declaring that he didn't want me living at home anymore. Thank God for Danielle, who took me in and let me live with her and Abby – and now her fiancé Ted.

"Since neither of my parents are really involved anymore; Danielle does everything for me. And Danielle is great, but she just doesn't always *get* all the things that need to be done as the stand-in-mom of a high school student. She's still trying to figure out pre-school most of the time," I joke.

"But what did she think you were going to do this summer?" Georgia asks.

"I don't think she thought about it. She's busy with work and Abby, and being pregnant again. She's amazing, but she really doesn't have that much time for me," I say, and then feel awful for saying anything bad about her since she pretty much saved my life.

"I think part of me was hoping that Ryan and I would do something together this summer, so I didn't really want to make any other plans," I admit.

"Oh," Jess says quietly.

"But I guess that didn't work out very well," I say.

"Can't you just babysit for Abby?" Georgia says helpfully.

"Not really. Gloria is her full-time nanny. So I could really only do it at night, which I don't want to do, because that's the only time I can see Ryan. And Gloria is there all the time, so if I don't find something to do during the day, I'm going to go crazy," I tell them, thinking about how long and depressing the summer will be with Gloria and Abby every day.

"You'll think of something," Jess says optimistically, making her way through her second drink.

"I hope so," I say, not too certain of my prospects, as I swallow almost a third of my drink in one icy gulp and pray that Danielle actually doesn't need me to babysit tonight.

Chapter 3 – Molly

"I just can't get over how everything feels like it's on top of each other," I grumble to Sabrina.

"That's what happens when you move from Colorado to New York," Sabrina laughs, as she pulls linens out of the moving box, one of the hundreds that are scattered around the house we moved into two days ago.

"I know Manhattan is crowded, but I thought the suburbs would be different! Our house is practically in our neighbor's yard," I complain to my sister.

"You actually have almost half an acre, which is a lot of land for Rye. And it wasn't like you were living on a ranch in Wyoming, you were living in Boulder," she reminds me.

"I know, I know. I'm sure it's going to be great. It's just going to take a little while to adjust," I concede.

"I've already adjusted," Derek jokes, as he walks into the room carrying Anna on his hip.

Derek is so easy-going; it's no big surprise that he feels just as comfortable here as he did back in Colorado. Although, it was *his* job that moved us here with only six weeks' notice, so even if he didn't like it, I'm sure he would put on a good show.

The opportunity was "too good to refuse" as they say, (although "they" aren't the ones who had to move, are they?) And when Derek presented it to me, it sounded pretty fantastic, especially the part about being a thirty minute train ride away from Sabrina; but now that it's real and I've left my job, my friends and my house, it doesn't seem quite so fantastic.

"Once you finish unpacking, you'll feel better," Sabrina says, taking another armload of towels out of the box.

"I think once I finish unpacking, I'm going to realize that I need to buy a lot more furniture. This house must be twice the size of our old house. It didn't seem so big when we looked at it before," I comment.

"That's because it had all of the previous owner's furniture in it. Now that it has our mismatched collection of Pottery Barn and Ikea, it *is* a little empty, but it's not that bad," Derek laughs.

"Luckily, your job came with a big raise," Sabrina says to Derek, looking around the spacious interior of the 1920's Tudor, that will hopefully feel like home one day soon.

Sabrina is certainly correct about the pay raise. I wish money didn't factor into the decision as much as it did, but Derek was killing himself as the top energy and natural resources associate at a firm in Denver and while the pay was fine, we weren't saving very much, let alone feeling comfortable enough to have another baby. Then along came this offer to move to New York and for Derek to run an entire team doing the same thing he had done before, but for five times his salary. I remember the night Derek came home and told me, he had to write down the number three times before I finally believed him. Now I can decide if I want to go back to work or not, we can easily save for Anna's college fund as well as retirement, and feel comfortable having another baby – hell, we can probably even buy a Range Rover, like everyone else in Rye! The trade offs may be that I don't have any friends, and need to start all over at the age of thirty-five, but for some financial security and Derek's happiness, it seems worth it.

"Can you stay for dinner?" I ask my baby sister, hoping to extend her stay, as well as prolong her unpacking assistance.

"Let me text Peter and see when he's going to be back from the hospital," Sabrina answers.

"You can invite him out here," Derek suggests.

"That's a great idea!" I exclaim. "Anna hasn't seen Uncle Peter in so long," I remind her, trying to use my three-year old daughter to make her feel guilty.

"He's *not* Uncle Peter," Sabrina says sharply.

"Whoa, take it easy," I say to Sabrina.

"Sorry," she says, twisting the 3.0-carat Tiffany cut engagement ring on her finger. "I just meant we aren't married *yet*, so he isn't *actually* Uncle Peter," she explains, trying to rationalize her outburst.

"No worries," Derek says easily, patting her on the shoulder as he passes by on his way into the kitchen.

Interesting that Sabrina yelled at me, but Derek is the one that absolves her - Derek has always had a soft spot for Sabrina, and is willing to tolerate a lot more from her; but she isn't his sister, so I guess that makes sense.

Sabrina's phone chimes and she looks down to read her incoming text. She reports back, "Peter is getting home around seven, but he's really tired, so I'll just stay here and eat with you guys," she says cheerfully.

"Are you sure? You don't want to go home and see him?" I question.

"I see him all the time, and he'll probably just go to bed. But my big sister just got to New York and she needs my help!" she says enthusiastically, ripping open another box.

As much as I wanted her to stay a few minutes ago; now her desire to be here makes me wonder if something else is going on.

***

I try to hold on to Anna's hand as we approach the playground at Bruce Park, but she runs toward the tiny slide, leaving me all alone. I still can't believe that I had to drive to another state to go to a park (even though it took less than fifteen minutes to get here), it still seems crazy to go to Connecticut for some swings. But Danielle swore that this is where a lot of her old friends from Rye used to go, and right now I don't have anyone else to ask, so I am at her mercy. It's funny how life works – Danielle used to just be my little sister's friend, and they both looked up to me and the older girls on the Army base when we were growing up; but now I look to her for realtor advice, playground tips, and I'm desperately hoping she might introduce me to a friend of hers from when she used to live here!

"Mama, watch me!" Anna demands, from her perch atop the mini pirate ship.

"Coming sweetie," I call out, walking over to her.

In the time it takes me to cross the playground, I see a larger boy, maybe five or six years old, reach over and grab Anna's stuffed dog out of her hand. Of course, Anna starts to cry immediately and the awful boy just holds it above his head, out of her reach.

I look around to see if anyone else saw what just happened. I'm hoping that one of the immaculately dressed blonde women in the group by the swings will be this boy's mother and she will run over and demand that he give the toy back to Anna, so I don't have to discipline someone else's child on my first day here. I look over at the group of five women, laughing hysterically at something one of them just said, but no one is looking at this little miscreant.

"Excuse me," I say calmly, "that dog belongs to my little girl. Can you please give it back to her?" I ask the flaxen terror.

"No," he yells at me, his little face twisted in malice.

Anna's screams only get louder, but she won't climb down the slide to me, as that will put her even further away from Doggy.

"That dog is hers, and she is very upset. Can you please give it to her," I try again, through gritted teeth.

"No way lady," he says, shaking his head.

I can't believe how brazen this little shit is being – he looks like he's part of the cast of the Sound of Music, yet he should be wearing horns and holding a pitch fork.

I take a deep breath and say in a voice I didn't even know I had, "if you don't give my daughter her dog, you're going to be very sorry you ever met me."

Suddenly, blonde boy drops the dog and starts crying and screaming, "Mommy, mommy, help me!"

One of the perfectly coiffed ladies runs over (although I'm not sure how she is able to run in her white skinny jeans and three inch high espadrille wedge sandals). "Thatcher, what's wrong?" she asks, as she approaches Anna's tormentor.

"This lady was so mean to me. She said she was going to hurt me," Thatcher says, pointing an angry finger at me.

"*What* did you say to my son?" Thatcher's mom asks me, in an accusatory tone.

Although I know this kid is evil, I can feel my face turning bright red and shame runs through me as I wonder how I am going to explain myself. "I didn't say I would hurt him. I would never say that," I stammer. "He took my daughter's toy dog and wouldn't give it back, and I was just trying to help her," I tell her, knowing I sound ridiculous.

"I didn't take the dog, I promise," Thatcher says, looking at his mom with big blue eyes and an angelic expression that we both know is a complete sham.

"I know you didn't sweetheart," she says to him, in a sympathetic tone. Then to me she says, "You should be ashamed of yourself."

"Come on Thatcher, we need to go anyway. Bye ladies, see you next week," Thatcher's mom says, as Thatcher climbs down the ladder and grabs his mother's hand.

There is a chorus of "Wait up!" and "I'm coming too!" as all but one of the other ladies grab their children and head toward their massive SUV's.

I stand there and watch Anna happily play with the faux steering wheel, holding Doggy happily under her arm, as if none of the events of the past ten minutes ever happened. I know that one of the other moms is still there, but I'm hoping she leaves soon, since I can't bear to be this close to her.

"It's not your fault. Thatcher is horrible, but she can't see it," says an unexpected voice.

"What?" I ask, shocked.

"Hi, I'm Jeannie Buhler," she says, holding out her hand with perfectly manicured light purple nails.

"I'm Molly," I reply, confused.

"Your little girl is so cute, how old is she?" Jeannie asks.

"Anna just turned three," I reply, always happy to talk about my daughter. And although I'm biased, Anna is objectively adorable. With her thick strawberry blonde ringlets (exactly like Sabrina) and her dimpled cheeks; she turns heads everywhere we go.

"My daughter, Lake, just turned 4! She's over there," she says, pointing to a little girl in pig-tails being pushed on the swings by a woman who looks too young to be a mom, but way too old to be her sister.

"*Lake?*" I ask. I don't want to be rude, but I'm honestly not sure if I heard her correctly.

"Yes, Lake. My husband wanted something unique, so we ended up with Lake. I hope she doesn't hate us when she's older, right?" Jeannie laughs, but I can tell she feels confident about her choice of name.

Unsure how to respond, I also just laugh a little, and make a weird "ha, hmm," sound, which isn't what I intended to do.

"I just wanted to apologize for my friend," Jeannie says. "I'm sure it wasn't anything you or your daughter did. She's really a nice person, she just doesn't know what to do with her son, I think she's in denial," Jeannie says.

"Thanks. That's very nice of you," I tell her.

"No problem," she says. "Nice to meet you," Jeannie says, giving me a little wave and walking back toward her daughter.

"Wait!" I call out. Suddenly I'm desperate to continue this conversation; the idea of spending the rest of the afternoon alone at the park with Anna (or worse, alone in the house unpacking boxes with Anna) seems too much to bear.

Jeannie turns around and looks at me expectantly, resplendent in her un-creased white shorts, navy linen halter-top and gold sandals. I almost change my mind as I take a quick peak at my Birkenstocks, khaki shorts and black Gap tank-top – I mean, seriously, do I even want to be friends with people who dress like this to come to the park?

Before I lose my nerve, I yell out, "Do you want to grab coffee or something?"

Jeannie stops walking, but gives me a look that lets me know it's not the norm to ask a stranger to coffee in the park.

"Sorry, I'm new here, we just moved from Colorado last week," I say, as if that will explain everything.

A smile appears across Jeannie's face, "oh you poor thing," she says. "Do you live near here?" she asks, anxiously.

"We live in Rye, but one of my sister's friends told me this was a good playground," I tell her.

"I live in Rye too!" Jeannie says excitedly. "What's your address?" she adds quickly.

I tell her the address, and find myself relieved when she says, "oh that's a *great* street," and looks at me with a new sense of respect.

"So far, it seems good," I say humbly. "I'm sure it will be even better when we are unpacked and we meet some more people," I laugh.

"I can help you with that," Jeannie says. "Here give me your number," she says, taking her phone out of her large tote bag (it looks really expensive, but other than Sabrina, no one I know carries fancy bags, so I'm terrible at recognizing brands).

I take my phone out of my black, industrial multi-purpose diaper bag, and wince as I notice the old formula stains. My bag seemed right at home on the playground in Boulder, but it looks old and dingy here; maybe Anna and I should stop at one of the nice shops in town to get a new bag on the way home...

"I can't do coffee today," Jeannie explains, "but I'll text you later this week and we can find a time to get together, okay?"

"That sounds great," I tell her. Even if she never actually texts me, at least I took the first step, I tell myself.

Chapter 4 – Sabrina

Manhattan in the summer is almost unrecognizable from its dark, miserable, twin of a few short months ago. There are nights in February when I vow to move to California every time I walk home from the subway and lose feeling in my fingers; but on a spectacular June evening like this, I can't imagine ever living anywhere else! From the size of the crowds spilling out of the bars and cafes onto the streets of Tribeca, I'm pretty sure everyone else in New York City feels exactly the same way I do right now.

One of the benefits of moving from the corporate world to non-profit is being able to leave work at 5:30 and actually enjoy nights like these. Peter's erratic schedule doesn't often match up with mine, but that's one of the pitfalls of dating a fourth year surgical resident. (Oh crap, I meant *being engaged to*, not just dating, I can't even get it right in my head – I had to correct myself twice at work today too!)

I would love to pop into one of these bars and grab a glass of wine and enjoy the beautiful evening, watching tourists wander up and down Greenwich Street. But, tonight is one of the few nights that Peter will be home early and I told him that we could start looking at our calendars to talk about wedding dates. Regardless of the beautiful weather, he wants to do that at home over take-out Indian food so he can relax on the couch.

My phone buzzes as I'm about to turn the corner onto our block.

Peter: So sorry! Just got called into another surgery. Home at 8 or 9? Love You!!

Sabrina: K – don't worry about it! xoxoxo

I'm disappointed that I won't see Peter tonight, but I have an odd feeling I can't quite place – it feels a little like relief. I just wasn't quite in the mood to sit inside and have a deep conversation about logistics, when there are so many other things I could be doing.

I know it's a long shot, but I quickly dial Danielle's number and wonder if there is any chance she can meet me for a drink.

She picks up on the third ring. "Hey Breen, what's going on?" she says, cheerfully.

"Hi! So, is there any chance I can convince you to come meet me for a drink? Pretty please?" I ask my best friend.

"Oh, you know I would love to, but Ted has a work dinner tonight, so it's just me and Abby," she apologizes.

"What about Gloria?" I ask, wondering where her nanny is for the evening.

"She leaves at seven, so by the time I met you, there wouldn't be any time before I had to get home."

"And Megan?" I plead.

"She's over at a friend's place studying for exams. Sorry sweetie," she apologizes.

"It's okay," I say, unconvincingly.

"I know it's not the same, but you're welcome to come over and hang out if you want. Abby goes to bed at 7:30, so we can order dinner and have a drink here," she offers.

"But you can't even *drink*," I complain.

"Um, *you* called *me*. What did you think I was going to have if we went out?" she laughs.

"But there would have been other people there drinking, now I have to be the lush drinking alone," I whine.

"Never bothered you before," Danielle replies. But since we've been friends more than half of our lives, I know this comment is meant to be funny and not offensive.

"Point taken. Okay, I'll get an Uber, and meet you at your place. It's probably going to take forever with traffic, but no way am I walking all the way back to the subway," I declare – Tribeca has a lot of things going for it, but proximity to the subway is not one of them.

"See you soon!" Danielle says.

***

"She's finally asleep!" Danielle exclaims, gently closing Abby's bedroom door and tiptoeing gracefully into the living room. No one would ever be able to tell that Danielle is four months pregnant, it might look like she ate an extra cookie or two, but other than that she looks amazing – I hope I look half as good when I'm pregnant (if that ever happens). Her secret isn't much of a secret; she runs marathons and triathlons all the time. Her slim five foot five frame is deceptive, because at first you think she is just another thin woman, but then you see her in a bathing suit or workout clothes and you realize she is all muscle, but the long lean kind you get from running, not the bulky kind. She also has this cute brunette pixie cute, that most women couldn't pull off, and it gives her an air of approachability and 'cuteness' that make both men and women love her.

"I don't know how you do it. I'm exhausted just watching you," I tell her, taking a big sip from my glass of Pinot Noir and tucking my feet further underneath my legs on the brown leather sofa.

"Tonight was particularly bad. Usually she goes to sleep without a fight, but I think she was excited to see you. Or else this is the beginning of the terrible two's. God help me if that is the case," Danielle worries, collapsing on the couch next to me.

"I'm sure it was just because Aunt Sabrina is here. Who could blame her for being excited?" I ask, in mock disbelief.

"Speaking of *Aunt Sabrina*, how is your sister settling in? How is the house? Does she like Rye?" Danielle asks.

"It's hard to say. I think it's too early to tell. So far she's just trying to get unpacked and figure out where the grocery store is," I joke.

"I feel so bad!" Danielle says.

"Why?"

"Because I feel like I made her move there, and gave her all of this advice and then I disappeared," she explains.

"I think Derek is the one who made Molly move here. But honestly, I think she is going to be fine. She just needs a few weeks and a few friends," I tell her.

"I'm not really in touch with anyone from Rye anymore, but maybe we'll go out there this weekend. Abby and Anna are about the same age, and it would be fun to see her and see the neighborhood," Danielle says.

"You're not thinking of moving back there are you?" I say, horrified at the idea.

Danielle pauses before she answers, but then says, "Megan still has a year of high school, so we wouldn't go anywhere before then, but at some point it might make sense for us to move. We're going to have two kids, and it might be nice to have more space and pre-schools that don't cost the same amount as college," she drifts off.

"You can't leave me!" I cry out, covering my mouth after I yell as I remember that Abby is sleeping. In a quieter voice I say, "You love the City! And this apartment is fantastic, people would kill for a place like this," I say, gesturing to the space around us.

Through a bizarre twist of fate, Danielle has a four-bedroom apartment on the Upper West Side. It isn't your traditional four-bedroom apartment, like the ones you see on sit-coms filmed in New York and think real people can actually afford. Dani's apartment came from the combination of two average size two-bedroom apartments – something that happens pretty frequently in upscale buildings, but the way that it happened was what was so unique!

Right about the time Abby was born and Dani got divorced she bought this apartment. Lucky for Danielle, her new neighbor Michelle happened to be separated from her husband, so she was temporarily staying in the apartment (a pied-à-terre Michelle had owned for over fifteen years). The two became really good friends and then Michelle patched everything up with her husband and moved back to Scarsdale. But then Megan (Danielle's ex-step-daughter) got into a horrible fight with her dad (not surprising, since Jim is such a jackass) and she came to live with Danielle.

Since Michelle didn't *need* the apartment anymore, and since she was also a billionaire (did I forget to mention that?) she sold Danielle the apartment for $5,000 or something ridiculous and also paid for the construction to have the apartments combined. So now, Danielle has the cheapest four-bedroom apartment in the history of Manhattan – how could she ever think of leaving?

"I know this place is great. Ted and I are crazy for even considering it. I just never imagined raising kids in the City," Dani says.

"Lots of people have kids in the City. Honestly, I can't go anywhere anymore without seeing a double stroller," I say, taking a huge sip of wine.

"I know. We really don't know what we're going to do yet. It's just something we talk about," Dani says, matching me sip for sip with her sparkling water.

"If you do move, maybe I can buy it from you," I joke.

"That would be perfect," Dani gushes. "You and Peter could move in here! And there's room for a baby. You guys will never leave Manhattan," Danielle declares.

"Don't get too far ahead of yourself," I tell her.

"Alright," she laughs. "We don't need to talk about kids yet, but we should certainly talk about your wedding!" she prods.

"There's not much to talk about," I say indifferently.

"What do you mean? You guys haven't talked about anything?" she questions, shifting her position on the couch, presumably to accommodate her tiny belly.

"Nope, not yet. We've only been engaged two weeks. We have soooo much time to plan. What's the rush?" I ask.

"There's no rush. Okay, there might be a tiny rush, if you want me to fit into a bridesmaid dress," she laughs.

"Oh crap, I hadn't even thought about that. We should definitely wait until after the baby comes," I tell her.

"I was kidding! You shouldn't plan around me! But I'm due in 5 months, so you probably aren't going to be able to get everything planned in that time anyway," she reasons.

"Of course not. I was thinking a longer engagement anyway. Maybe a year and a half or two years," I tell her.

"Is Peter okay with that?" she asks.

"I'm sure he'll be fine. We were supposed to talk about it tonight, but he got called into surgery. Really, he's still got another year of residency, so it probably doesn't make sense to even think about doing it before then anyway," I say, feeling a weight lift off my chest as I realize there won't be major changes taking place anytime soon.

Chapter 5 – Megan

Only one more test to go, I tell myself, trying to make the studying more bearable. But my joy is quickly diminished when I remember that as soon as exams are done on Tuesday, all of my friends will be gone for the summer and I'll be stuck here alone every day with Abby and Gloria.

I roll over on my bed and stare blankly at the ceiling; although there aren't any answers to either my chemistry test or my summer dilemma written up there, this sluggish act still makes me feel a little better. A glance around my room reveals a mess that needs to be cleaned up, but also the amazing transformation that has taken place over the past two years since I moved out of my Dad's house in Rye and moved in here with Danielle. Everything I own is now here in this room. Some things, like my clothes and books and pictures, were brought over from the house; but everything else, including my mahogany sleigh bed, matching dresser, night table and desk, as well as the bedding and rug were brand new, just for this room.

My dad was so happy to get rid of me that he gladly paid to furnish my new home in Danielle's apartment. I still don't know the exact details of the arrangement they worked out, but I know that he pays for all of my Dalton school fees and then there is also some sort of separate account where he puts all of the money for me and Abby, so Danielle can use that to pay for stuff for us. I think

Abby's stuff might be separate, since he absolved himself of any real responsibility before she was even born (poor kid!) but my arrangement is a little trickier. With college approaching next year, I'm guessing I'm going to need to know more about it, but Danielle has told me "not to worry" a few times, and once when she was really mad at him, she said "your dad may be an asshole, but he is filthy rich, I promise sweetie, you will never have to worry about money – I've made damn sure of that."

I roll back over on my blue and purple tie-dyed duvet cover and prop myself up on my elbows, attempting to get comfortable to face my textbook for another round. I sneak a peek at my phone hoping to see the little red bubble next to my text message app indicating a new text from Ryan, but no such luck. He said he had a lot of work to do this weekend, but I hoped he was exaggerating – seems like he wasn't. When he interned at his dad's office two years ago, he was in a back room somewhere transferring paper files to digital records, and he couldn't wait to get out of the office; but now that he's in college, his dad has given him his own project and he's even working with clients, so Ryan is taking it seriously. I am really proud of him, it's great that his dad appreciates how brilliant he is, but hopefully it doesn't take over his whole summer, since it *is* just a summer internship at a boring investment bank.

Even if I don't have a job or friends here this summer, at least I'll have Ryan. Besides, I'm sure the excitement of his job will wear off soon and we'll have most of the nights and weekends together. Maybe I could even convince Danielle to let me go on a trip with him. Ugh, okay, chemistry first, then I can plan our romantic summer.

***

Ryan: u up?

Megan: barely

Ryan: sorry it's so late. I worked longer than I thought and then a couple guys were going out for drinks, so I went with them. Sorry I didn't call

Megan: it's okay

Ryan: u free tmrw night? have some work news

Megan: sorry, chem test on Tues, so need to study. Tues night? we can celebrate the end of the year and beginning of summer!!

Ryan: k. good luck! xoxo

Megan: xoxo

***

"I'm a Senior!" I yell into the phone, before Danielle even has the chance to say "Hi."

"Does that mean it went well?" Danielle laughs.

I readjust the phone with my chin and shoulder, so I can get my sunglasses out of my backpack while walking, without losing Danielle. "I think it went pretty well, but more importantly, my Junior year is now done, which means I'm a Senior!" I shout with glee.

A couple of people turn to stare at me as I cross Madison Avenue yelling happily into my phone, but it's Manhattan, so I'm hardly the strangest one here. I'm probably not even the most unusual person on this block right now!

46

"Congratulations!" Danielle says. "We should do something tonight to celebrate. Where do you want to go?" she asks.

"Sorry, I'm already having dinner with Ryan tonight. But we can do something tomorrow? Or this weekend?" I offer.

"Okay, we'll figure it out. Will you still be there when I get home from work tonight?" she asks. Danielle is far from an overprotective parent, in fact she's more like a really cool aunt, so it never bothers me when she asks where I'm going or when I'll be home the same way it bothers my friends.

"I'm not sure. I haven't heard from Ryan yet today. I'm secretly hoping he'll leave work early today so we can hang out this afternoon, but that's probably not going to happen," I admit.

"Don't get your hopes up, you know he can't just leave work whenever he wants. Hopefully I'll see you tonight, and if not I'll see you in the morning. And no pressure, but we should probably figure out what you're going to do between now and September," Danielle mentions.

"I know, I know. I'm thinking about it," I tell her, although the only thing I'm really thinking about is how much time I can spend with Ryan.

"Congratulations again Megan – I can't believe you're a senior!" she says.

"I know, me either!" I squeal.

***

I see Ryan waiting at the table of Rye Bar and Grill before he sees me and I get the same fluttery feeling I always get in my stomach when I haven't seen him for a few days, even after we've been together for two years.

Sometimes I still can't believe that he's my boyfriend, but I'm not the same insecure Freshman I was when we met, constantly questioning why the most popular boy in school would want to date me.

Still, the word that always pops into my head when I think of Ryan is *beautiful*. I know that the word is traditionally reserved for women, but Ryan is definitely beautiful - although there is nothing delicate or feminine about him. He is over six feet tall and weighs just under two hundred pounds, but it is all muscle, from years of ice hockey and lacrosse. Ryan's brown eyes and brown hair are both the color of milk chocolate, and he has a perpetual tan, even though he always wears sunscreen. He has also been stopped on the street and mistaken for an Abercrombie & Fitch model (so my former insecurity is not totally crazy).

Ryan looks up from his menu and waves as he sees me lingering in the front entryway, hopefully he thinks I just couldn't find him and not that I was staring at him!

"Congrats!" Ryan says as he stands up to give me a kiss on the lips and then wraps me in a full bear hug.

"Thanks," I murmur into his chest, deeply inhaling the mixture of deodorant and aftershave and general Ryan-smell.

"Thanks so much for meeting me out here. My dad wanted me to take the train home with him so we could talk on the ride, and it would have been hard to get back into the City," he explains.

"That's okay," I say, even though I had hoped we could meet in the City and then go back to his sister's empty apartment (ever since he had to give up his dorm room for the summer, it has been quite a struggle to find somewhere to be alone, together.)

"Let's order and then I can tell you my news," Ryan says excitedly.

"Okay," I say, eager to hear what he is so excited about.

Ryan flags down the waitress and we both order our usual dinners – a cheeseburger for Ryan and lobster salad for me; we also order two iced teas, Ryan will be twenty in six months and some places will serve him without ID, but this isn't one of them, so he won't even try – and it would be embarrassing to get shot down since he's sure to know people here.

Once the waitress takes our menus and brings the drinks, Ryan picks up his tea, "a toast to finishing your Junior year at your fancy school," he says with a big smile.

"Cheers!" I say, clinking my sweaty pint glass against his and then taking a sip of the pleasantly bitter drink.

Ryan raises his glass again for another toast and I copy him, unsure what he is going to say.

"Here's to my dad finally giving me some responsibility and putting me on a real deal this summer!" Ryan says, clinking his glass against mine again.

"That's great sweetie, I say. But I thought you were already on a real deal?" I ask, unsure why he's so enthusiastic.

"No, no," he says, shaking his head. "I've been helping out with a project, but I've mainly been doing research and background stuff, not real time deal stuff. But my dad thinks I've done a great job and they need some extra help on this huge acquisition and I'm going to get to work on it!" he says, beaming with pride.

"That's amazing!" I tell him, reaching across the table to squeeze his hand. I'm still not sure what he's going to be doing or why it's different than what he was doing, or why he's excited, but if he's happy then I'm happy. I feel like this might mean he's going to be busier than I would like, but I try to keep the smile plastered on my face, because I don't want to be selfish.

"There is one more thing," Ryan says, looking down at the table.

"What is it?" I ask, getting a bad feeling.

"The deal is in London," he says quietly.

"What?" I say so loudly that the people at the table next to us look over.

"I know Meg, that part sucks. But I couldn't say no. There are no other college kids who get this opportunity. The rest of the interns on the team are all in business school. It's so great for me," he says.

"But what about us?" I ask.

"It's just for the summer, and then I'll be back at school and it will be like before," he says confidently.

"When do you have to leave?" I ask, feeling the tears forming in the back of my eyes.

"Tomorrow night," he says sheepishly.

"Tomorrow night?!" I yell back, feeling like I've been punched in the stomach. "How can you do this to me?" I ask him, realizing how pathetic I sound, but not caring. I can feel the stares of the people at the tables around us boring into me like daggers; I know they are staring because I have been on their side before and it's impossible *not* to stare at the couple having a fight in the middle of the restaurant.

"Calm down Meg, it's going to be fine," Ryan says, glancing around at the other diners with his charming smile, hoping to convince them that there's nothing to see here.

"How is it going to be fine?" I ask, my voice still raised; but slightly lower than before.

"It's only two months. This is such a huge opportunity for me, and it will look great on my resume. I really thought you would be happy for me," Ryan says, clearly disappointed in me.

I feel horrible for my initial reaction, but I don't know if I can put on a good enough act to pretend I am happy for him, when I am watching my entire summer blow up in my face, and probably our whole relationship.

I take a deep breath before I respond, tuck my hair behind my ears and readjust my white denim skirt (which has ridden up quite a bit) to stall for time. "I *am* really happy for you. It's just that we've never been apart for two months, and I was looking forward to spending the summer together. I have no idea what I'm doing and you have everything all planned out and you're doing it without me," I complain.

Ryan reaches across the table and takes my hand in his and says, "The summer is going to fly by, and then we are going to be back together like nothing ever happened, okay?"

"Promise?" I ask weakly.

"Promise," Ryan says.

I feel my heart breaking at the prospect of a summer apart, but I have to believe we are strong enough to get through it.

Chapter 6 – Heather

"Why do you look so fancy?" Kevin asks with a little whistle, as I come out of the closet wearing an orange Escada sundress and Prada sandals. I've taken to getting dressed in the walk-in closet whenever Kevin is home so I can arrange the prosthesis in my bra without him seeing. Of course he knows it's there, but maybe if he doesn't have to actually see it, he'll forget about it.

"I RSVP'd to this women's business fundraiser thing months ago, and then I forgot about it, but I feel like it's too late to cancel," I sigh.

"And you feel okay to go?" Kevin questions, while he proceeds to get himself dressed in the middle of our bedroom. Unlike me, Kevin has nothing to hide, made clear as he proudly struts across the room in his boxer briefs showing off the results of his daily gym routine and natural athletic build.

"I feel fine," I reply, already tired at the idea of a full day in the City socializing.

"It could be fun to have a ladies lunch," Kevin says, pantomiming drinking a cup of tea with his pinkie raised. I would be annoyed, but I know Kevin is joking, so I just smile and walk into the bathroom to start on my makeup – another daunting task having spent the majority of the past six months au natural.

"Have a great time," Kevin says, poking his head into the bathroom. He is already fully dressed and on his way out, while I am still working on concealer.

"I'll try," I say. "I'm going to get the girls to school and then head over to the train. I'm going to leave myself extra time," I explain.

"Just enjoy yourself. And you should definitely take an Uber home. You don't want to push yourself too much. You should actually take one on the way there!" he urges.

"Okay. I'll think about it," I reply, appreciating the advice, but hating that a ladies' lunch and round-trip on the train will be "too much" for me, when I used to put in the same number of hours that he did five days a week.

***

I find my name amongst the sea of creamy white place cards perched atop the pale blue tablecloth in the hotel lobby. I try to catch a glimpse of other familiar names, but unfortunately the trip from Bronxville to Grand Central to the Pierre has zapped all of my energy. I've been done with chemo for over a month, so I don't understand why I always feel like shit all the time, but I guess that's just another one of the fun perks of this fucking disease. I hope table number eight is where they put all the forty-three-year old PR execs on medical leave coping with cancer, so we can commiserate; if not, I'm really not sure what I'm going to talk about.

I take my seat at the beautifully set table, observing the powerful women around me standing in groups of twos and threes, playing the opening game of 'who's who' and trying to figure out the most important people to network with over the next two hours. I glance at the menu laid carefully on top of my plate and notice the speakers listed between each of the courses. The keynote speaker for the day is a woman from the first company where I worked. I'm sure she wouldn't remember me, since I was right out of college and only there for two years, but even in her mid-thirties she was already on the management team – I'm not surprised to see that she is now the CEO.

"Heather, is that you?" comes from the voice of a woman sliding into the chair next to me.

"Hi! Yes it's me!" I say with enthusiasm. I know we used to do all the PR for her tech company, but that was a couple years ago and now I am blanking on her name. She is wearing a nametag, but it's on her other side, and it will be really awkward if I try to look at it.

"Sabrina," she says, reaching out her hand for mine, and saving me from embarrassment. "We worked together when I was at Salesforce," she offers.

"Right, of course," I say, glad to have it confirmed. I would love to say I remember her for all the brilliant discussions we had, but the thing I remember most about her is her beautiful strawberry blonde hair and porcelain skin; she reminded me of a sexy China Doll the way she used to toss her hair back and forth in meetings. I think I also remember her having a reputation for being quite tough (in a good way) and I once heard a rumor about her and some guy at work, but I'm not even sure if it was true.

"How have you been?" Sabrina asks.

I know she is just making conversation, but this question is nearly impossible for me to answer truthfully, I mean not with an answer anyone wants to hear. I hadn't really given any thought to making small talk; but this is only my first conversation and I'm failing miserably.

"Things have been better," I say vaguely.

"Sorry to hear that," Sabrina says sincerely, taking a sip of her water at the awkward pause I've created in the conversation.

While she is drinking I notice the gigantic diamond ring on the hand that is holding her water glass. Considering the size of it and how it catches the light from everything around us, it would be impossible for me to miss it!

"It looks like things are going very well with *you!*" I say enthusiastically, happy to change the conversation.

"Yes, they are! Did you hear about the endowment we just got? It's going to make such a big difference for the program! And we will double in size by the end of the year!" she says excitedly. Sabrina gives a quick wave to someone behind me and then returns with her full attention.

"I was actually talking about your engagement ring," I confess, "but the endowment sounds amazing. I take it you're not at Salesforce anymore?" I ask, feeling very out of the loop.

"Oh this?" she says, casually holding up her left hand and moving it away from her as if it had a large wart on it, rather than a ring worth more than many annual salaries. "I just got engaged a couple weeks ago, but we aren't going to get married for a while. I started at this amazing non-profit about two years ago and it has been life changing. I began as the program director, but now I'm the CEO," she says with a mix of modesty and pride.

"That's incredible! What do they do?" I ask. I just notice that the majority of the women have taken their seats, which probably means the first speaker will begin soon, but I'm dying to hear about party girl Sabrina's career one-eighty, it seems so unlike what I know about her!

"We match up sixth, seventh and eighth grade girls with female mentors at jobs throughout the city, to show girls what successful women look like. Initially, we started with the schools where there are the lowest graduation rates, with students who have lower levels of parental involvement at home. Although we continue to focus there, we have now expanded the program throughout the City to a range of schools, since we have found that girls of all socio-economic backgrounds can benefit from a strong female mentor; or actually as many strong female mentors as we can expose them to," Sabrina tells me.

"Wow, that's amazing," I say, staring at Sabrina in awe.

"We didn't have the money before, but we should have more soon with this new endowment. I'd love to talk to you about some PR work," Sabrina says, gracefully placing her napkin over her navy linen skirt as the waiter puts what looks like a spinach salad in front of her. Meanwhile, the waiter is waiting patiently as I fumble with my napkin and try to maintain eye-contact with Sabrina. The women at our table are probably wondering the last time I ate and carried on a conversation at the same time.

"I would love to work on that with you, but I'm actually out on medical leave right now," I tell her, embarrassed, as if cancer was somehow my fault.

"Oh, I'm so sorry," Sabrina says. "Let me know when you're back, or if you want me to call someone else at the firm," she adds, turning back toward the table to start her salad.

Oh shit. What if she thinks I have something contagious? She's probably sitting there eating her salad and wondering "why is Heather on medical leave?" but she can't ask what's wrong with me.

"It's just cancer," I blurt out, realizing only after I say it how ridiculous it must sound; there's no such thing as *"just* cancer."

"Oh Heather, I'm so sorry!" Sabrina says, giving me the familiar look of pity and sadness I have come to know so well.

"It's okay. I mean of course it isn't okay, but I'm through pretty much all of the hard stuff," I assure her.

We sit in silence for a few moments. I know I should be paying attention to the empowering words of the woman speaking, but I'm finding it hard to be inspired today.

Sabrina places her arm on my shoulder and leans in toward me. "I'm really so sorry, Heather. Please let me know if there is anything I can do for you," she tells me. I've heard this so many times, and I know it's just what people say, but it feels sincere coming from Sabrina, something I wouldn't have expected.

"Thanks so much," I tell her. "I'm hoping to be back to normal soon. I'm going to rest for the summer and then hopefully I'll be ready to get back to my life in the fall."

"That sounds like a good plan," she concurs.

"Well, it would be a good plan if I could actually get everything planned. We are supposed to leave next week and I'm not at all ready," I complain.

"Where are you going?" Sabrina asks.

"We are going to the Cape for the summer. We usually go for two weeks, but this summer we are going for two months, so that I can relax. My husband thought it would be a great idea, for me to get away for the summer, but he doesn't realize how much work it is to actually get ready to go away for two months! And the worst part is that the only way I'll be able to relax is if I find a babysitter to come with us and I haven't found anyone yet," I confess. I'm embarrassed at exposing my lack of organization, but it feels good to unburden myself.

"I'm sure you'll find someone," Sabrina says hopefully, but I can tell she doesn't like my odds.

"I can't imagine anyone I'd actually want would be available for the whole summer at this point. I should never have left it to the last minute, but with the chemo, the last few months have been such a blur, I couldn't get anything done. Now the only people left will be people who couldn't get anyone else to hire them, and I'm pretty sure I won't want them either," I moan, realizing for the first time how dire my situation has become.

"Unless, her plans for the summer fell through!" Sabrina says excitedly.

"Huh?" I question.

"I don't want to get your hopes up. But I may have someone for you. She just finished her Junior year at Dalton and she is fantastic. It's my best friend's daughter -sort-of. That part is a little complicated; but she is amazing! I was talking to my friend this morning and it looks like her plans for the summer have completely fallen apart. It's sad for her, but maybe it could work out for you!" Sabrina says.

"Oh my God, I don't want to let myself get too excited. Can you give me her name? Can I call her?" I ask eagerly.

"Let me give my friend a quick call first. I'll call her after lunch and then I'll let you know. Hopefully this will all work out!"

"Fingers crossed!" I say, actually holding up both hands to show Sabrina my crossed fingers like a seven-year-old girl, and feeling optimistic for the first time in so long I can't even remember.

Chapter 7 – Molly

"What's your plan for the day?" Derek asks, cautiously. I bit his head off last time he suggested I get out of the house, and yesterday when he intimated that I wasn't as far along on the unpacking as he thought I would be, I burst into tears; so he's either very brave or very stupid for broaching this topic again.

"Actually, I'm going to have lunch with that lady I met at the park," I say smugly.

"That's great!" Derek exclaims, with the level of enthusiasm usually reserved for news of a promotion or pregnancy.

"What do you think I should wear?" I ask him. I take one more big stretch and then swing both legs over the side of the bed, resigned that it is time to get up and start the day. I'm amazed that Anna isn't up yet and in here asking to watch a show – she rarely sleeps past seven.

"Is this a date?" Derek jokes. "Should I be worried?" he laughs. Derek wanders into the bathroom to brush his teeth. I've never understood why he waits to brush his teeth until he's fully dressed in his suit; I think the odds of spilling toothpaste would be far greater at that point, but when I mentioned it once he looked at me like I was crazy, like it was the only natural time to brush your teeth in the morning. Just add it to the list of idiosyncrasies and things you learn to live with in marriage.

"Of course it's not a date," I yell over the running water. "But, it seems everyone here dresses differently than people in Boulder. I think I may need to buy a few things to fit in better. I wonder if I have time to get something this morning before lunch?" I think out loud, more to myself than to Derek.

"I can't imagine it matters what you're wearing, but if you want to go get a new outfit, than go get something. We're making the big bucks now," Derek laughs.

***

I keep waiting to get a call from American Express about the unusual activity on my card, or to have my card declined, but for better or worse my little gold card successfully lets me spend $3,000 in seventy-five minutes. I wish I could say I got a whole new wardrobe for that amount of money, but to maximize my time, I went to the local "mall" (although The Westchester is nicer than any mall I've ever been to) and the stores they have don't have a lot of bargains. Honestly, if I'm looking for new clothes to fit in with the ladies I saw at the park, I need expensive clothes.

I got four t-shirts, three pair of shorts, two dresses, two pair of pants and one sweater for $3,000. Looking at the clothes spread out on my bed, I'm surprised there isn't more here – it felt like so much when I was shopping; but the saleswoman convinced me these were all key staples that I *needed* to have, and I'm sure I can mix and match them with some of the clothes in my closet. Although, I'm not sure anything in my closet goes with a $200 t-shirt...

It's too late for second thoughts now. I rip the tags off of a new grey fitted t-shirt that is as soft as silk, and a pair of black Marc Jacob shorts. I look in the full-length mirror in my closet and see exactly what the saleswoman meant – these clothes *do* fit me perfectly! I look at least ten pounds lighter than I did in my baggy Gap cargo shorts and Old Navy tank top. It occurs to me that I look just like Sabrina! Hmmm, not quite as striking (I have dirty blonde hair in place of her strawberry blonde, and I'm missing something else – maybe cheekbones?) Sabrina and I actually have pretty similar figures, but she always looks great because of her clothes; I'm never wearing anything baggy again!

Oh no! What am I going to wear on my feet?! I was in such a hurry in the store; it didn't occur to me that none of my shoes would go with these new clothes. I glance at my bulky Birkenstocks and Reef flip-flops lying on the floor, mocking me with their lack of sophistication.

It's 11:50. I'm supposed to be at Jeannie's house at 12:30. I really don't want to be late, but I can't wear my old shoes with these clothes – they ruin the whole look!

I grab my phone and text Jeannie before I can re-think.

Molly: Hi Jeannie! I'm running 5-10 mins late. So sorry! Can I bring anything?

Jeannie types back immediately.

Jeannie: no prob! don't bring anything – see you soon!

"Anna, sweetie, are you ready?" I call down the hall optimistically, as I make my way down the long Berber-carpeted hallway toward her room.

"Hi Mama," Anna beams up at me as I enter her room. She is sitting in the center of her nursery-rhyme area rug, surrounded by hundreds of Duplo blocks.

"Let's go sweetie. It's time to get your shoes on," I tell her.

"I wanna stay here and play!" Anna yells. She was such a champ at the mall this morning, and I feel terrible dragging her away when all she wants to do is play quietly in her room; but if we don't leave now, I won't have time to run to the shoe store before lunch.

"Come on Anna," I say, scooping her up from the floor as her cries start to turn into a full on meltdown.

"I don wanna go!" Anna yells, as she kicks and screams against me while I carry her down the stairs, praying that we don't both fall down the whole flight.

"If you're a good girl, you can have a cookie in the car," I say, fully accepting my role in this bribery exchange.

"Two cookies," Anna sniffles.

"One cookie in the car, and one more cookie if you're good in the store," I counter, utilizing my negotiating skills.

"Okay," Anna accepts.

***

The shoes may not be quite as fancy as the clothes, but they are a vast improvement over my worn-out Birks.

And I know it was meant to be, because there was an open parking spot right in front of Shoes 'n More in downtown Rye! I tried on six pairs of black sandals and was back in the car with this pair of Vince mules in ten minutes. I have to admit that they aren't nearly as comfortable as any of my other shoes, but they look great with the shorts!

I hold Anna's hand as we walk up the slate walkway to Jeannie's house. The house is a very different style than ours; I'm not great with names, but I think this would be called Colonial or maybe Georgian? I know our house is a Tudor, but I didn't know that before the realtor told us. I can't tell if it's bigger than ours (although it probably is), but it's definitely more imposing – maybe it's the massive front porch, or the circular driveway, or the double front doors with the giant doorknocker? I can't tell what it is, but Jeannie's house definitely screams "money" in a way that ours does not.

"Come in!" Jeannie says, appearing at the door before I even have a chance to knock. "I'm so glad you and little Anna could make it."

"Thank you so much for having us," I gush, immediately noticing her two-story foyer and stunning decorating. I think of my front hall still filled with boxes and our hall table from Ikea and I cringe at the idea of Jeannie ever coming to my house for lunch.

Jeannie bends down to face Anna, "do you want to go see what toys we have in the playroom?" she asks.

"Uh huh," Anna nods shyly.

"Greta, come meet Anna," Jeannie beckons.

The young woman from the park miraculously appears in the foyer as soon as she is summoned.

"Hi Anna, I'm Greta. Do you want to come play with us?" she asks, with a mild accent (German would be my guess).

"Uh huh," Anna nods again, and takes her hand.

"Lake's in there and so are the twins," Jeannie says. I'm not sure if she's telling *me* that or Anna...

"Ah, now you can relax! Do you want something to drink? Red? White?" Jeannie asks, as she walks out of the foyer and I only assume I am supposed to follow.

"Are you sure the kids are okay in there?" I question, as I enter Jeannie's magnificent kitchen, a vision in white wood, stainless steel and gray marble.

"They're great! That's why the au pairs are here. They have plenty of toys and snacks and three German girls to look after them," a black haired woman says to me.

"Hi," I say to the stranger in the kitchen. I hope my shock at finding another person here isn't apparent. I don't know why I thought it would just be Jeannie and me (or why I care), but I realize I am a little disappointed that she has invited someone else.

"I totally see what you mean," the woman says to Jeannie, after looking me up and down, but before I can gather my thoughts and think to be offended, the black-haired woman says, "Hi, I'm Lisa. You must be Molly." She takes a sip from her white wine, without making an effort to move from her perch on the stool to come shake my hand, although maybe women in Rye don't shake hands...

"Hi Lisa, so nice to meet you. Sorry, who did you say was with the kids? I think I missed that." I'm still hovering near the entrance to the kitchen archway; I can't believe Anna went with a stranger so willingly, and I'm sure she's going to come running in here any second, so I don't want to get too comfortable.

"Jeannie's au pair, Greta, and both of my au pairs are in there. I promise you, the kids are just fine. And I took their phones away," Lisa says, pointing to a stack of iPhones on the counter, "So, I guarantee they are playing with the kids and not just texting and playing candy crush," she says snidely.

"Oh, okay. Maybe I'll go check on Anna in a bit, but I guess I'll just have a splash of white right now if that's what you're both having," I say, making my move toward the enormous marble island where both ladies are sitting with their wine and what appears to be a plate of celery and mini rice cakes.

Jeannie pours me a generous glass of wine (which could never be mistaken for a splash) and points to the plate with the instructions to "help myself." My visions of eating mac and cheese and then sitting on the playroom floor swapping stories about the trials of motherhood with Jeannie, while Lake and Anna play around us, are crumbling around me. Since Anna was born, I have been over to many friends' houses for lunch with kids, and they all look pretty much the same, but they've never looked anything like this. I say a little prayer that I had the foresight to go shopping today and congratulate myself on springing for the designer shoes.

Jeannie and Lisa are both wearing sundresses that look like something I would wear out to a fancy dinner (I'm sure I couldn't afford either dress, but it's the type of thing I might wear to dinner). I can't imagine putting on a dress and heels to go over to a friends' house for lunch (or for celery), but I guess a few weeks ago I wouldn't have imagined spending $300 on a pair of designer shorts to wear to lunch, so who knows?

"Jeannie told me you just moved to town. You live on a great street. How do you like Rye so far?" Lisa asks.

Once again, I feel like I've passed a test with my address, but instead of being annoyed at the obvious shallow nature of the test, I'm happy to find approval with someone as glamorous as Lisa.

"So far, so good," I say, trying to be chipper. "Moving is always an adjustment," I add.

"Who are you using to decorate?" Jeannie asks.

"What?" I reply, unsure what she means.

"You must have a lot of vision. I walked through it when it was on the market the first time and I just kept thinking how much work it needed. I'm sure you're going to want to gut the kitchen, but you can probably wait until next year after you've done the rest of the house," Lisa says casually.

"We are just trying to get settled first and then we're going to figure it out," I say helplessly. Derek and I hadn't given any thought to making changes to the house. In fact, we told our friends in Boulder that one of the best things about the new house was that we wouldn't have to do anything to it!

"You don't want to wait too long. There can be a long wait for some of the best decorators, and then, as you know, all the custom stuff takes forever, so you're going to want to start ordering or you won't have anything done for Christmas!" Jeannie says, horrified.

I take another look around Jeannie's kitchen and realize why she would think I would want to make changes to mine. I was thrilled to have granite instead of Formica and hardwood instead of laminate, but looking around here, it's becoming pretty obvious to me that what I thought was high-quality this morning, looks cheap and worn a few hours later.

***

"So, how was your day?" Derek asks, as he comes down the stairs after reading Anna her bedtime story. Derek raced in just as I was putting Anna to bed twenty minutes ago, so I haven't really seen him yet.

"It was good. I had lunch at that woman's house," I remind him.

"Oh right! How was that? Were you dressed appropriately?" he laughs, grabbing a bottle of beer from the fridge.

"I was, but *only* because I bought a new outfit! These ladies are not messing around," I tell him.

"I think you're just being self conscious. I'm sure you're fine the way you are," Derek says lovingly, giving me a kiss on the head as he walks by me on his way to the kitchen table.

"I promise, I'm not being modest. There were two women at lunch today, and they both looked better than I would look to go out on a Saturday night, and this was for a lunch play-date with toddlers," I emphasize.

"Hmmm," Derek says, already absorbed in something on his laptop.

"I hope you're okay with grilled cheese and tomato soup for dinner. I meant to get to the store today, but I was actually at Jeannie's house for three hours, and then Anna was exhausted and needed a nap," I justify.

"I'm fine with whatever," Derek says, absentmindedly brushing his hand through his curly brown hair, not even looking up from his computer.

"Is everything okay?" I ask him, making my way over to the table with our plates. I tried to arrange the soup and sandwiches so they look more like a dinner of comfort food and less like something off the kids' menu, but I'm not sure I succeeded.

"Yeah, it's okay. Just had a long day, and I still have a lot of work to do," Derek says, sounding tired.

"Sorry," I tell him, not sure what else to say. I can't remember Derek ever bringing work home with him in Colorado, but in New York, he seems to have work to do every night. I guess that's part of the new job and having more responsibility, but it might take time to adjust.

"It's okay. All part of the job," he says, echoing my thoughts, and giving me his trademark smile, revealing perfect white teeth that could rival any Hollywood stars'.

We sit in silence for a moment and then I ask the question I have been thinking about all afternoon. I have thought about many different ways to bring up the subject, but after careful consideration I decide just to ask him.

"Do you think we should talk to a decorator to help with the house?" I blurt out.

Derek pauses midway in his tomato soup dunk to look at me. "What do we need to do to the house?" he asks, perplexed.

"I was just thinking that we could use some help picking paint colors and maybe I could use some advice on furniture?" I suggest.

"What are we painting? I thought we said we loved everything about this house and one of the things we loved was that we didn't need to do anything. And even if we did need to paint or buy furniture, why would you need help? We painted the whole house in Boulder and it looked great," Derek declares.

"I guess so. This place is just so much bigger; it's a little daunting. And you should have seen Jeannie's house today, it was impeccable, almost like a museum – nothing like this," I say, looking around at the light wood cabinets, knowing I could never host a white-wine lunch in this kitchen.

"Who would want to live in a museum?" Derek asks. "Thanks for dinner. I'm going to go to my office and try and get some work done. I have a couple more hours left," Derek says, grabbing his computer and beer and leaving me to clean up (although with this half-ass dinner there really isn't much to clean).

There's no way she could have known, but Jeannie's timing seems uncanny. As soon as Derek leaves the room, I get the following text:

Jeannie: Here are the names and numbers of the designers I told you about. Call ASAP – there's probably a waitlist – I'll call tomorrow and put in a good word for you – Rick Norson 914-712-2342 Tiffany Maryen 914-897-1451
Let's have lunch next week!

It's going to be so embarrassing to tell her that I can't call them because my husband doesn't want me to use a decorator. Or even worse, that he doesn't want me to make *any* changes to the house – specifically when Jeannie and Lisa both told me how ugly they think the house is right now. Maybe it wouldn't hurt to talk to one of them, especially if Jeannie has gone to the trouble to call them for me. I'll just call and see what they have to say and then I can tell them that I'm not interested – it can't cost anything for a phone call…

Molly: Thanks so much! I'll call first thing tomorrow! Would love to have lunch next week!

Chapter 8 – Megan

"Can I come in?" Danielle asks, knocking lightly on my partially opened door.

"It's open," I reply, staring blankly at the same page of the US Weekly I've been looking at for the last twenty minutes – I honestly don't care "who wore it better," but I'm too depressed to turn the page.

"Mind if I sit down?" Danielle asks, motioning to the corner of my unmade bed. Sometimes I wonder what it would be like if I still lived with my mom. I can't imagine she would be polite and cautious like Danielle, always worried she's going to overstep her role as former-step-mom. Most of the time I love that she's like an awesome big sister, but sometimes, like tonight, it would be nice if she had a strong opinion, or at least gave me a kick in the ass and told me to get out of bed and stop moping.

"Sure, have a seat," I tell her.

"Sabrina just called," Danielle says.

"Okay," I reply. I don't know why this is newsworthy; sometimes they talk three or four times a day. I hope I have a friend like Sabrina when I'm older; she's so cool! She wears the most amazing clothes, and talks about how much she goes out, and her fiancé is so hot!

"Sabrina had an interesting opportunity that you might want to hear about," she says thoughtfully.

"What kind of opportunity?" I ask, rolling onto my side to face Danielle and abandoning my trashy magazine for the moment.

"She has a former business contact, who is looking for a babysitter for the summer," Danielle says.

"Ugh, I don't want to babysit this summer. If I wanted to babysit I would just stay here and sit for Abby all summer and I wouldn't even have to leave the house," I complain, rolling back away from her. I know I'm being a bitch, but I can't help it. My entire summer is ruined and now Danielle and Sabrina think they can fix it by finding me a stupid babysitting job.

"So, you're just going to sit on your bed and read cheap magazines all summer?" Danielle asks.

"Maybe," I reply sarcastically.

"What if I told you that the babysitting job was in Cape Cod? Would that be more interesting?" Danielle asks, being nicer than I deserve.

"What do you mean? How would I do that?" I ask, sitting up and hugging my knees, but giving her my full attention.

"You'd have to call Sabrina to get all of the information, but I think this woman is looking for someone to come with them for the summer and help take care of her children. You would live with them in their house," she says.

"Would I have to work all the time? Would I have time off to go to the beach? How many kids are there? How much would I get paid? Would I have my own room?" I ask, firing off questions as quickly as I think of them. I'm not sure if this is something that I want to do, but the introduction of a tangible option to get out of the City for the summer is incredibly appealing.

"Whoa, slow down," Danielle laughs. Let's call Sabrina right now and see what she knows.

Thankfully Sabrina picks up on the second ring, because I'm too curious to wait until later.

"Hi Breen, Megan and I are both here, do you have a minute?" Danielle asks, with the phone on speaker.

"Sure, what's up?" Sabrina asks.

"I just told Megan about the job on the Cape and she wants to know more," Danielle explains.

"Right, of course. I'll tell you what Heather told me, and then if you want more information, I'll tell Heather you're interested and you can call her for a phone interview or whatever she wants to do," Sabrina says.

"I'm sure she'll need to meet Megan in person for an interview as well," Danielle adds.

"Actually, I think she said they're leaving tomorrow or the next day, so I'm not even certain if there would be time, but let's find out if you're interested first," Sabrina says. "Megan, what do you want to know?"

"Danielle didn't tell me very much. Just that some lady you used to know is looking for a babysitter on the Cape for the summer. So, I want to know everything. How many kids? How old they are? How much I would have to work? Would I have free time? Things like that..." I say to Sabrina.

I hear a shuffling noise on Sabrina's end, like she's looking through papers, and then she comes back on the phone.

"Here's what she told me when I saw her at lunch the other day. Heather has two girls, one is eleven and the other is seven. They are renting a house for two months and her husband is coming for most of the weekends and I think two weeks at the end of August, but for the rest of the time, it will just be her and the girls and she needs some help with them during the day..."

I cut Sabrina off to ask a question. "Aren't they a little old to need a babysitter all day? What does she need help with?"

"Heather has breast cancer. She just finished her chemotherapy treatments, but she said she still feels tired and she isn't sure she is going to be able to keep up with the girls all summer and take them to the beach every day, on bike rides, and do all the stuff that the girls like to do. And she wants to be able to rest without feeling like she is letting them down," Sabrina informs us.

"Oh," I reply, not knowing what else to say.

"So, I think Heather would be around a lot of the time, but then some times she would want you to take the girls so she could rest. She did say that you would have your own room and your own bathroom and use of a car, and she's offering $2,000 a week," Sabrina tells me, reading from her notes.

"Are you serious? That's crazy!" Danielle says to Sabrina. To me, she says, "I know your dad has put money into your trust and takes care of school, but you can't touch a lot of that money until after college. I don't think you're going to find another way to make $16,000 for spending money for college."

"What's the catch?" I ask Sabrina.

"What do you mean?" she replies.

"There has to be something wrong with her or the kids, or something? No one offers that much money for a babysitting job with that many perks if there isn't a catch," I explain.

"Honestly, I think she is just desperate to find someone. I don't know her that well, but from what I do know of her, she is great. I don't know the kids at all, so maybe they're awful? I think they have a lot of money, so the money isn't the issue and she's just hoping that offering a lot of money will make it more appealing to you. But Megan, you'll have to talk to her to figure it out for yourself, and ultimately you'll have to make the call," Sabrina says.

"Okay. Let me think about it," I tell her.

"All right, guys. I have to go. I'll send you Heather's info so you can text her or give her a call, but like I said, I think she is leaving tomorrow or the next day, so do something soon," Sabrina reminds me.

"Thanks so much, Breen!" Danielle says, ending the call.

"So what do you think?" Danielle asks me, shifting on the bed so she is sitting up against the headboard. She is still in her suit pants, but has changed out of her blouse into a t-shirt. I hadn't noticed her outfit when she first came in, but I guess that means she really did come to get me as soon as she got off the phone with Sabrina, even though she was midway through changing her work clothes.

"I don't know what to think. What do you think I should do?" I ask, throwing the question back to her.

"It's not my decision. I already know what I'm doing this summer – it's pretty boring actually, I'm going to go to work every day in the stifling Manhattan heat, while I get more uncomfortable and my belly gets bigger and bigger, and if I'm lucky I'll go out to the Hamptons one or two weekends, and maybe for a week in August. That's about it," she says, shrugging her shoulders at this fait accompli.

"I just want to spend the summer with Ryan," I sniffle, the tears welling up in my eyes again.

"I know honey," Danielle says, wrapping her arms around me, while I soak her shirt with tears.

"Why did he have to go to London? Why doesn't he love me?" I ask her, through heaving sobs, all the emotions I've been holding in since dinner three nights ago pouring out now.

"Shhh, shhh," Danielle says, rubbing my back and shushing me, like she used to do to Abby when she was a baby.

78

I cry in her lap for what feels like hours, until I have no more tears left; I may even be dehydrated.

"I'm going to call her," I tell Danielle, when I pick my tear-stained face off her shoulder.

"Heather?" Danielle confirms.

"Yes. What do I have to lose?" I ask.

"I think that's a great idea," Danielle says.

"Do you think it's too late to call?" I ask.

"It's only nine o'clock. Ordinarily, I might say it's a little late, but since she may be leaving tomorrow and we know she is desperate for a babysitter, I think she will be thrilled to hear from you this late."

Chapter 9 – Sabrina

Sometimes when I watch Peter sleep, I can't believe he's real. I don't mean that I can't believe he's a real person or anything, I just can't believe that he's in my bed and that we live together and that we are going to be waking up together every day for the rest of our lives...

It definitely isn't because he isn't appealing to look at; he's definitely the most attractive man I've ever been with (and that's saying something, because I've been with a lot of guys). Oh wait, there was that one male model in Hawaii, okay, but other than him, Peter is definitely the hottest guy. Oh, I forgot about the bartender from Kansas City, he was ridiculous, but other than that, it's absolutely Peter.

I look at his chiseled face, peaceful in sleep, but usually set in determination. He's either concentrating over a medical journal, or working out, or engaged in a political discussion; he's always "on", but in a good way, it's rare to see him relaxed. I can't see his beautiful green eyes, but I know they are there, one of his most striking features against his olive skin and his chestnut-colored hair. The sheets are down around his waist revealing the top of his pajama bottoms and his bare muscular chest and stomach; even with his demanding schedule at the hospital, he makes time to work out enough to look like a beach lifeguard. I often wonder what his patients must think when they first meet him; he looks like he is an actor playing a doctor, rather than an actual surgeon who went to Columbia medical school. Ah, I just remembered one more guy who is a little hotter than Peter - that actor I slept with in LA, but I think that's it. That was the problem with all the travel I used to do. But other than those three, that's it, Peter is honest-to-God the fourth hottest guy – and he's also really smart, and those other guys were dumb as rocks.

Maybe this won't be that scary, I tell myself. We have been together two years; and if anyone asked me two years ago if I thought that was possible, I would have said they were crazy. People get married all the time, it's just part of growing up. It's not like I want to date anyone else right now, but the thought of *never* dating anyone else (or *never* having sex with anyone else) is the part that I'm having trouble figuring out.

"How long have you been up?" Peter asks sleepily, rolling over and draping his arm across my body.

"Just a couple minutes," I say, trying to snap out of my previous thoughts and back into reality.

"What time is it?" Peter asks, trying to find his phone on the nightstand.

"It's only 6:30. You can probably even go back to sleep," I suggest.

"I don't have early rounds today, but I want to go for a run before it gets too hot," he says through a yawn.

"What time are you going in?" Peter asks.

"I was going to get in the shower in just a minute. I have a board meeting at eleven, but I wanted to do a little more prep work first," I tell him, scooting towards the edge of the bed to make good on my word.

"You have plenty of time before eleven," Peter says, moving his hand to my inner thigh.

At the touch of his hand, my whole body tingles. I don't even need to look, but I do, and see his pajamas straining against his hard-on, the head of it so ready it is already poking out of his waistband and lying against his stomach, just waiting for me. I reach over and lightly stroke the tip and Peter groans in delight, and then pushes me over on my back and takes my flimsy tank top off all in one swift motion. I lie back and put my hands over my head as he takes my nipple in his mouth and uses his free hand to lightly rub between my legs, but still over my underwear, teasing me with every motion. I can't take the anticipation and I raise my hips off the bed to let him know that I'm ready; Peter is enjoying his game, but he complies and slowly removes my black silk thong and then plunges his finger inside me and I let out a moan of delight as I orgasm from just his touch.

Peter can't take it any longer either and he replaces his finger with what I've been waiting for and thrusts inside me, while supporting himself on top of me with his powerful bronzed arms. He moves inside me and I reach around and grab his firm ass and push him deeper and deeper and we move faster and faster until we explode at the same time, then he collapses on top of me, covering my face and neck in kisses.

"I love you so much, Sabrina. I can't believe I'm lucky enough to be the guy who gets to spend the rest of my life with you," Peter whispers into my ear.

"I love you too," I say to him, trying to match his enthusiasm.

***

Heather: Thank you so much!!!!

Sabrina: You're welcome – for what?

Heather: Megan took the job!

Sabrina: That's great! I'm so glad it worked out!

Heather: We had to do the interview by Face Time, since we left this morning, but she seems great!

Sabrina: She is great! Hopefully you can relax this summer with her there.

Heather: That's the plan. I already feel so relieved.

Sabrina: When does she arrive?

Heather: She's flying up on Sunday. Kevin is driving us up now and he will be there tomorrow and over the weekend, so I should be okay until then ☺

Sabrina: Let me know if you need anything else! Have a great summer!

Heather: Thanks so much!

"Wow!" I say out-loud, to no one in particular, even though there are three people sitting in my office, now staring at me.

"What happened?" Pam asks, one of the new interns helping me prepare for the board meeting.

"Oh nothing. Just some successful match-making," I tell her.

"Who did you set up?" Pam asks, with far more candor than I would ever have had with a former boss, but maybe that is the difference between for-profit and non-profit, or maybe that's just the problem with brazen twenty-three-year olds right now.

"Oh, it isn't like *that*. I just helped a former colleague find a babysitter for the summer," I tell her. I realize I should probably stop talking since Pam would likely kill for the chance to make $2,000 a week considering her salary here, even if it meant using her Ivy-league education to supervise sandcastles and bike rides.

I want to call Danielle to get more info, but I have way too much to do before the meeting – I'll have to wait until this afternoon.

My phone chirps again, and I assume it is Heather with another comment, so I grab it, even though I should be focusing on the changes for the presentation.

Jessie: Are you still going to the alumni thing tonight?

Oh crap, I totally forgot about that! I told Jessie I would go months ago when we got the email, but then I never put it in my calendar. I'm about to write back that I can't make it, when she texts again.

Jessie: You can't bail on me! You promised!

Oh shit. Peter has to work late anyway, and I haven't seen her in forever. It's always fun to see who shows up at these things; and if it sucks, then I'll just leave early, or Jessie and I can leave and go get drinks on our own.

Sabrina: I'll be there! What time does it start? Where is it again?

Jessie: You totally forgot, didn't you?

Sabrina: Maybe. But I'll be there!

Jessie: 6:30. Monkey Bar

Sabrina: Really? I don't think I've been there in 10 years!

Jessie: See you tonight!

Sabrina: Can't wait

"Sabrina, can I print this version?" Pam asks me, balancing her voice between impatience and concern. She is clearly worried that we won't have enough time, but she doesn't have enough experience with me to know that I could fly through this meeting without any material and the board would still be amazed and impressed by my every word. I know I sound cocky, but it's true.

"Sure, go ahead and print it, and bind ten copies," I tell Pam, already thinking past the meeting ahead to tonight and wondering who will be there from Yale class of 2007. It's hard to believe we've been out of school for over ten years. I look down at my left hand and realize this will be the first time I've seen everyone (or anyone from school) since I've been engaged. I know many people from my class are already married, or married with kids, some of them have come full circle and have gotten divorced and are single again; but I've always been fun, flirty and single – I'm not sure I know how to *be* engaged.

Chapter 10 – Molly

"Thanks so much for letting me leave Anna at your house while we go to the studio," I say to Jeannie, as we hurry out of Jeannie's house and get back into her silver Escalade, which is idling outside in the driveway.

"It's no problem," Jeannie says, but I can't tell if she means it, or if she's slightly annoyed with me, most likely the latter.

When Jeannie came to pick me up this morning to go meet with one of the decorators at his studio, Anna and I were dressed and ready to go. Jeannie tried unsuccessfully to hide her shock, when she said, "What is *she* doing here?"

I apologized profusely and explained that I didn't have any babysitters in Rye yet. But really it hadn't even occurred to me that Anna wouldn't be welcome! I assumed she would bring Lake, and I would bring Anna and the girls would play on the floor while we talked to the decorator.

I'm not sure I've ever been in a car like this. It looks like a truck on the outside; I mean plenty of people in Boulder have Suburbans, but the inside is like a private lounge crossed with a first class airplane cabin. It is also the cleanest car I've even been in that wasn't in a car dealership; I would be mortified if she ever rode in my car, with goldfish crumbs and dry cereal everywhere.

Jeannie breaks the silence. "I should have offered earlier to have Greta watch both the girls, I wasn't thinking," she prostrates herself.

"No, no, don't be silly. It's totally my mistake. I need to start looking for some babysitters in the area, maybe some local high school girls," I wonder out loud.

"Have you ever thought about getting an au pair?" Jeannie asks.

"Oh, I don't think I need an au pair," I say, careful not to say too much more at the risk of offending her.

"I didn't think I needed one at first either," Jeannie says, "but after our full-time nanny left when Lake was two, it was necessary," Jeannie tells me.

"Oh, did you work until she turned two?" I ask her, thinking I've found a connection, since I worked full-time until a few months ago when we found out we were moving here.

"No, why do you ask?" Jeannie asks.

"Nevermind," I say, feeling lost in the conversation.

Jeannie seems unfazed and keeps going as she barrels expertly through the backstreets of Rye on our way to Greenwich. "I just think you should consider it. Even if you start the process now, it could take a few months before your au pair arrives, and you're going to have to interview a lot of them before you find one you like. There's no harm in signing up and starting the process. It's forty hours of babysitting a week, but you'll go through that in no time, I promise. Greta works about fifty or sixty hours most weeks, but she loves the overtime pay," Jeannie says confidently.

"Okay, I'll think about it," I say, not quite sure how else to answer.

"It's also *a lot* cheaper than getting a babysitter by the hour and it's *so* much easier than always having to call and find someone," she says, in full saleswoman role.

I know it's crass, but I ask anyway, "So how much is it? I mean, how much does an au pair cost?" I ask, wincing as the words are out of my mouth.

"I don't actually know, my husband pays all the bills. I just know he was thrilled when we went from a nanny to an au pair and he told me it was really cheap," she says, pulling in to a parking spot at the decorator's studio.

"Rick and I go way back, so let me start off," Jeannie says, as we walk through the parking lot and approach the door to the large glass house that must be where Rick comes up with all of his fancy decorating ideas.

"Jeannie!" Rick yells, as we walk inside, and a tall, handsome, extremely slender man in skinny jeans and a black t-shirt runs over to envelop Jeannie in a hug, and then takes a step back to kiss her on both cheeks.

"It's so good to see you!" Jeannie gushes. "I have another project for you, but you-know-who says I have to wait until next month," she says flirtatiously. I can't possibly imagine what else she could have left in her house to decorate, but maybe there is some corner that hasn't been touched.

"I can't wait!" Rick says, matching her tone.

"But until then, my friend Molly has a pretty sizable project for you," Jeannie says.

I try not to choke at Jeannie's introduction, which leaves me with a weird, dry coughing noise, when Rick reaches out his hand to introduce himself.

"Hi Molly, it's nice to meet you. Any friend of Jeannie's is a friend of mine," he says, still looking at Jeannie.

"Hi Rick. It's so nice of you to take the time to meet with me. I'm not sure quite how sizable the project really is. We just bought a house in Rye, and I'm looking for a little help," I tell him.

"It's the Tudor that the Martins used to live in," Jeannie explains to Rick, which is interesting because I had no idea she knew the previous owners.

"Oh that's a great house. It has great bones – a lot of potential," Rick says to me. "And it's a great street!"

"That's what I hear," I say, trying to keep a positive attitude.

"I usually wouldn't have time for a project of that size, but I actually just had a project moved to the fall, so I have some availability," Rick tells us.

"That's amazing!" Jeannie says, clapping her hands.

"I can come out to the house tomorrow around ten and take a look around and we can go from there. Sound good?" Rick says.

"Sounds great! Thank you so much!" Jeannie answers.

Just as I'm about to say something, Rick's phone rings, and he tells us that he has to take the call, but he's looking forward to seeing us tomorrow, and then he answers his phone and disappears behind a wall of fabric samples.

"This is so exciting!" Jeannie says, as we get back in the car.

"It is," I say, a little stunned at what transpired so quickly, and very unsure about what I just agreed to. I want to ask Jeannie if there is a fee associated with Rick coming out to the house, but I'm embarrassed after all she's done for me.

"I'll bring Greta and Lake with me tomorrow, since I know you won't have anyone to watch Anna, and we'll want to be able to spend time with Rick without being interrupted," Jeannie says, in a serious voice.

"That would be great," I reply, because what else I can say?

Chapter 11 – Heather

The traffic inched so slowly approaching Bourne Bridge, that I thought we might spend the whole summer on that two-lane road of hell. Every summer as we crawl past the Christmas Tree Shop, I wonder why that ridiculous store is the first thing to greet us on Cape Cod. But now we are sailing along Route 6, losing cars at every exit, as eager travelers leave the highway in search of their vacation homes. Most of these cars will be back on the road next Saturday on change-over day when their rental is over and they have to head back to reality – their cars filled with dirty laundry, empty coolers and sunburned faces. But I won't have to be on the other side of the highway until Labor Day – I can't believe it!

We usually come for two weeks, and even that feels luxurious, but the idea of two months is making me giddy. With every mile I put behind me, I feel stronger. I roll down my window to let in the fresh air, hoping to get a whiff of the ocean, even though Route 6 is a little too far from the beach for a taste of salt.

Before I know it, we are twisting through the streets of Brewster, past Kate's Fried Seafood & Ice Cream, the firehouse, the library, the town hall, and so many new restaurants and shops that weren't here years ago. I hear the girls whispering in the backseat, but I'm choosing to ignore them. They are probably saying that it looks smaller than Chatham, but I know they will love it once they give it a chance.

Kevin dutifully follows the GPS on his phone so he doesn't miss a turn; I want to tell him to look around and enjoy his surroundings, but I know he is anxious to get to the house and get us in and unpacked. I used to know every street in this town when we came here growing up, and of course we've been here for dinner or ice cream a few times over the last several summers. But I guess I don't really know Brewster anymore, because I've almost told Kevin to turn a few times, and I've been wrong every time.

"I think this is the street," Kevin announces, as we turn onto the road that leads to Swift Lane. I hold my breath and hope that the house is as good as it looked online.

"That house is *really* small," Brooke says as we pass one of the first houses on the street.

"There are houses of all different sizes on the street," I tell her, optimistically.

"And that one looks *so* old," Brooke adds, obnoxiously.

"Watch it, Brooke," Kevin warns, from his place behind the wheel.

"There are a variety of houses on the street. Some are the original houses, and some are much newer," I tell the girls, praying hard now that our house is as advertised. I know that I should be annoyed with Brooke, but I was thinking the exact same things as we drove by those houses.

The paved road comes to an end and the road narrows as we drive onto dusty Swift Lane. There are only a few houses on the road and I spot ours immediately; it looks even better in person than it did online! Kevin pulls into the driveway, and I practically jump out of the car.

"Be careful!" Kevin calls after me.

"I'm fine," I assure him. "Girls, come on," I tell them.

"Where are we going?" Brooke complains, but I can tell by her voice that she is already relieved about the size and age of the house.

"Just come on! Kevin, you too!" I call out.

"But what about all the stuff?" He protests.

"We'll come get it in a minute. Just come with me," I plead.

"I'm coming!" Caitlin yells, tumbling out of the car and appearing at my side in her tiny denim shorts, pink tank top and purple flip flops.

Slowly, Kevin and Brooke extract themselves from our over-packed Range Rover and join us in the backyard of our summer house.

"Are you ready?" I ask.

"For what?" Brooke questions.

"Come with me," I say, leading them around the side of the house and through the gate into our front yard.

Once the house is no longer blocking the view, it's pretty hard to hide my big surprise, but the view doesn't really come into focus until we get a few feet into the front yard.

"The ocean's right there!" Caitlin screams. "We have our own stairs and our own beach!" she yells, running to the edge of the yard to make her discovery.

"It's the Bay, but yes, pretty great, right?" I say.

Kevin has already found a rocking chair on the front porch. "This is pretty nice," he says, no longer in a rush to get the bags from the car.

Brooke hasn't said anything yet, but I'm going to take her silence as approval. She's going to have a hard time arguing that this isn't nicer than the house we rented in Chatham for the last five years. The house there was fine, but it was an average three-bedroom house with a ten-minute walk to the beach – nothing compared to this.

I finally let myself exhale and hope that I can start to heal this summer.

***

"What do you need, honey?" I ask Brooke. I still have my back to the door, but I can feel her hovering in the doorway and I know she's there.

"When's the babysitter going to be here?" Brooke asks.

"Her name is Megan, and she is going to be here tomorrow. Dad is going to get her from the airport in the morning," I tell her, even though I know Brooke already knows all of this.

My entire body aches from the exhaustion of unpacking and getting moved in over the last thirty-six hours, but we are so close to being settled, that I don't want to stop. I know I shouldn't overdo it, but it will feel so good when everything's done. I stand up from my position crouched over the dresser drawers and reach my arms over my head, arching my back and feeling my muscles complain about being overworked.

"But what if I don't like her," Brooke says, trying hard to maintain her composure.

"Why don't you think you'll like her? We talked to her on Face Time and she seemed great," I remind Brooke.

"But that was because she was trying to impress you. What if she gets here and she's different?" Brooke asks me.

"How is the house so far?" I ask her.

"I guess it's fine," she says stubbornly.

"You know it's a lot better than fine, it's fantastic! I saw you run out of here this morning before breakfast and you and Dad were in the water in two minutes. How are you going to complain about that?" I challenge her.

"Fine. The house is really nice. I'll admit it's better than the other house, are you happy? But that doesn't mean Megan is going to be great," she states defiantly, crossing her slender arms across her chest.

"Please just give her a chance. You didn't think you were going to like it here, and you do. So maybe Megan will be good too, okay?" I say.

"Okay," she mumbles.

"And remember, if Megan isn't here, you aren't going to be able to run down to the beach and swim before breakfast, because I don't want you out there alone," I remind her.

I can't hear what she says clearly, because she has already started to walk away, but I'm pretty sure what she says is, "the only reason it was fun is because it was Dad, I am *never* going for a swim with Megan."

Dear God, please let Megan be as good as, or better than Sabrina said, or this is going to be a loooong summer.

Chapter 12 – Megan

It looks like a "tornado hit my room," as my mom used to say. There are clothes covering every surface in the room, suitcases open on the floor overflowing with my belongings (with no chance of closing) and I'm not even close to being ready.

"How's it going in here?" Danielle asks, poking her head into the warzone.

"Terrible. I don't know how to pack for two months in two bags! I can't fit half of the stuff I want to bring. But I don't even know what I'm really going to need, so that makes it even harder," I lament.

"I think you need a bathing suit and some shorts and t-shirts. What else do you need?" Danielle asks.

"I don't know. But what if it gets cold? Or what if I actually want to go out in my free time? Or maybe we'll do something other than go to the beach..." I remind her.

"Clearly you need more than a bathing suit, I'm just saying that you probably don't need too much stuff. And there are stores in Cape Cod, you could also shop there. Especially with all the money you'll be making," she teases.

"Okay, I'll take some of this stuff out and just pack the basics," I say, starting to remove flimsy dresses and bulky hoodies from my suitcase and throwing them into the large pile of clothes on my bed.

"Are you nervous about being away for two months," Danielle asks, taking a seat on my bed and starting to fold the mountain of discarded clothes.

"I'm a little nervous about living with Heather and the two girls, but honestly only a tiny bit. As you know, I've moved around quite a bit the last few years," I say, giving her a big smile, "so I think that has taken away a lot of the stress about this type of situation."

"I guess that makes sense," Danielle reasons.

"Over the last four years, I've lived with my mom and her crazy boyfriend, then with you and my dad, then my dad and Petra, and here with you and Abby and now with Ted too. I think that amount of change means I'm ready for anything," I joke.

"That reminds me, did you happen to tell your dad that you will being going to the Cape for the summer?" Danielle asks nervously, clearly not wanting to have to talk to him herself.

"I sent him a text. I don't think he really cares. He's too busy trying to sleep with anything that moves in London," I say, with a note of disgust in my voice.

"Megan" Danielle says, with a warning tone.

"What?" I ask. "It's true."

"He's still your father," she says. But I know she is only saying what she thinks she is supposed to say as my surrogate mom/ caretaker, because she despises him more than I do.

"He wrote back and said that it sounded great, but that's all he said," I tell her.

"Do you know if he is planning to come back here at all this summer, or if he is staying in London?" Danielle asks.

"I talked to Kyle a few days ago and he said that Dad was staying in Europe all summer. I mean, he may be back in New York for meetings, but he hasn't told us the last several times he's been back, so I don't know why this would be any different," I say with disdain.

"So Kyle is already out in Wyoming? How does he like it?" Danielle asks.

"He said it was going well so far. I guess the ranch is pretty cool, so he's having fun with the horses and it's a nice break from school. He didn't mention Bill, but they got along better over Christmas, so that's probably okay too," I tell her.

"You know, maybe you could take a trip out there before school starts? I'm sure your mom would love it," Danielle suggests, as she has many times before.

"I don't want to talk about it right now. Let's finish packing. Do you think I'll need this?" I ask, holding up a short, white halter dress.

"That will look great with a tan, throw it in," Danielle says, helpfully.

Danielle and I continue to pack in companionable silence while I think about her suggestion to go out to Wyoming. Of course, I have thought about it – I think about it all the time. Although I love Danielle and I've adjusted to my unique living situation, it's still bizarre that my mom lives in Wyoming on a ranch with her new husband Bill, while my dad picked up everything last year and went to run his firm's office in London, taking my little brother with him.

Obviously, he didn't have time to actually be a real dad to my younger brother Kyle, so he threw him in boarding school in England, and now he's sending him back to live with my mom for the summer. Kyle and I are closer now than we ever were when we lived together. I'm not sure if it's because we're older, or if we've united in a joint hatred of our father and the need to adapt to living conditions that might have put us in social services if it weren't for Danielle and a lot of money.

I've mostly gotten over the divorce and forgiven my mom for choosing Bill and leaving us to run off and start over out West; but the key word is *mostly*. When I really think about it, I get angry all over again, and I'm so tired of being angry. The last year and a half with Danielle has helped me forgive my mom and move on. I haven't forgiven my dad, and I don't have any plans on doing that; but Ryan is what's really helped me. He made me feel loved and special and let me know that whatever issues my parents had were their issues, not mine. Just thinking about him makes my chest hurt and I can feel the tears coming again.

"Hey Danielle, I'm going to try and give Ryan a call, okay? It's late in London, but I want to catch him before he goes to sleep," I tell her.

"Of course! Tell him I say hello. I should probably see if Ted needs any help with Abby in the bath. I told him I would be right back, but that was a long time ago," she laughs.

"I'm sure Ted is doing just fine. Although, on second thought, Abby has him wrapped around her little finger, so she may have convinced him to bring ice cream or her iPad into the bath – you should probably get in there right now," I joke. Ted is one of the nicest guys I've ever met (although the bar was pretty low), and after everything Danielle went through with my Dad, I'm so glad that she found him.

"You're totally right! Who knows what Abby has persuaded him to do," she chuckles, as she leaves my room and closes the door behind her, giving me privacy to call Ryan.

The phone rings once, twice, a third time, and then goes to voicemail. "Hey, it's me. I wanted to catch you before you went to sleep, but I guess I'm too late. Just thinking about you. I miss you so much! I leave for Cape Cod tomorrow morning. I wish you were here. I love you." I hang up before I start crying on the phone, bitterly disappointed that I won't get to talk to him tonight.

A few minutes later, as I'm actually zipping one of my suitcases closed, I hear my phone chime.

Ryan: Sorry I missed your call – really loud in this club. Have a great trip tomorrow. xo

What the hell? He is still out at one in the morning in London at a club – who is he with at a club? And he can *text* me back, but he can't step outside to call me? I start to text him back, but I don't know what to say. I don't want to start a fight with him over a text message, but am I just supposed to be okay with that? Is this how it is going to be the whole summer?

Megan: I'll be up late packing, if you want to give me a call. xoxoxoxo

When I go to sleep three hours later, with my phone on my pillow, Ryan still hasn't called.

Chapter 13 – Sabrina

I have so much work to get done today, but I can't get myself to focus. So far my procrastination has led to the purchase of two pairs of shoes, a beach bag, and yet another pair of white jeans (it's impossible to have too many). It's hard to imagine what I did before online shopping. I sit at my desk and when I'm having trouble coming up with the right words for my email, I'm on the Saks site with the click of my mouse, and five minutes later, I've spent $600 – just like that! Luckily I don't do this every day, or it would be a very expensive distraction.

I try again to pay attention to the email that I'm supposed to be writing to all of the mentors about the summer get-together next week; but I know the real reason I can't concentrate is the Facebook notification I received this morning. It's only a simple friend request, nothing to freak out about, but it's from Parker...

Until I saw him the other night at Monkey Bar, I honestly hadn't thought about him since graduation. Okay, maybe a few times the first year we were out of school, when I would sit and stare at his picture and wonder why he broke up with me the last week of Senior year. He said it was because he was moving to San Francisco and he didn't want to be "tied down" with a long distance relationship; but I was convinced there was more to it. I definitely haven't thought about him in the last *five* years

– and then *bam*, there he was at the bar last night, back in Manhattan and so happy to see me.

It was fun to catch up, and I will admit that I was quite happy I ended up having time to go home and change and re-do my hair and makeup before meeting Jessie. I know it doesn't matter, but it's always better to run into your ex-boyfriend in a black halter top, then in a rumpled suit. I was sure I would never hear from him again, and then this morning on the way to work I got a Facebook notification that he wants to be my friend. I'm sure it doesn't mean anything – I bet he's one of those people that has two thousand friends on Facebook and never posts anything or even checks it.

Finally I can't take it anymore and I log onto my account from my computer. I never check Facebook at work, and if I do, it's usually a quick peek on my phone while I am waiting for the elevator, but if I'm going to do it, I might as well go for it. I click on the 'accept' button and it takes me to his profile page. Obviously, the first thing I see is his picture. I know I just saw him the other night, but seeing his smiling face right here on my computer feels so much more personal than when we were all crowded around the dark bar.

Parker looks a little older than he did ten years ago, but I would recognize him anywhere. His dark brown hair is a little shorter than it was in college, and it looks windblown in this picture (I think he's on a mountain). He is wearing sunglasses, but I know his bright blue eyes are underneath, with long lashes, that some would say are wasted on a guy, but they aren't wasted on him. He seems to be more tanned than usual in the picture, but he always used to have color on his face from any of the outdoor activities he did – skiing, or mountain biking, or sailing – I think my mom described him as an "outdoorsy" guy. The best part of the picture is his smile. It's almost like he's laughing, but not quite. I wonder who took the picture, who he's looking at like that – I bet it's his girlfriend. I bet they are hiking together on some mountain and when they got to the top, she took his picture. Then they climbed back down and had wild sex, while still wearing their hiking boots. Oh my God – what is wrong with me?! I'm looking at his profile picture and suddenly I'm jealous of the imaginary girl who took the picture? I have got to get a grip.

The next thing I notice about his page is that he only has 97 friends. So, either he doesn't have a lot of *actual* friends, or he is selective about his Facebook friends. I quickly check his relationship status and notice that it says "single." It could mean that he's dating someone and it isn't serious, and *of course* it doesn't matter to me, but I am a tiny bit relieved. I wonder what my relationship status says? I know that I changed it to "in a relationship" a while ago when Peter and I moved in together, but I don't think I ever changed it to "engaged." Hmmm, it seems silly to change it right now, but I should remember to do that later.

Suddenly I hear, "What are you looking at so intently?" And I nearly jump out of my seat! I shut down my entire Internet browser, because I can't close the Facebook window fast enough. Even though my computer screen faces away from my office door, I feel like I have been caught doing something illicit – I can sense my cheeks burning.

"You scared the crap out of me!" I yell at Theresa, my administrative assistant, not meaning for it to come out so harshly.

"Sorry!" she apologizes. "But you were staring so hard at your screen, I thought you might damage your eyeballs. My mom told me that could happen," she advises me, nodding vigorously.

"No, I'm sorry, it's not your fault. I guess I was just absorbed in something," I confess.

"It was wedding dresses, wasn't it? I bet it was wedding dresses!" she gushes.

"No, it wasn't dresses," I admonish her, but then realize it would be so much easier if I said it was something wedding related, since apparently as a recently engaged woman, I'm supposed to be crazy about all-things-wedding and I will be forgiven any transgressions as long as they are white and covered in lace.

"Let me know when you do want to look at dresses. Sometimes, I buy the bridal magazines just to flip through them," she confesses.

Theresa would make the perfect bride. Maybe I should ask her to plan the wedding? I know it's not entirely work related, but it's helping me, and isn't anything that helps me technically her job?

"Did you need something?" I ask Theresa, reminding her that she originally came in here and scared the hell out of me.

"Oh right, sorry," she giggles. "You just got a call from someone named Parker Avery, when you were on the other line. He said you would know what it was in reference to. I was coming to give you the message," she says, walking over to my desk and handing me a yellow post-it note.

"Do you know what he's calling about? Is it about the wedding?" Theresa probes, desperate for more details about the "Big Day" and constantly disappointed by my lack of information and enthusiasm.

"I'm not sure I know why he's calling, but it's definitely not about the wedding," I promise her.

***

Peter has another late shift at the hospital tonight, so I decide to pick up some sushi at the place around the corner from our apartment on my way home. People always say things like, "it must be so hard that Peter has to work so many nights," and "I couldn't imagine if my boyfriend was gone all the time." But honestly, I think one of the best parts about our relationship is that we have so much independence. I know Peter is looking forward to the day when he has more seniority and doesn't have to work such crappy hours; but, I can't imagine what I would do if we spent seven nights a week together.

As I settle onto the couch with my spicy tuna rolls and glass of Pinot Grigio, I decide to give Danielle a quick call to see if she's heard anything from Megan.

"Hey, Dani, how are you? Do you have time to talk?" I ask her. This is now my first question since Abby was born, because at least half of the time she cuts me off right away and tells me she doesn't have time and she'll have to call me back.

"I actually *do* have time. Abby is asleep and Ted is out with some guys from work, so I was just about to pour myself some seltzer and find something mindless to watch on TV," she says.

"That's pretty much my plan for the night as well, only not the seltzer. I'm deciding between *The Bachelor* and *The Voice*," I tell her.

"Those are pretty much the same level of mindlessness. Although, I don't know how you can still watch *The Bachelor*. Honestly, I don't even know how it's still on!" Dani exclaims.

"It's so bad that it's good. The whole thing is a trainwreck; that's what makes it great. Anyhow, I just wanted to check and see if you had heard from Megan yet. I was going to text her, but I didn't want to bother her," I admit.

"She texted me this morning when her plane landed, and then another quick text letting me know she got to the house, but I haven't heard from her since then. I'm going to wait until tomorrow to call her, but I'm hoping to hear from her tonight. I'm going to let her get settled and spend some time with the kids before I bug her," Dani laughs.

"Tell her I say hi," I add.

"Okay, will do. Alright, I'll talk to you tomorrow," Danielle says, ready to hang up the phone.

"Wait. Actually there is something else," I say, reluctantly.

"What is it?" Danielle asks.

"Parker was at the alumni event the other night," I reveal.

"Oh, the guy you dated at Yale?" she asks, casually.

Sometimes I forget that even though Danielle and I were best friends in high school, we lost touch in college and for several years afterward. She knows the details of so much of my life, but there are a few years where there are a lot of holes, and in times like these, it's really annoying!

"Yes, he's the one. The guy who broke up with me right before graduation and moved to California," I remind her.

"Was it good to see him? Or was it weird?" She asks.

I'm suddenly regretting bringing this up at all. I know she is trying to be supportive, but I need to talk to someone who knows Parker - someone who knew me and Parker as a couple, and knows why this is such a big deal. It's too hard if I have to explain our relationship and why getting a phone call from Parker Avery is monumental.

"It was fine. He's still really hot," I tell her, because I can't think of anything else to say.

"I bet it felt great to wave that big diamond ring in his face, right?" Danielle asks.

"Yeah, totally. All right, I think my sushi is starting to get warm. Have a good night," I tell her.

"You too!" Danielle says, in a chipper voice as she ends the call.

I don't know what it would have felt like if I waved my ring in Parker's face, because instead I kept my left hand in my pocket the entire night.

Chapter 14 – Molly

"I'm so glad you could come up here for dinner. Thanks again for changing plans at the last minute," I say to Sabrina.

"It's not a problem," my sister assures me. "And this way I get to see Anna," Sabrina gushes, giving Anna another squeeze, as Anna giggles in her lap and looks adoringly up at her aunt.

"Derek's hours are getting crazy. He was sure he would be home so I could take the train in to the City, but then he called this afternoon and said he would be late again," I tell Sabrina, while opening cabinet after cabinet, searching for my cheese grater – I've finally unpacked, but now I can't remember where I put anything.

"I wouldn't call working until 6:30, crazy hours. I wouldn't even say that's working late," Sabrina says, looking at her watch.

"No, I know this isn't that late, but he was there until 10, one night last week!" I tell her.

"Molly, this is New York. People work twenty-four hours a day. I have friends who sleep on their couches for an hour or two, multiple nights a week, when they are working on a big deal. I think you and Derek just need to adjust to a different pace," she advises me.

"I guess so," I say, unconvincingly – now I'm hunting for my Dutch oven, having found the grater.

"So how is everything else?" Sabrina asks, looking up from her intent play-doh activity with Anna.

"Everything else is pretty good. I made a new friend," I tell her, proudly.

"That's great," Sabrina says, earnestly, understanding that it really *is* a big deal to make a new friend at this age in a new place. "And it looks like you are all unpacked and settled. The house looks great," she adds.

"Really? Do you think so?" I question.

"Of course. Why, you don't think it looks good?" She asks.

"It's okay, but it could use a lot of work," I tell her.

"Really? I thought you guys weren't planning on doing anything?" Sabrina asks.

"I guess we weren't, but now that we're here, I realize that there is actually a lot that needs to be done. Mostly cosmetic stuff, just some design work on the main floor – I don't think we're going to do any of the structural stuff until next year," I say, repeating what Rick said yesterday.

"That sounds like it could be expensive," Sabrina says.

"I don't think it will be too bad. The painting and rugs and furniture probably won't cost too much. The kitchen might be more expensive, but we won't do that until next year after Derek gets his bonus," I say, remembering what Jeannie told me about the big bonus that her husband always gets in February.

"This is a great kitchen!" Sabrina says, looking around the room, gesturing with her arms.

"It's fine for now, but it's a little dated," I tell her. "Okay, enough about me, let's talk wedding!" I say, excitedly, dumping a box of linguini into the pot of boiling water.

"There's not much to tell," Sabrina says, casually.

"Have you talked about a date? Do you know what type of wedding you want to have? Places book up so quickly, you're going to have to get going," I advise her.

"That's what everyone keeps saying," Sabrina says, absentmindedly rolling a long piece of green play-doh into a snake.

"What does Peter want to do?" I probe.

"I think he wants a traditional wedding," Sabrina says.

"What does that mean?" I ask.

"I don't know. Probably get married in a church and then have a fancy party in a hotel afterward?" she says, but its more of a question.

"Have you guys even talked about it?" I ask with disbelief.

"Not really. But we've only been engaged for a month," she says defensively.

"I used to talk to Derek about weddings every time we went to a wedding, and that was years before we were engaged," I tell Sabrina.

"Yes, but that's because you and Derek have been together since you were twenty-two. It's different," she says.

"I don't think it's that different. Have you ever been to a wedding with Peter?" I ask her.

"Yes, we've been to a few."

"And when you were there, didn't you ever talk about what you liked, or what you didn't like, or what you might do at your own wedding someday?" I ask, incredulous.

"Nope, not that I can remember," she tells me.

"Wow. That's just so weird!" I say, finding it hard to believe that we can be related. I was planning my wedding shortly after Derek and I started dating, even though we were way too young to get married; by the time we actually got engaged, all I had to do was iron out the details. I can't even imagine what I would have done if I had the type of budget Sabrina and Peter must have for their wedding with Peter's family money and whatever Sabrina is contributing from her vast savings!

"Then I guess I'm weird," she admits.

"Would you want to get married in a church? When was the last time you were even in a church?" I ask her.

"I don't know - maybe in high school? I kind of assume that Peter's mom would want that. You know his sister got married at The Plaza with like five hundred people a few years ago. I know the ceremony was at some church beforehand, but I have no idea which one," she says, seeming very displeased with this idea.

"But that doesn't mean that you have to do the same thing. I always pictured you getting married on an island somewhere under a few palm trees," I share with her.

"Really?" she asks, intrigued.

"Don't worry, the palm trees were attached to a very fancy resort," I assure her.

"Phew," she laughs. "That definitely sounds better than five hundred people at The Plaza. I wonder what Peter would think about it..."

"There's only one way to find out," I say.

"I guess you're right," Sabrina says.

Chapter 15 – Megan

The drive to the house was a little awkward at first, but then it turned out that the dad (he insisted I call him Kevin), went to Dalton for high school, so we actually had a lot to talk about. He seems like a really nice guy and a genuinely nice dad, which makes him totally different than my dad. When I meet other people's parents, I always expect them to be somewhat like my mom and dad (selfish, narcissistic, or lecherous in my dad's case), so I am surprised when I find parents who seem to genuinely care about their kids – if that isn't fucked up, I don't know what is!

When we pulled up in the driveway behind the house, the mom (Heather), was standing by the side of the gate with one of the girls, and they were both waving to us. From the Face Time call, it looked like it was the younger one (Caitlin), but I wasn't sure at the time.

On the call, Heather had described the house as a beach house, but I know that can mean a lot of different things. I was happy to see the traditional gray-shingled house with clean white trim similar to those that we'd stayed in on the Vineyard.

The last two hours have been a complete blur of meeting Caitlin and Brooke, getting a tour of the house, running up and down the steps to the beach playing chase with Caitlin, and now I am finally in my room getting a chance to unpack before we all head down to the beach for the afternoon. I offered to help make lunch (it felt like the right thing to do), but Heather assured me there would be plenty of days for that, and I should take the chance while Kevin is still here, to get settled.

My room is beautiful. I think this entire house was just built, or re-built or something – everything in it feels brand new. My room is much bigger than my room at Danielle's, and I have a huge window with a view of the water. The whole room is decorated in blues and grays, and all of the furniture is white wood that is meant to look old. There are large sea-shells placed strategically on the dresser and on the nightstands; they would look tacky somewhere else, but this close to the beach, they're perfect. I also have my own bathroom attached to the bedroom – Brooke and Caitlin are sharing a bathroom, but they also have pretty great rooms, so I hope they won't mind.

I maneuver my suitcase onto the bed to attempt to put everything away – if I'm going to be here for the whole summer, I might as well get comfortable. As I unzip my bag, I remember what a terrible job I did packing for this trip; unfortunately nothing has magically improved since I closed the bag. I'm also reminded of my unanswered texts and calls from Ryan last night. In my rush to get to the airport this morning, I wasn't able to dwell on it, but now I am. I check my phone and see a few texts from Danielle, and my heart soars as I see one from Ryan.

Ryan: Hope you have a good trip. Super busy here. I'll try to call soon! Love you.

It wasn't what I was hoping for, but I guess it's better than nothing. I try to remind myself that he's overwhelmed at work trying to impress his dad, while I'm getting ready to go play in the sand.

117

Megan: It's great here. Just got to the Cape! Maybe we can talk tonight? I love you!! xoxxoxo

***

The whole family is gathered around the center island in the kitchen, laughing hysterically, when I walk down the stairs. I try to turn around and creep back up, so I'm not the fifth wheel, but Heather spots me.

"Megan, come here," she says, trying to catch her breath. "Caitlin was just telling this story about a dead crab from last summer. I guess it doesn't sound that funny when you say it that way. Anyway, I think we are all set to take everything down to the beach," Heather says, changing the subject.

"Caitlin, take the bag with the toys and the little cooler. Brooke, take the towels and the boogie boards. I've got the chairs and umbrellas. Megan, can you take the big cooler and that other beach bag?" Kevin asks me, as we all file out onto the deck.

"Sure, no problem," I reply, hoisting the large bags onto my shoulders, happy to have something to do.

"What am I taking?" Heather asks, looking around at all of us with our arms full.

"Just grab your book," Kevin says to her.

"Let me take something," she requests, sounding annoyed.

"We've got it all, right guys?" Kevin asks.

"Yes!" We all reply in unison, not wanting to disappoint him.

"Fine. Whatever. But when you're gone, I'm going to carry this stuff and I'm going to be just fine," Heather says to Kevin, breezing past him on her way to the beach stairs.

"Megan, hold up a minute," Kevin says to me.

My shoulders are starting to ache a little from the weight of the bags, but of course I have no choice in my response. "Of course, what is it?"

"I know Heather looks like she is doing well, but she is still really tired and fragile. I don't want her carrying things up and down these stairs, okay? You might have to take a few extra trips, but that's why you're here this summer, right?" Kevin pleads.

"Right. Of course," I promise. He seems so much more serious than he did this morning in the car, or a few minutes ago in the kitchen. I can't tell because of his sunglasses, but I think I see tears in his eyes.

"I'm just really worried about her being on her own this summer, and I think she's going to push herself too hard once I leave. On the one-hand, I think the time away will be great for her to relax, because she loves the beach so much, but on the other hand, I wish she were closer to home so I could be there to help," he confides in me.

This man that I've known for five hours is pouring his heart out to me about his sick wife, and I'm really not sure how I should respond. I thought I was here to take care of two pre-teen girls, and the excessive pay was because they were late finding a sitter; but now I'm wondering if Kevin is the one who decided on the rate to cover his guilt and try to ensure a substitute caregiver in his absence.

"I promise I'll do whatever I can to help. I'll check in with you during the week and let you know how everything is going," I hear myself saying; eager to please him and erase the concerned look from his face.

"That would be amazing," Kevin says, a smile of relief spreading across his face.

I adjust the bags on my shoulders and grimace as the heavy cooler digs into a new spot. "We should probably get down there, before they think we ate all the food," I joke, hoping he gets the message.

"Right, let's go," Kevin says, stepping aside and letting me go in front of him down the wooden stairs leading us directly to the private beach twenty feet below.

"Do you need a hand with that?" Heather calls out, as I make my way to the bottom of the stairs.

"No! I'm good!" I yell out, a little too firmly. Kevin is only a few steps behind me, and I want to make sure he knows that I'm handling the situation – it's too soon for me to mess up.

I walk the few steps over to the place where Heather and the girls have set up; although it doesn't look too appealing yet since Kevin has the chairs and umbrellas. It's more of a spot on the sand where Heather is standing, surrounded by all of the bags and towels that the girls have dropped before they ran into the water.

I try not to stare, but Heather's long blonde hair from earlier is nowhere to be found and she is sporting a blonde buzz-cut; similar to what my brother had when he was really little.

"Oh, the hair," Heather says, when she catches me looking. "The wig is just too hot down here in the sun. I was also a little worried it might blow away, and then what would I do?" she laughs, poking fun at herself.

"Oh, no. Um, I mean, I didn't..." I stumble, unable to find the right words.

"Megan, don't worry about it. You weren't expecting it, it's not a big deal. The girls are still getting used to it too, and they've had months! But I promise, this is a big improvement over the baldhead I've been sporting. It's finally starting to grow back, but I think I'm going to stick to the wig until it get's a little longer. Besides, it's a pretty great wig – nicer than my old hair used to be," she says, dramatically.

"It's beautiful," I say, still lacking the right words.

"Where do you want to sit, sweetie?" Kevin says, coming up behind Heather and putting his arms around her waist.

"Anywhere is fine with me. The tide is on its way out, so we can go a little closer to the water," Heather says.

"Okay Megan, let's grab the stuff, you can follow me. We'll make a second trip for the rest of it," Kevin says, and starts walking toward the ocean.

"I *can* help," Heather says, with a hint of annoyance.

"Don't worry about it, we've got it," Kevin says.

"Fine," Heather says, picking up her book and rolling her eyes.

"Isn't everything going to get wet?" I ask Kevin as he drops the chairs in the soft sand about five feet from the water.

"Nope. That's the beauty of the Bay and low tide. It's going to keep going out for the next few hours, in a little while you won't even recognize this beach. And then when you come back tomorrow morning at high tide, the water will be up to here," Kevin points to his waist," it's crazy.

"Wow," I say, thinking I'll have to see it to believe it.

A few minutes later, Kevin has constructed a fortress of shade, expertly arranging the umbrellas around the chairs to block the sun from every angle. I'm guessing it's going to take me a little longer than he did to set it up like this tomorrow, but I'm pretty sure I can figure it out.

Lunch is a blur. As quickly as Heather and I can unpack the cooler and hand out the food, Caitlin and Brooke have gobbled down their sandwiches, edamame and watermelon and are ready to go back into the water. I'm still unwrapping my hummus wrap, when Caitlin starts pleading with me. "Megan, please, please come in with us! You haven't been in yet, let's go find hermit crabs!" she begs.

"Um, sure," I reply, wrapping up my sandwich and putting it back in the cooler for later.

"I'll just stay here, if *you're* going to go," Brooke says.

"Let Megan finish her lunch," Kevin says to Caitlin. "I'll come in with you. I won't get to look for crabs tomorrow, and Megan has all summer," he says, giving me a friendly look.

"Yay!" Brooke says, clearly responding to her dad coming in with her, not to me being here all summer.

"I'll be there in a couple minutes," I promise Caitlin, not saying anything to Brooke.

The three of them head off toward the water, which is now at least twenty-five feet away from us and moving quickly, just as Kevin said it would.

"Don't worry about Brooke," Heather says, putting her hand on my arm. "She'll warm up soon," she promises.

"I'm sure she will," I say, not sure at all.

"I'm going to miss Kevin when he goes back tomorrow, but I promise you won't be stuck taking care of me. He's just being overprotective, but I feel great. Just being on the Cape makes me feel so much stronger. Of course I still want your help with the girls, but I think I'm going to be able to do a lot more this summer than I thought I could," Heather says, flashing me a conspiratorial grin.

"That's great," I respond, trying to match her smile. Oh my God, what have I gotten myself into!

Chapter 16 – Heather

The first few days with Kevin gone, were a little awkward. Or maybe that isn't quite the right word, but it felt a little weird having a stranger in the house. I know I was doing my best to make sure Megan felt comfortable and included, but I also wasn't used to having another person in the house twenty-four-hours a day, so I had trouble relaxing, even though that was the whole point of having her here.

I got up early the first two mornings to make a big breakfast for everyone, and then when Megan offered to clean up, I shooed her away and told her to go outside and play with Caitlin. But then as I was scrubbing the waffle iron, and watching them play Frisbee on the front lawn, I was annoyed that I had been left alone with the dishes.

I'm not sure that I'm thankful for Brooke's outburst at dinner last night, but I think it did finally get a lot out on the table and Megan lost her role as houseguest, and officially earned her stripes as babysitter, employee and superstar. It was hard to describe to Kevin on the phone, because I didn't want to own up to the parts where I was doing all of the work and admit that things hadn't gotten off to a great start, but if I could have told him, this part of the conversation would have been the best to recap.

Brooke: "Megan, why are you even here? You sit around all day and let my mother wait on you and you totally ignore me and play games with Caitlin. You're mean and no fun. You should just go home."

Me: "Brooke, please don't be rude. Megan, I'm so sorry, we're so happy you're here."

Megan: "Heather, please don't apologize. Actually Brooke brings up a point that I've wanted to mention, but didn't know how to say it. I really would like to help out more; I should be helping with meals and in the kitchen – and you definitely don't need to be taking care of me; I'm here so that you can take care of yourself and get better. But Brooke, as far as you and I are concerned - you know that I have been trying with you since the minute I got here. If you want to have a terrible attitude and ruin your own summer, that's fine, but I'm not going to let you get in the way of your mom's recovery. Caitlin and I are having a great time, and if you would stop being such a pain in the ass, you would realize that you could be having a great time too. Oh my God Heather, I shouldn't have said that, I'm sorry."

Me: "Please don't apologize. I think what you said was perfect. Brooke, you heard Megan. Starting tomorrow, Megan's in charge, got it? I'm going to sleep late and then go into town for the afternoon, maybe I'll go get a massage. But Megan seems to have it under control here, so if you have a problem with that, then you're going to be the one who suffers."

***

Now it's ten in the morning and I'm sitting outside of Eat Cake 4 Breakfast (my favorite coffee place on the Cape), enjoying a massive cinnamon roll and large latte. I still have some weight to put back on from everything I lost

125

during chemo – I'm not sure that daily pastries are exactly what my oncologist had in mind, but after months of nausea and vomiting, I have certainly earned it. Once my clothes are no longer loose, then I'll have to resume a more 'balanced' diet, but until then, I plan to eat a steady regime of carbs and more carbs.

Megan and the girls seemed to be off to a good start when I left them this morning. Megan was pouring bowls of cereal for all three of them and unloading the dishwasher, and they were already dressed in bathing suits, ready for the beach. I was going to suggest that they go for a bike ride, or try something different today, but it's Megan's first day on her own, so it's probably easiest if she stays close to home. It would be a stretch to say that Brooke was all-smiles when I left, but she was being polite to Megan, and she wasn't hiding in her room, so I'm going to call that a success.

"Are you using that chair?" a voice asks me, interrupting my thoughts.

I look up to see a man in a fitted bright yellow biking outfit and matching helmet, with his hand on the chair next to mine.

"No, I'm not using that one," I reply.

"Okay, great," he says, settling himself into the chair. I had expected him to move the chair over a little before sitting down, but it looks like that isn't going to happen.

The strange bike man takes a long sip from his iced coffee, and then unbuckles his helmet, revealing a head covered in matted down, sweaty jet black hair – but even with the sweat and the funny outfit, he's pretty cute, he's also at least ten years younger than I am, if not more.

"Have you been out on the trails today?" he asks me. Eat Cake 4 Breakfast happens to be right next door to a bike rental shop, which is also at one of the easy places to enter and exit the Cape Cod Rail Trail, a relatively flat bike trail that's over twenty miles long and goes through the middle of the Cape.

"No, just having some breakfast," I tell him, a little embarrassed of my gluttony in the face of his recent workout, but I'll get over it.

"It's a great day for a ride, perfect temperature," he says, draining the rest of his iced coffee in a few sips.

"I hadn't really thought about biking today," I tell him.

"What *are* you doing today?" he asks. "I mean, after you finish your breakfast?" he says, with a smile I wasn't expecting.

I'm sure he's just making conversation, but it feels a little bit like he's flirting. I can't imagine why he would be flirting with me – maybe it's been so long since that's happened that I don't even remember what it feels like. I catch a glimpse of my reflection in the storefront behind him, and am pleasantly surprised at what I see. My dirty-blonde hair (well, my wig) is pulled back in a bun on top of my head, but it looks chic with wispy pieces framing my oval face, instead of the messy birds-nest my real hair used to look like when I attempted a bun. It's only been a few days, but I can already see that I have a nice healthy glow on my face from the sun. It helps that I tan easily, and in comparison to the ghostly gray color I've had these past few months, any other shade would be an improvement! This morning I grabbed a gray tank top and black capri leggings off the chair in my bedroom; but looking at them now, I see my long lithe body in the reflection, not a scrawny cancer patient.

"I don't know, I hadn't made much of a plan past my giant cinnamon roll," I joke, choosing to embrace my breakfast choice.

"Have you been to Brewster before?" my new biker friend asks.

"I have, but it's been a long time," I reply.

"I'm partial to the bikes, but you could also go kayaking. They rent kayaks here too," he says, pointing to the bike store.

"I don't think I'm going to rent a kayak," I say, laughing at the idea, trying to imagine how that would even work.

"Maybe another day," he says.

"Maybe I *will* go for a bike ride," I say.

"There you go. Now you have a plan," he says, looking pleased.

I can't imagine what Kevin would say if he knew I was doing this. Actually I know what he would say – he would be furious! He would say that I'm not ready for this and I should go take a nap. But I don't feel tired – I'm so fucking sick of being tired!

"I'm going to see about a bike rental," I say to the stranger, "have a good day!"

"Enjoy your bike ride. Maybe we'll do that kayak trip another day," he says, and winks at me.

"Yeah, sure," I say laughing. I'm sure I'll never see him again, but I'm glad he gave me this idea, and if I'm being honest with myself, it was nice to feel like an attractive woman today, and not Kevin's frail wife, if only for a few minutes.

Chapter 17 – Sabrina

"What do you want to do on this beautiful Saturday?" Peter asks, stretching out lazily on the bed.

"I don't know. I hadn't really thought about it," I reply, which isn't exactly the truth. My plan is to go to a nine am Soul Cycle class, followed by a pedicure, and then hopefully a mimosa-filled brunch with Jessie, and an afternoon walk in the park with Danielle and Abby – I've really designed quite a nice Saturday for myself.

"This is the first weekend I haven't had to work in forever; I'm so happy that we get to spend it together," Peter gushes.

"I actually did have a couple of things I was going to do today," I confess, "but, I can try and move them around," I tell Peter.

"Sabrina, I feel like we haven't seen each other in ages. I've been looking forward to this weekend forever," Peter says, looking at me with his big green eyes.

"Yeah, me too," I say quickly, as I watch my perfectly laid out day shatter into pieces. I reach for my phone to cancel my Soul Cycle class and text Jessie and Danielle about my change of plans. I forgot that Peter was going to be home this weekend; I've gotten used to him being at the hospital almost every Saturday, and then sleeping all day Sunday, so I've become accustomed to planning my weekends without him. But now that I think about it, I do have a vague memory of discussions about this weekend – I think we even talked about going away, and then decided that it would be more fun to stay in the City for some reason.

"We could go to brunch at the Boat Basin? Walk along the Highline? Go to MoMa? Or we could do a picnic in Central Park?" Peter says, winking at me, trying to remind me of our first "real" date.

"Hmmm, any of those sound fine with me," I reply, trying to get excited about the day and trying not to look at my chipped toenail polish and wonder how Peter would react if I suggested we get our nails done together.

"We could go look at wedding places?" Peter says, propping himself up on his elbow and giving me an optimistic look.

"Wait, what do you mean?" I spit out, taken by surprise.

Peter finds this funny for some reason and just laughs as he gets out of bed, stretching his tanned, muscular body on his way into the shower. "I meant we could go look at places where we might want to have the wedding. That's something engaged couples typically do," he replies.

"Don't you need an appointment?" I ask, remembering hearing about Danielle's wedding and all of the ridiculous scheduling – she even needed an appointment to try on a dress.

"I have no idea," Peter calls back from the bathroom. "But we could still look at the lobbies of some places, even if we can't see the ballrooms, it would give us an idea of what we like. Several of the places are right around the Park, so maybe we do that, and then we could go for a walk, or have lunch, sound good?" Peter yells out from his steamy shower.

"What places are you thinking about?" I ask him, already knowing what he will say.

"I don't know – the Plaza, the Pierre, the Mandarin, the Peninsula – you know the typical places," Peter replies.

At least I can tell Molly that I was right; Peter is thinking of exactly the same type of wedding that his sister had. I'm not really upset about it, because I don't care that much. But ever since I talked to Molly, I've been thinking about the idea of an island wedding without all the pomp and circumstance, and although still a little scary, it seems manageable.

"You know that those places are only "typical" for your family," I say to Peter, trying to be humorous.

"Hey, that's not fair," he says, trying to look hurt, staring at me from his position in front of the sink, where he is now lathering up with shaving cream, with a towel secured dangerously low around his hips.

"You know I think your parents are great, I'm just saying that there *are* other places to get married," I challenge.

"Oh really? So are we actually going to have a conversation about the wedding?" Peter asks, his tone bordering between playful and sarcastic.

"We *just* got engaged," I retort.

"So what are these *other* places to which you refer?" Peter says with a smile. "I do know that there are other hotels in New York, but I just kind of assumed it would be one of those, it doesn't have to be – Sabrina, this is *our* wedding, we should get married wherever we decide," Peter says, lovingly.

"Do you mean that?" I ask him.

"Of course. There are all sorts of great event spaces and boutique hotels – remember that thing we went to last year at the Library? Maybe we could do something like that – we could rent out the Library, or one of the museums! It would be different, but I bet my parents would come around to that," Peter says, getting excited.

"What if we didn't do it in New York?" I ask, twisting the sheets around my hands absentmindedly.

"What do you mean? Where else would we do it?" Peter asks, confused.

"Maybe Hawaii? Or another island?" I ask cautiously.

"Oh," Peter says, pausing to digest this information. "Don't you think that would be too hard for everyone?" Peter asks.

"We don't need to invite a lot of people, we could only invite immediate family and a few close friends," I tell him.

"I don't know..." Peter says.

"Never mind," I say, cutting him off. "It's not a big deal."

"We can talk about it. I just always pictured a big black-tie wedding," he says, stepping back into the bedroom and casually dropping his towel on the bed as he heads over to the dresser to pick his clothes. I've seen it all too many times to count at this point, but his smooth olive skin and molded physique is still a distraction – it's hard to reconcile the manly man I'm looking at, with the guy telling me about the dream wedding he's envisioning.

"That's fine. It's not a big deal; a hotel is fine. Besides, I'm sure your parents would die at the idea of a small island wedding," I joke.

"Maybe if you could get us Richard Branson's island?" he retorts, with a grin.

"I'll see what I can do," I reply, smiling, happy to be done with the potential confrontation.

"So, should we go look at a few places today? Just one or two? Then we'll go get brunch. And maybe while we're up by the Park we should see if Danielle and Ted are free, that could be fun," Peter says.

"Sure, that sounds great, I'll text Danielle now," I say, feeling myself relax at the idea of a double date, and the chance of reclaiming my boozy brunch.

***

Fourteen hours later, Peter is sleeping soundly beside me after a long, action-packed day. It ended up being a lot more fun than I expected, and it was nice spending the entire day together after so many weeks of only seeing each other in one or two hour windows. Thankfully, only a small part of the day was wedding focused. After brunch at Norma's, we stopped by the Plaza and the Mandarin just to look around the common areas, and we poked our heads into the ballroom at the Mandarin. Peter said he felt like it would be repeating his sister's wedding, so he crossed off the Plaza, and he liked the Mandarin, but wants to keep looking. I know it is very "un-bridesy" of me, but I really think they are all pretty much the same.

Considering what I great day we had, I should be happy to curl up and go to sleep, like Peter already is, but I can't turn my brain off. I grab my phone from the gray oak nightstand, where it perpetually lives, even though every article I read (on my phone) tells me that I should not keep my phone in the bedroom. I scroll through a couple work emails and flag a few to respond to in the morning, then I open Facebook, which I knew I was going to do, even though I pretended that wasn't why I grabbed my phone.

In the darkness of our bedroom, the blue light glows brightly, displaying pictures of babies with food on their faces, political rants, vacation images and articles about things I could easily get sucked into just from the headline. But I quickly scroll through the distractions, no longer caring about the pretense of updates. When I don't see anything, I go directly to his page. Parker's last update is from two days ago; it's a picture of him and another guy on a sailboat somewhere near the Hamptons. There are a few likes and comments on the photo – I could just add a comment to the photo - that would be harmless, it would be something that a college friend would do, right? Before I can talk myself out of it, I write, "Which one of you is the captain?" and push send.

Ugh! Why did I write that? What does that even mean? Maybe he won't notice it. I don't read half of the comments I get on Facebook.

Just as I'm about to turn off my phone, so I can't do any more damage, I get an alert that flashes up from Facebook Messenger:

Parker Avery: Of course I'm the captain. But you knew that ☺

I try to calm the flutters in my stomach as I figure out what I should write back, or if I should write back, and if it's wrong to send a harmless message back to Parker, while I'm lying in bed with Peter...

Chapter 18 – Molly

I wish I had something else to wear today. Jeannie's already seen all of my new clothes, at least the ones that would be suitable for a "casual" meeting with Rick to go over his initial ideas for the living room. I throw on an old pair of jeans (with genuine holes, instead of the kind that cost $300 for a machine to make) and a black tank top, and hope that the look is edgy and not trashy.

Anna wanders into my bedroom clutching her stuffed dog. "Watch Sesame?" Anna asks, hopefully.

"Yes, sweetie, you can watch Sesame Street," I reply, and I delight in the shocked look on her face. She's so used to hearing "No," that she isn't quite sure how to react.

I still haven't made much progress on babysitters, because I've decided that I want an au pair, so I don't want to spend a lot of time looking for sitters. I called the local au pair lady that Jeannie recommended, but she won't meet with me without Derek, because she needs to interview the whole family, and I'm having trouble finding a time that works for him. If I'm being honest, I haven't mentioned it to him yet. I was hoping to get it all sorted out and then just tell him about it, but it doesn't seem like I can do it that way.

But for today, I have figured it out! I am going to put Anna in front of the TV before Jeannie and Rick get here. She'll have a snack and Sesame Street, and be occupied for the whole time. I know that I made snide remarks back in Boulder about people using the television as a babysitter, so I probably owe a few people an apology.

"Let's go sweetie," I say to Anna, intent on having her quiet and hidden away before Jeannie arrives.

"Okay Mama," Anna replies, beaming up at me, clearly on best behavior because of the recent TV news.

Anna and I wander slowly down the stairs into the makeshift playroom. The previous owners used this room as an office combined with a storage room, but I think it is technically the maid's room. It is a smallish bedroom right behind the kitchen and it has its own bathroom – for us it is the perfect playroom. Anna runs over to her little green chair with the pink A embroidered on the back and snuggles into the seat, hugging her dog securely to her chest. Although toys surround her, Anna's eyes are already glued to the 40-inch television that is mounted on the wall (blessedly left here by the people before us). I find Sesame Street on the DVR; Anna's face lights up and she begins singing along to the theme song within seconds. I hand her a sippy-cup full of milk and a bowl of goldfish and quickly make my escape.

It's 9:28, assuming Rick and Jeannie are on time; I should have almost the full hour with them without any interruptions from Anna. I mentally pat myself on the back for handling everything so well. On schedule, the doorbell chimes at exactly 9:30 (Jeannie is disturbingly prompt). I glance down again at my wanna-be-trendy outfit and have second thoughts, but know that it's too late to do anything about it now.

Jeannie and Rick are huddled together on the welcome mat When I open the door, laughing about something that I can only hope is not related to me or my house.

"Hi darling," Jeannie says, greeting me with a kiss on each cheek as she breezes past me on her way into the front hall. Two kisses are new for Jeannie, but I'm pretty sure I'm not supposed to mention that.

"Hi Molly, lovely to see you again," Rick says, following suit with two kisses of his own, but at least I was prepared for his. "I'm so excited to start our project together," he adds, looking around the foyer, almost like he's trying to remember where he is. The last time Rick was here, he was only here for about fifteen minutes, but he said that was all he needed to "get a feel for the transformation that was necessary."

"Me too," I reply eagerly. It's at that point that I notice all the books and binders Rick is carrying, so I add, "Do you want to go into the living room, so you can put those down?"

"That would be great. We just need to go over a teensy bit of paperwork first and then we can get started with the fun stuff," Rick tells me.

"Oh right, of course," I say. I had been dreading this part, since Rick never mentioned how much this was going to cost and I was too embarrassed to ask Jeannie. I'm not sure what I'm going to say to him now if it costs more than I can afford, but I can only hope that it isn't too pricey.

"Take a quick look at this," Rick says, handing me a few very expensive feeling pieces of paper clipped together with a gold paperclip.

"Just sign it, so we can start looking at all the books," Jeannie urges, from her spot on the gray microsuede sofa – I happen to like that couch, but I have a feeling it will be going away very shortly.

I glance at the first page, but really I'm only looking for the dollar amount. I scan all the paragraphs until I find it, and almost let out a sigh of relief - $7,500. Obviously it's not free, but I was worried it would be so much more expensive. Derek's making a lot of money now, and I can justify this expense to transform our home.

"Everything look good?" Rick asks, holding up a pen.

"Yes, it's fine," I say, grabbing the pen from him and skipping to the last page to hastily sign my name. "Let's start!" I say eagerly.

"If you could just grab a check," Rick says, uncomfortably, "then we won't have to worry about that later..."

"Oh right! Of course, I'm sorry, let me go grab my purse," I apologize, backing out of the room, feeling foolish.

In the kitchen, I can hear the faint sounds of Big Bird and Grover from the playroom. I wonder if I should peek my head in to check on Anna, but decide to leave well enough alone and get back to Rick and Jeannie, while Anna is still happily occupied.

Back in the living room, I hand Rick the check and he tucks it into the back pocket of his black jeans. Then he claps his hands twice, as if to get our attention, and announces, "Let's begin!"

"Okay!" Jeannie and I say in unison.

"We're going to start with this side of the living room today, and then maybe we can assess the foyer if there's time, but I'm not sure if that's possible," he says, looking at the shiny Cartier on his wrist. "Maybe we'll just do one area a day until we're done with the planning, sound good?" he asks.

"Um, alright," I answer feebly, thinking of all the Sesame Street Anna is going to be watching.

"I may not be able to make it every day, but I should be able to be here most mornings," Jeannie replies, consulting the calendar on her phone.

I don't know when Jeannie went from being the introduction to Rick, to a key member of my design team; but I'm not going to complain, since having her here means I have a friend to hang out with almost every day. I'm not sure if Jeannie's interest is due to her love for home renovation or if she really likes hanging out with me, but I'm not going to question it.

Rick continues, "for this room, we are going to begin by selecting the sofa, and then we will create the room around it. These books are just to give you some ideas, but let's start with this one," he says, placing a massive, glossy album in my lap. Jeannie quickly appears at my side, so she can flip pages with me, not wanting to miss a single glamour shot of a sectional or loveseat.

"That one's beautiful!" she exclaims, pointing at a gray overstuffed couch, that honestly doesn't look *that* different from the one Jeannie was just sitting on – I guess it's a little nicer, but I think it's kind of similar.

"Jeannie, you have a beautiful eye!" Rick praises her. "That would look spectacular in here. It is stunning in the gray silk. That style just started coming in silk," Rick adds.

I scan the page for a price, but the only thing I can find is "contact your dealer for pricing" written in fine print at the bottom of the page.

"What do you think of this one?" Rick asks me.

I want to ask him how much it costs, and I also want to ask if it's really that different from the couch I already have, but I know I would embarrass Jeannie if I asked either of those questions, so instead I hear myself say, "I love it!"

"That's fantastic. Now I don't want to make this decision yet, but I'm thinking grays and purples – how does that sound to you?" Rick asks, opening a book with pictures of chairs.

"That sounds perfect!" Jeannie says, clapping her manicured hands. "Right Molly?"

"Right," I answer, trying to remember if Derek hates purple or just really doesn't like it.

Chapter 19 – Megan

"Go get ready for the beach, while I clean up from breakfast," I tell the girls, accidentally brushing toast crumbs off the counter and onto the floor – oops. Luckily Heather is already gone for the morning, so she isn't here to see my poor kitchen skills; she seems to be sticking to this new routine of getting up and out of the house early.

"Okay!" Caitlin chirps, happily bringing her plate to the sink, then turning to skip to the stairs, still in her rainbow nightgown with messy braids hanging down her back.

"Isn't there anything else we can do?" Brooke complains. She is also still in her pajamas, but those consist of a Taylor Swift t-shirt and a striped pair of lounge pants, which appear to be three or four inches too short for her tall and lanky frame.

"You don't want to go to the beach?" I question.

"We've been doing the same thing, every single day. Why can't we do something else?" Brooke whines.

"Sure. We can do something else. What do you want to do?" I ask, slightly worried how Brooke will respond. She has definitely warmed to me over the last few days, but she is a little moody, and it's unclear what will set her off.

"I want to go to Chatham," Brooke says.

"Okay, um, sure. Let me text your mom and make sure she's okay with that," I reply.

"Why do you need to ask her? Where is she anyway?" Brooke asks.

"I don't know. But I think I should check with her, if we're going to leave Brewster," I tell Brooke. "Why don't you go get dressed, while I check with her," I suggest, hoping Brooke will leave the kitchen and not watch me the whole time.

When I grab my phone, I notice a text from Kevin that must have come in after I went to bed last night:

Kevin: How's it going? How's Heather doing? Has she been resting? Anything else to report?

He texted a few days ago, but I was able to write back honestly and say that we had been at the beach most of the day and Heather had relaxed in the house that afternoon. Now I'm not sure what to say! I don't know where Heather has been going in the morning, but I don't think he wants to hear that she disappears every day for four or five hours and then comes back and meets us at the beach or takes a nap and then plays a board game with the girls before we have dinner.

Kevin had an emergency at work and has to stay home for the weekend, instead of coming up here. The girls were pretty upset yesterday when Heather told them, but they seem to have recovered. I couldn't tell how Heather felt, she was pretty unemotional when she delivered the news; but she was up and out early this morning in a cute workout outfit.

I text Kevin back the most truthful reply I can manage:

Megan: Everything here is good! Sorry you can't come up for the weekend – the girls really miss you ☺

After I send it, I re-read my message and wonder if it's too personal. I barely know this guy, and he's my boss; I probably shouldn't be sending emojis and going off-topic.

Kevin: Glad to hear it – keep an eye on her and make sure she takes it easy! Tell the girls I miss them too!

Megan: Okay!

I guess he didn't read anything into it; and my vague reply seemed to do the trick, at least for now. I'm not sure I'm going to be able to keep this up, but Kevin will be up here next weekend and then hopefully he'll see how well Heather is feeling and he'll stop worrying about her.

That reminds me that I need to text Heather and ask if I can take the girls to Chatham. I've only driven to the General Store for a few groceries and twice to JT's for ice cream. Luckily I spent most of last summer driving Ryan's jeep around Rye, so I feel pretty comfortable driving – if any of my other Dalton friends had gotten this job, they would be hopeless! One negative about kids from Manhattan is that most of us don't learn to drive until college or sometimes later.

 I don't know if Heather is somewhere where she can quickly text me back, but for Brooke's sake, and mine, I'm hoping that she is.

Megan: Hi Heather! Would it be okay if I took the girls to Chatham this morning? Brooke really wants to go.

Immediately, a response appears on my screen.

Heather: Sure – sounds great – have fun!

Heather: There's cash in the top drawer of my dresser. Take money for lunch, shopping, etc.

Before I can ask how much, she writes again.

Heather: $200 should be good – give the girls some spending money. See you this afternoon!

Megan: Great, thanks!

Wow, that was easier than I could have imagined. I find myself looking forward to the day as well; it will be nice to change up our routine.

I scroll up at my older texts to make sure I didn't miss anything else from last night or earlier this morning, but there's nothing else there. Ryan did try to call a few days ago, but I was looking for hermit crabs with Caitlin, and by the time I tried to call him back, it went straight to voicemail. Since then, there have only been a handful of bland texts where he tells me how busy he is and wishes he has more time to call. I'm trying to be supportive and understand the extent of his hectic schedule, but I really don't get how he doesn't have time for a phone call or Face Time – I mean how busy can someone be?

***

Downtown Chatham looks exactly as Brooke described. The main street is a winding array of boutiques, t-shirt shops and restaurants, with happy, suntanned tourists wandering in and out of the stores enjoying a beautiful morning away from the real world. Immediately, I realize the challenge that I'm going to face today, as Brooke begs me to walk down to the Lighthouse to see if any of her friends are hanging out there and Caitlin wants to go the other way to Chatham Penny Candy to start spending her money. Since it isn't even eleven o'clock, I tell Caitlin that it is too early for candy, and she begrudgingly agrees to walk down toward the Lighthouse, if I promise we can go to the candy store later.

I didn't realize that the Lighthouse was essentially the beach, but I figure that out as we round the corner on Main Street and the waters of Chatham Harbor open up before us. Brooke takes off running down the sidewalk and embraces two girls at the top of the steps leading to Lighthouse Beach. I can't imagine that it is a coincidence that these girls just happen to be here at the same time we are; I don't know why she didn't just tell me she wanted to come here to meet her friends – did she think I wouldn't have taken her? Oh crap, unless she isn't supposed to be hanging out with these girls – I can't deal with any more secrets with this family.

"Hey Brooke, are these your friends?" I say, stating the obvious, when Caitlin and I catch up to her.

"Um, yeah. We were going to try and run into each other. Is it okay if we hang out for a little bit?" Brooke asks sweetly.

"Sure. But we didn't bring suits or towels," I say, alluding to her friends in their rather small bikinis.

"I threw mine on, under my clothes," Brooke says, taking off her t-shirt to reveal an equally small bikini that I have not seen her wear on the beach in Brewster.

"You could have told *us*," I say, feeling annoyed.

"Sorry," she says sheepishly.

"That's okay," Caitlin says, definitely being the bigger person. "I can still play in the sand in my clothes. C'mon Megan, let's go make sand castles!" she says, tugging my arm in the direction of the stairs.

"We'll stay for an hour," I say to Brooke, as she follows us down the stairs, already ignoring me and laughing with her friends.

Luckily, it's not that crowded yet, and it's not too hot today. It would have been nice to be in a swimsuit, but it's not *that* big of a deal to sit here in shorts and a tank top. It actually gives me an excuse not to go in the water. I put my foot in and the water feels about twenty degrees colder than the water over in the Bay near our beach. Maybe I should be thankful that Brooke didn't tell me to wear a suit – I know Caitlin wouldn't mind the cold, but I'm perfectly happy on land.

Just as I'm using my hands to shovel out sand for the castle's moat, I hear a deep voice say, "would you like a shovel for that?"

I turn around and shield my eyes with my right hand to block the sun, so I can see where the voice is coming from, and I see a really hot, tall, dark-skinned guy, probably about my age or a little older, in light blue board shorts, holding a yellow plastic shovel.

"Sure," I answer.

"Here you go," he hands me the shovel, and then takes a seat next to me.

"Do you just go around handing out beach toys to strangers?" I ask him playfully. Before Ryan, an interaction like this would have made me too nervous to speak; but now that I have a boyfriend, I don't get anxious around hot guys the way that I used to, because I don't think of them like *that*. I mean it's almost like a girl is sitting down next to me, I don't even notice what he looks like (okay, I'm not blind or dead, I can't help but notice that he is freaking gorgeous, but that's just because I'm human, it doesn't mean anything.)

"I'm very judicious about handing out my shovels," he replies, smiling, revealing beautiful white teeth.

"So, how am I so lucky?" I ask, matching his flirtatious tone, without trying.

"You're making a huge mess of that moat without one, so it was the least I could do before you ruined your sister's castle any further," he deadpans.

"It's not that bad," I say, looking at the moat, and then re-evaluating. "Okay, maybe it's pretty bad. But she isn't my sister. I'm her babysitter, so she'll probably forgive me," I suggest.

The hot stranger doesn't seem to have a response to this, and it's at this point that I realize that I don't see Caitlin anywhere. She was right next to me when he sat down; but now she is gone and a quick scan of the area provides no results.

"Shit!" I exclaim, standing up, and looking furiously to the right and the left, craning my neck, like this will help me find her.

"What's wrong?" he says.

"I can't find Caitlin!" I tell him, starting to panic.

"Is that the girl you're babysitting?" he asks, calmly, but with concern.

"Yes!" I say, my voice laced with fear.

"Is that her?" he asks, pointing to a group of girls sitting about twenty feet to our left.

"Oh my God, yes, that's her!" I say, my heartbeat still racing. "How did I miss her?" I ask him, and myself.

"She was wearing a sweatshirt before, and it looks like she took it off," he says, pointing to the purple object at my feet. "I think you were focused on that," he says.

"How did *you* possibly find her," I ask, both amazed and slightly annoyed.

"My little brother used to run away all the time, so I've got plenty of practice," he says.

"Thank you so much, I really appreciate it. I don't know what I would have done..." I say, my voice trailing off.

"You would have found her thirty seconds after I did," he says.

"I'm Megan, by the way," I say, offering my hand for him to shake, which feels oddly formal.

"I'm Brad," he says, reaching out to grab my hand and although his hand is almost twice the size of mine, he shakes it with just the right amount of pressure, not trying to crush me like some guys, and not too loose like some men who think they'll break a girls' hand if they actually shake it – clearly he's had good handshake training.

"Have you been to Chatham before?" I ask, trying to think of something to say.

"We come every year. You?" he asks.

"This is my first time," I reply.

"A Chatham virgin, hmmm," he says, raising his eyebrows as he looks at me.

I can feel the blush spread across my cheeks and my chest and I can only hope that Brad doesn't notice his effect on me, but that seems unlikely.

"This is my first summer in Cape Cod," I say, hoping to move the conversation along, but realizing that I have opened the door to another virgin comment.

"Where are you staying?" Brad asks, mercifully letting the comment go.

"We're in Brewster," I answer.

"How do you like it so far?" he asks.

"It's only been about a week, but I like it," I reply.

"How much longer are you staying?" he asks.

"We're here until the end of August," I tell him, wondering why I'm sharing all of this with a complete stranger.

"Then you'll definitely have to come back to Chatham," he says, flashing his smile again.

"Will I?" I ask, trying hard not to flirt, but failing miserably.

"In my humble opinion, Chatham is the best place on the Cape, or at least one of the best places, and you can't just come to Lighthouse Beach and say you've seen all there is to see. You need a native to show you around," he claims.

"A native? So you're from here?" I question.

"I'm from Boston, but I do have a house here, and I've been coming here since the summer I was born," he says.

"And when was that?" I ask.

"Is that another way of asking how old I am?" he says.

"Maybe," I reply.

"I'm eighteen. Graduated from high school last month. You?" he asks.

"I'm seventeen. I'll be a senior this fall," I say, feeling young and wishing I could also say I was "off to college in the fall."

"Can we go get candy now? Please? We've been here forever!" Caitlin complains, appearing at my side out of nowhere.

"Don't you want to finish our sandcastle?" I ask hopefully, not quite ready to leave.

"Not really. It kind of sucks anyway," she says, kicking it with her barefoot.

Brad tries to stifle a laugh, but it still comes out, and then I join him, since Caitlin is just telling the truth.

"Okay, let's go find Brooke and we'll go get candy and then we'll get lunch," I tell her.

"Let's go," Caitlin whines, pulling my arm and dragging me in Brooke's direction – Caitlin is going to pull my arm out of the socket at this rate.

"Bye," I say to Brad, as I half-stumble, half run across the beach.

"Bye, Megan," Brad calls out.

I try to ignore the pit in my stomach as I leave the beach. I have a boyfriend, so I shouldn't care about some stranger that I talked to for twenty minutes. Besides, he isn't even in the same town, it's not like it would even make sense to try to be friends with him this summer. I take out my phone to check for any texts or voicemails from Ryan, but of course, there's nothing there.

Chapter 20 – Heather

I pull into the parking lot of the bike shop and feel a mixture of guilt and excitement when I see the black Land Cruiser parked out front. This is my sixth bike ride in the past eight days, but only the second time I've been here at the same time as Jasper (since our first encounter). Somehow I wasn't surprised when he told me his name was Jasper; a fact I learned a few days ago while enjoying a well-earned iced coffee after my ride.

"You can't get enough, can you?" Jasper jokes, as I approach the front porch of the bike rental shop.

Jasper has clearly just finished his bike ride; he is walking his bike back to his truck, his face and forearms glistening with sweat.

"It's nice to exercise outside," I say, trying to act like this much exercise is normal for me, as well as hide my disappointment that he is leaving just as I arrive.

"Mind if I join you?" he asks.

"Didn't you just finish?" I ask, surprised.

"It wasn't that long of a ride," he says modestly, "I could go out again," Jasper says with a grin.

"Sure, I'd love the company, let me just get my bike," I tell him, walking toward the shop.

"Do you rent every time?" Jasper asks.

"Um, yeah, it's just easier," I explain.

"Doesn't that get expensive?" he inquires.

If only he knew that this was my sixth bike rental in barely a week, and not just the third time he's seen me rent, he would know just how expensive it is!

"I'm making sure I like it before I buy something," I lie.

"You know, I think I have an extra bike back at my house if you want to borrow it?" he offers.

"That's so nice of you, but then I'd have to get a bike rack, and that feels like such a commitment," I joke.

"Let me know if you change your mind," he says, clearly thinking I'm crazy. I *am* crazy, but not for the reasons he thinks. It would definitely make a lot more financial sense to buy a bike, but how would I explain that to Megan and the girls, and Kevin!

"I'll wait over there," Jasper says, pointing to the side of the building near the trail. "Come out when you have your bike," he says kindly.

I exit the shop feeling a little foolish in my helmet, but secure in the knowledge that my wig is firmly in place underneath it.

"You ready?" Jasper asks, perched on his bike seat, with one foot already on the pedal, his quads straining against his bike shorts.

"Ready to go," I reply. As I fall in line behind him on the hill leading down to the trail, I reconsider the wisdom in this decision. Other than being able to stare at Jasper's butt for the length of our ride, it's not like we're going to be able to talk; and the chances of me being able to keep up with him are slim to none.

***

An hour and a half later, my fears have been put to rest as we ride our bikes up the exit path in Brewster. I'm sure Jasper was just being nice, but he rode at a very manageable pace the whole time, without making it obvious how little work he was doing. We didn't talk a lot, given the single file nature of the bike trail, but we exchanged some witty banter and then rode the rest of the way in companionable silence.

"I'll grab us coffees while you return your bike," Jasper says, rolling his super high-tech bike over to strap on the back of his truck.

"That would be great," I call back, quickly looking at my watch to see how long I've been gone – I promised the girls I would take them to get ice cream this afternoon, but I should have at least another half an hour before I have to go.

"I got you an iced coffee, I hope that's okay," Jasper says, as I slide onto the metal rocking chair. "It looked like you had whole milk the other day, so that's what I got."

"Wow, thanks. That's pretty observant of you," I remark, wondering how it is that Jasper knew to get whole milk, when half of the time Kevin will get me skim or half and half.

"Do you live out here, or are you just visiting?" I ask, trying to figure out the answer to the question that's been bugging me all week.

"I come here every summer. I live in Manhattan, but I'm pretty lucky that I can work from anywhere, so I come up here from Memorial Day to Labor Day. I've been doing it for the last ten years," Jasper says, matter-o-factly.

"What kind of work do you do that you can work from anywhere?" I ask, fascinated by this type of mobility. I can't imagine either Kevin or I away from our office for three months (except under my present circumstances).

"I'm a writer," Jasper says, somewhat modestly.

"What do you write?" I ask, "Would I have read anything you've written?"

"I write YA books," he says, with a hint of bashfulness.

"My daughter reads a ton of those!" I say excitedly, forgetting that until now he didn't know I had kids or a husband. I guess he still doesn't know I have a husband; my rings are too big after all the weight I lost during chemo, so I have 'single hands.'

"Has she read anything by Erika Swartz?" he asks.

"Yes, she has. I think she's read a few of her books," I tell him, trying to remember all the titles and authors from the bookshelves in Brooke's room.

"That's me," Jasper says, pointing to himself with his free hand.

"What?" I ask, trying to make the connection.

"I write under a pen name. I found that I had more success with agents, and then with readers of YA, as a female author, so I just stuck with it. Besides, then I don't have to wear a disguise to avoid the paparazzi," he jokes.

"Wait, really?" I start to ask, confused.

"No, I'm kidding," he laughs. "It's not like authors have a big problem with that anyway. Maybe if you're JK Rowling, but other than that..."

"I can't wait to tell my daughter that I met you, she's going to think it's so cool! Oh, can I tell her that you're a man?" I ask.

"Sure, it's fine. It's just a pen name, not a secret identity," Jasper laughs. "How old is she?" Jasper questions.

"I have two daughters. Brooke is eleven – almost twelve, as she reminds me every day. And Caitlin is seven," I tell him, happy to have this 'secret' revealed.

"So who's with them when you are doing all of your biking?" Jasper asks, playfully.

"I brought a babysitter with me for the summer; she's a senior in high school, her name is Megan. It gives me a little more flexibility," I tell him. I take a sip of my creamy iced coffee and think about the answer I gave Jasper. He didn't ask about a husband, or significant other, and I *did* give a completely truthful answer; but I know if Kevin were in my shoes and did the same thing, I wouldn't be happy.

"That's gotta be a pretty great babysitting job - free trip to the Cape for the whole summer? You must really like Megan," Jasper notes.

"I do. I'm just getting to know her, but she seems great." I can tell by the look on Jasper's face, that he is incredibly confused. "It's a long story, but I waited too long to find someone. Luckily, a friend of mine found Megan for me, so it all worked out," I tell him, leaving out all the details.

"That's great. Now that I know you have all this free time, we are definitely going to go kayaking," Jasper says.

"I don't know..." I answer.

"Friday. We're going," he says definitively.

"Um, okay, sure," I reply, thinking this is probably the part when I tell him that I have a husband.

"Do you want me to pick you up?" Jasper asks, casually.

"No, I'll drive, just tell me where to meet you and I'll meet you there," I tell him, trying to figure out what I've signed up for.

"Sounds good, let's meet at nine at Chatham Kayak," Jasper instructs.

"Okay, I'll be there," I say, taking the last swallow of my coffee, and standing up to signal my departure. "I have to get home, but thanks for the ride and the coffee," I tell him.

"My pleasure. Enjoy the rest of your afternoon. I'll see you in the morning," Jasper calls out, "Don't forget your bathing suit!"

***

It's Saturday morning and Brooke and Caitlin have been staring out the family room window all morning waiting for Kevin to arrive. I told him that I could come get him at the airport, but he thought it would be easier this way. Or as he said, "you should rest up for the weekend, you wouldn't want to get too tired driving all the way to Hyannis." Hopefully when he sees me this weekend, he'll realize how well I'm doing, and he can stop being so overprotective.

"He's here!" Caitlin screams, hearing his taxi pull into the shell-lined driveway.

Before I can acknowledge the comment, both girls have run out the side door and are less-than-patiently waiting for him to grab his bags from the trunk. It's been a long time since Kevin and I have been apart for eleven days, especially since I got sick, but I think it's been good for both of us to have a little space. It took me forever to fall asleep last night, as I lay in bed wondering if it would be awkward to see him again, and how to tell him about my new hobbies, but relief washes over me as I watch him sling his leather duffel bag over his shoulder and head toward the house – he's my husband of sixteen years, everything's going to be fine.

"Daddy, let's go swimming," Caitlin says, pulling Kevin by the arm, as she practically drags him inside.

"No, he said he was going to show me something on his iPad," Brooke protests, pulling on his other arm, as if Kevin were the wishbone.

"Girls, give me just a minute to say hi to your mom," Kevin laughs, pretending to be a little annoyed, but loving the attention.

"Hey there," Kevin says, shaking himself free of our daughters and walking over to where I am perched on the white wooden stool in the kitchen.

"Hey, yourself," I say, standing up to give him a kiss, and finding a thin layer of stubble above his top lip.

"You look really tan," he comments.

"I know, right?" I reply, thinking the same thing as I was getting ready this morning – how nice and healthy my tan looks against my honey-blonde wig.

"I'm just worried you aren't using enough sunscreen," Kevin says, definitely not the comment I hoped he would make.

"I promise I'm using sunscreen. I think we just all got used to how ghostly I looked, so you forgot what I look like with some sun," I say, trying to lighten the mood.

"Just be careful," he warns.

"What do you want to do today?" I ask, changing the subject.

"I thought we were going to the beach?" he asks, confused.

"Right, of course. I just meant if there was anything else you wanted to do, since you haven't been here," I say, trying to tread lightly.

"I'd love a lobster roll," he says. "And obviously ice cream."

"Obviously," I laugh.

"I was thinking I might go for a bike ride. Maybe see if Caitlin or Brooke want to come with me," he says, looking over toward the toile-covered couch where the girls are already both absorbed in their iPads, the excitement of Kevin's arrival a distant memory.

"A bike ride would be great. I'd love to do that," I say, silently thanking Kevin for making this so easy for me.

"Oh Heather, you couldn't possibly go on a bike ride, that would be way too much exertion for you," Kevin says sympathetically.

"I'm really feeling pretty good. I think it would be good for me. I've been getting a lot of rest and some exercise and I think I'm up for it," I challenge him.

"You know what the doctor said. You're supposed to be resting. Don't you remember what she said? It's just not safe," he says, his tone a mix of concern and warning.

"Doctors don't know everything," I say, mostly under my breath.

"Heather, she saved your life, I think she knows what she's talking about," Kevin says, signaling the end of the conversation.

"Who's ready to go to the beach?" Kevin yells. "Last one dressed is a rotten egg," he says, grabbing his bag and running up the stairs.

The girls try to push each other out of the way to beat him up the stairs and I can hear happy screams and laughter as they compete to get dressed. Even Brooke is in on the childish competition, her roller-coaster tween mood on a high today. I trudge up the stairs to join them, but my spirits are certainly much lower than they were a few minutes ago, all thoughts of telling Kevin about my biking and kayaking squashed before they could begin. The only thing that brightens my mood is the thought of paddle boarding with Jasper on Tuesday morning – kayaking was so much fun, I can't wait to see what our next outing brings.

Chapter 21 – Sabrina

I feel terrible for canceling lunch with Molly today, especially since my afternoon appointment just got rescheduled, but it would have been too last minute for her to have gotten the train into the City anyway. I feel a little guilty that I'm sneaking in a coffee with Danielle in my newfound free hour, but not *that* guilty.

"I can't believe you got a table," Danielle says, sliding into her chair with an iced decaf latte. She looks adorable in a navy and white short sleeve maternity dress, highlighting her tiny bump.

"It wasn't that crowded fifteen minutes ago. Must be the mid-afternoon coffee rush," I comment, looking around the packed Midtown Starbucks and the line that now extends out the door.

"Lucky us," Danielle remarks, placing her phone face up on the table so she doesn't miss anything while she is away from the office.

"Have you heard from Megan this week?" I ask, curious how she is doing with her summer job, especially since I feel responsible for her getting the job – for better or worse.

"Actually, she called last night and we talked for a while. It was a nice change from all of the one-line texts," Danielle remarks.

"So, is everything still going well?" I ask anxiously,

"She's having a really good time. She loves the girls and she really likes Heather. She said the dad seems oddly over-protective of Heather, but it's not that big of a deal. He's only there on the weekends, and that's when she has most of her time off," Danielle says, sipping her latte and glancing at her watch to check the time.

"That's great! I'm so glad it worked out," I reply, relieved that my matchmaking was successful.

"Yes, that was so great of you to connect her with Heather," Danielle adds. "The only thing that worries me is that she seems really upset about Ryan."

"Because he's in London?" I ask.

"I think it would be okay if they were talking, but she says she has only talked to him a couple times since she's been there, and they were really short conversations, and he barely texts her," Danielle tells me.

"Oh, that sucks," I say. "Long distance can be hard. But they're young. Maybe it will be good for her if he's being such a jerk – she can move on without feeling bad about it."

"I don't think that's what's happening at all," Danielle says, clearly annoyed with my response. "Ryan is a great guy – I wouldn't want them to break up. And I don't think he's being a jerk, I just think he's having a hard time with the new job and the time zones. I know it is hard for Megan, but it's only until the end of August. I tried to get her to see his side of it, and I think she felt a little better," Danielle says.

I know I am treading in dangerous waters, but I decide to dive in. "Why are you defending him? They've been together a long time, if he can't figure out how to keep in touch with his girlfriend over the summer, then I'm guessing he's found someone else. I know we all love Ryan, but maybe he isn't perfect. Megan is young and away for the summer, she should use the time to explore her options," I tell Danielle, worried I've said too much.

"He would never cheat on her!" Danielle says defensively – her sensitivity to infidelity coming through. "And just because they are having a bit of a tough time, doesn't mean they should break up. It's hard to be in a relationship, it takes a lot of work, but you don't throw it away just because it gets a little challenging," Danielle says.

"Are we still talking about Megan? Or is there something you want to say to me?" I boldly ask Danielle. Although she is my best friend, there are certain areas where we have always had trouble communicating, and we have a tendency to fight like sisters.

"I *was* talking about Megan," Danielle says cautiously, "But I'd be lying if I said I wasn't a little concerned about you as well," she admits.

"Peter and I are fine," I reply quickly.

"Okay, I'm glad to hear it. You just don't seem very excited about the wedding. And when we were all together this weekend, you just seemed a little *off,*" Danielle says.

"I promise, everything is fine. I'm just not into weddings the way most people are. Peter wants a big fancy wedding and that's fine. In fact, I was thinking I could let his mom plan the whole thing and I can show up on the big day," I tell her.

"You don't *really* want that, do you?" Danielle asks, taking another look at her watch and then picking up her phone to check something.

"Do you have to go?" I ask, realizing that I should probably also get back to work.

"Yeah, I should probably get back," she says, putting her phone back in her bag and taking the last sip of her latte.

"Me too," I reply.

As we walk outside, the sun practically blinds me as I search around in my bag for my sunglasses (brand new from Prada, a little gift to myself). Although I love the summer, I could do without ninety-five degree days when I'm in a suit; but I'll take it over the misery of winter any day.

"Seriously Breen, do you really want your future mother-in-law planning your wedding?" Danielle asks, unwilling to drop the topic.

"I don't know - probably not. But it might make the whole thing so much easier. Then she'll get the wedding she wants for Peter and I won't have to do anything," I say, vocalizing what I've been thinking about since the weekend.

"Be careful what you wish for," Danielle warns.

"I know," I reply.

"Thanks for meeting me on such short notice," I say to her as I pull her in and give her a hug, feeling the hard protrusion of her little belly against my own.

"Of course," she says, giving me a head-tilt that conveys too much concern for my comfort.

"By the way, did you ever hear from that guy Parker again?" Danielle asks, apparently remembering that I told her he had called.

"I don't think so. Maybe he tried to call me again, but I'd have to check," I say casually, hoping the sunglasses conceal my big fat lie. I don't like lying to Danielle, but especially after the lecture I just received, I know she would never understand.

***

Thanks to an insane afternoon at the office after my coffee with Danielle, I'm able to resist checking my Facebook account for the rest of the day. I barely had time to wonder if Parker replied to my message from last night, although it's possible I thought about it a *few* times.

After being home for the last several nights, Peter is at the hospital working the night shift and I think he said he has to be there all day tomorrow, but I can't quite remember what he told me this morning – I was running late after my Pilates class and barely had time to shower.

At 8:30, I'm the last one in the office, so I carelessly open Facebook on my computer, and hold my breath as I wait to see if Parker replied. I'm more excited than I should be to see his return message waiting for me:

PA: Let's get a drink sometime…

Before I can think better of it, I write back. It says that he's online, but I'm sure he won't reply right away.

SM: How about tonight?

Instantly, I see the dots blinking, indicating that Parker is typing. I drum my fingers on my desk and wait, unsure how he will reply.

PA: Sounds good to me. Where do you want to go?

Oh crap, this is really happening. It's just a drink, but I have the same butterflies I used to have when Parker would walk into the dining hall – I feel nineteen again.

SM: There's a wine bar close to my office on 51st – Aldo Sohm – meet there at 9?

I definitely would not have chosen this outfit today if I thought there was any chance I was going to meet up with Parker tonight. It happens to be one of my favorite suits, a white Tahari pantsuit paired with a black silk camisole, but it isn't quite what I pictured wearing if I saw Parker again. Before I can spend more time fantasizing about the perfect outfit to make him realize I look even better now than I did in college, he writes back.

PA: I'll be there.

And with that, it's done – I'm having drinks with Parker tonight, just the two of us. I know that my recent fascination needs to come to an end, but I want to see for one night what it would be like if Parker didn't dump me, and then I'll be done with it.

***

Parker is waiting for me at the bar when I stroll in at 9:15. Although it's close to my office, I decided it would be better to kill time going over emails at my desk than getting here early and looking lonely with my glass of wine when he walked in.

"You look stunning," Parker says, as I walk up to the empty seat beside him.

"You don't look so bad yourself," I reply, which is truly an understatement. He is wearing a light green button down and jeans; I assumed he would come straight from work, but he looks a little casual for any desk job. Although, I honestly don't know where he works, so maybe this *is* what he wears to the office.

"What are you drinking?" he asks, pointing at the wine list.

"I'd love a glass of Shiraz," I reply. I take the opportunity before sitting down to take my jacket off and place it on the stool next to me; if I have to be in a suit, I might as well show off my arms, so he knows what he's missing. I cross my legs in my seat and position my left hand underneath my thigh as I try to get comfortable – it really doesn't look as awkward as I thought it might. I rationalize that I'm still wearing the ring, I just don't want that to be the focus of our conversation, and besides, I want another hour or two to keep playing this out.

"Isn't it crazy how life works," Parker begins. "Who would have thought that we would be sitting here together after all this time?"

Feeling emboldened, I reply, "it's not really that crazy. We were together for three years. I would argue it's crazy that we *haven't* seen each other in ten years, considering our history."

"Touché," Parker replies, holding up his glass and toasting me, before taking a drink.

I return the gesture and wait to see if he has anything else to offer. There are so many things I have thought about saying to him over the years, but now that we are here together, I don't know where to start.

"I should have gotten in touch sooner. Hell, I should never have left you in the first place, I regret that every day, but I can't change anything about the past," Parker admits, staring at me with his bright blue eyes.

I can't believe he just said that. I have been waiting to hear that since the day he left me. I was hoping over the course of the evening he might offer something of an apology, or seem a little jealous, but never in my wildest dreams did I imagine he would actually say that. I know he deserves a response, but what am I supposed to say to that?

"Everything works out for the best," I manage to say.

"Did it?" he asks, refusing to take his eyes off of me.

"You're obviously doing well," I say to him, although I don't know what I'm basing that on, other than a few great Facebook photos. "And I couldn't be better," I tell him, giving him my best smile.

"Then I'm glad to hear it. I want you to be happy Sabrina," he says earnestly.

"I am," I say, my voice wavering. Without thinking, I reach for my glass with my left hand this time, and notice a look of surprise on Parker's face as the light catches off the large stone.

"I didn't realize you were engaged. So who's the lucky guy?" he asks.

"Oh, um, yeah, I'm engaged," I say awkwardly, the way some people might say, "Oh, this rash isn't that bad."

"Congratulations," he says, offering his glass again, this time for a proper toast.

"Thanks. So what about you?" I ask, wishing I had been able to prolong the discovery a little longer, but resigned to this new reality.

"Nope. I'm still single. There was one girl out in California that I dated for a couple years, but that's pretty much it for anything serious," he admits.

I try not to think about all of the 'non-serious' women there have probably been in his life – hard to imagine he has a lot of lonely nights. "So no one in New York?" I inquire.

"Only you," he says, his eyes shining.

"Ha-ha," I reply.

"I'm serious. I moved back to New York for work, but I'd be lying if I didn't say that I hoped to find you here," he tells me. "I've gone to the last few alumni events hoping to see you, and my hard work finally paid off," he smiles.

The butterflies in my stomach are on full alert at this point; thankfully we haven't eaten anything, because I'm pretty sure I would throw up.

"Why didn't you call me? Or email me? Or something? If you've been thinking about me all this time, why didn't you say anything?" I ask, trying to make sense of it all.

"Sometimes it takes a while to figure out what you want. But now that I have, here I am," he says with certainty.

"But I'm engaged," I reply helplessly.

"So I see. And if you're really happy, then that's all I want for you, and I'll leave you alone," he tells me.

"We can still be friends," I say, realizing how lame that line actually sounds.

"I don't know if I can do it. I'm not sure I can just sit by and watch you with some other guy. I know it's completely unfair, but I don't think I can do it," he says sadly.

Before I realize what's happening, Parker gives me a kiss on the cheek, whispers goodbye in my ear and is on his way out the door. I can't believe he left me again! It's different this time, but it doesn't feel that way – how did I let this happen? I replay the events of the last twenty minutes over and over in my head and wish I had them recorded so I could listen to him saying what a huge mistake he made – or maybe I'm the one making the mistake...

Chapter 22 – Molly

I'm not going to try and read anything into it, but I'm starting to wonder if it's something about me. First, Sabrina cancelled lunch a few days ago, then Rick had to cancel our visit to the Persian rug store, and now Jeannie just called to cancel our coffee date this morning. I'm sure it's just a coincidence, but it's definitely not good for my ego.

The day stretches out in front of me. It's just Anna and me for the whole day, with nothing to break up the eleven hours until her bedtime. I don't remember feeling like this in Boulder when I had the rare opportunity to spend a whole day at home with her, but maybe that's because it didn't happen very often – there was work, friends, and play dates, and of course Derek was around a lot more.

"Mama, wanna watch Sesame," Anna says, tugging on the hem of my shorts, as if she is also bored of me.

"It's too early for TV, honey," I try to explain. Although I can understand that she might have a difficult time appreciating this, since watching multiple episodes of Sesame Street in the morning has become a regular part of her routine, while I am busy with Jeannie, or Rick, or anything else.

Anna's face scrunches up, and I can see the tears starting to well up in her eyes, she is seconds away from a full-blown meltdown.

"Okay, sweetie, let's watch a few minutes of Sesame, while Mommy tries to figure out what we are going to do," I tell her. Anna only hears the part where I tell her she has won the TV battle, and she runs into the playroom to get settled on her special chair. I wish I hadn't caved so quickly, but I couldn't bear a tantrum. I'll sit in here with her while she watches (bonding time), and I'll do a little searching on my phone to find a good activity for us today.

After forty-five minutes of searching the Mommy Poppins website, along with multiple other Westchester and Connecticut kid and family sites, I determine that Anna is either too young or old for every activity, or that all the great activities are happening on other days.

"More Sesame?" Anna asks hopefully, after the credits begin to roll at the end of the first show.

How is it possibly over so soon? All right, I can figure this out.

"Anna, what should we do together?" I ask her.

"Sesame!" she answers effusively, her strawberry-blonde ponytails bobbing along with her head.

"What about going to the park?" I ask her, unable to come up with anything else.

"Okay. Let's go park. I watch more Sesame later," she says confidently – I wish she wasn't right, but we both know she is.

***

Bruce Park is a little emptier than it was the last time we were here. Jeannie mentioned that things start to empty out in July and everything is totally dead in August because everyone is on Nantucket, or the Vineyard, or the Hamptons, or sailing their yachts somewhere. I know we won't be going on vacation this summer since Derek is still getting settled at work, but listening to Jeannie talk about her fabulous plans makes me wish we could get away, even if only for a long weekend.

I look around to see if I notice any familiar faces, but realize how ridiculous that is, since I only know six people in the tri-state area. And if I did see Jeannie here, it would mean she was lying about having a doctors' appointment and not being able to meet for coffee, so I should be glad she isn't here. Anna has run off toward the sandbox, not usually my favorite park activity, but today I'm happy to sit on the side of the sand and watch her play (I have to remember to shake out her shoes before we get in the car).

A young woman sits down a couple feet away from me, from the looks of it, she's an au pair or a babysitter – even with all the 'work' some ladies seem to have done around here, she still looks too young to be a mom.

"She's adorable," the woman says, nodding toward Anna.

"Oh, thanks," I reply. "She just turned three," I tell her, even though she didn't ask.

"Is she your only child?" the woman inquires.

"Yes, she is. For now," I add, "we'll probably start thinking about having another one soon," I tell this complete stranger, although she didn't ask and I'm sure she doesn't care.

"Do you live around here?" she asks.

"We live pretty close by, in Rye," I tell her. "Do you live around here?" I ask, making conversation.

"Yes, I live very close, in Port Chester. But the family I work for lives right here in Greenwich," she answers, confirming my guess that she's a nanny.

"Oh, how nice," I answer, unsure what else to say. I'm not sure I know exactly where Port Chester is, but I think I saw signs for it on my drive here today, so it can't be too far.

"Brevin is one of the kids in the family," she points at the little boy sitting in the opposite end of the sandbox, pouring sand all over his pants. "I also take care of Lilly, Ben and Maxwell, they're seven," she says, pointing at children that look like triplets over on the slide. "They have 4 kids and the mom is pregnant again," she confides in me.

"Wow, that's a big family," I reply.

"Do you have a nanny?" she asks pointedly.

"No. It's just Anna, so I don't have a nanny. But I was thinking about getting an au pair," I tell her, voicing the thought that Jeannie keeps pushing and Derek is uninterested in discussing.

"I know a lot of the au pairs in town. They aren't as focused as the real nannies. Most of them are just here to have a good time in the US for a year, and they don't always care about the kids," she warns me.

"Sorry, I didn't mean anything by that," she adds apologetically.

"Oh, that's okay," I reply, wondering about the earnestness of the girls I've already skyped with in Budapest and Copenhagen.

"I know this may sound crazy, but by any chance would you consider hiring me?" she blurts out.

The look of shock on my face must say it all, because she quickly backtracks. "I mean of course you would have to interview me, and talk to my references. Oh, and I should probably introduce myself, I'm Hannah," she says, holding out her hand for me to shake.

"I'm Molly," I reply, slightly baffled. "Hannah, didn't you just tell me that you have a job working for another family?" I ask, pointing at the sand-covered boy across from me.

"I do. I know this sounds outrageous; I'm so unhappy with my current job, but I can't quit because I need the money for school," she answers, looking crestfallen.

Although it's none of my business, this girl and her brazen approach to job-hunting intrigue me. "What's wrong with your current job?" I ask, looking forward to some gossip to spice up my day.

"I probably shouldn't say anything. I don't want to talk about another family," she says, absentmindedly chewing on a hangnail.

"I completely understand, that's very respectful of you," I tell her. After a long pause, I say, "You don't have to tell me, but I don't know them. I just moved here a few weeks ago, and I barely know anyone in Rye, let alone in Greenwich. I'm happy to listen if you want to talk."

I know I shouldn't pry, but now I'm really curious about her job issues and this unknown family. Taking another look at her, I see that she's probably younger than I initially thought, maybe only twenty. She's a little plain, with mousy brown hair down to the middle of her back and parted in the center. She also looks exhausted, much more so than any college student should – maybe it's the pressure of school and money-worries and watching four kids (I know that's more than I could handle).

"It's just that the mom keeps extending my hours. Initially I was supposed to work twenty hours a week, so I would have time to study, but it feels like every time I turn around, she keeps increasing my hours and she doesn't pay me for them," she laments.

"Have you talked to her about it?" I ask, thinking that it may just be an oversight from a busy mom.

"I've tried to talk to her about it, but she never has time. Some weeks I work thirty hours and sometimes almost forty – she will come home two or three hours later than she says she will, but then when she gets home, she says that she needs to go lie down because she's exhausted, or nauseous from morning sickness. A month ago, she told me that she would try to be better about her schedule, but nothing's changed," she tells me.

"That sounds terrible, I'm sorry. But have you tried talking to the dad, or threatening to quit?" I suggest, in full problem solving mode.

"The dad is never there. And the few times I have seen him, he looks at me like he can't even remember who I am or what I'm doing there – I swear he doesn't even know my name!" Hannah says.

"Hmmm," I say, nodding along.

"And I did threaten to quit, but she told me that she would give me a terrible reference and make sure I never worked in Greenwich again," she says. Then she adds in almost a whisper, "she said she would tell everyone that I had sex with her husband and that's why she fired me. No one would ever hire me if they thought I did that," she says, tears starting to form in her light brown eyes.

"That's awful!" I exclaim, shocked that anyone would do that.

"I'm sorry to dump this on you. It's not your problem. You must think I'm ridiculous. But you look so nice and your daughter seems so lovely, so when you said you didn't live in Greenwich and that you might be looking for an au pair, I thought I would ask," she says, apologetically.

"How many hours a week would you want to work?" I ask Hannah.

"Twenty would be perfect, but I would work fifteen or twenty-five – I'm really flexible," she says hopefully.

"And how much do you make an hour?" I ask her, the wheels spinning in my head.

"I make $20 an hour right now, but I would take $17 or $18, especially if you only have one daughter."

I quickly do the math and realize that $400 is about the same amount I would have paid an au pair, but now I wouldn't have to deal with someone living in our house, and best of all, I wouldn't have to go through the interview process with the au pairs, and the home visits, and Derek wouldn't have to be involved at all!

"When could you start?" I ask Hannah, realizing that this is a crazy decision, but feeling confident about it.

"I would have to give two weeks notice, so I couldn't start until then. But I'm guessing once I tell her I'm leaving, she won't even want me to stay for the rest of the day, let alone come back for two weeks," Hannah says with glee.

"That sounds good to me," I tell her, wondering if I need to officially offer her the job, or if she gets it.

"So, I have the job?" Hannah confirms.

"Yes, I guess you do," I reply, amazed at what just transpired.

"Let me get your phone number and I'll text you later today when I find out what she says," Hannah says, taking a battered iPhone out of her shorts pocket.

"Great," I say, getting out my phone to exchange numbers, feeling a surreal quality to the whole interaction, but also thrilled that I hired someone so easily and soon I can start going to exercise classes with Jeannie and shopping, and maybe even make more friends in my free-time.

"Thank you so much!" Hannah gushes. "I promise you won't regret it."

I hadn't thought about regretting my decision until she mentioned it, but I'm so excited to tell Jeannie my big news, that I can't even think about regrets.

Chapter 23 – Megan

The house is so much calmer this morning with Kevin gone. It was really nice of them to give me so much time off this weekend, but considering I have no friends, it wasn't all that exciting to have free time – there's only so much time I can spend at the Brewster coffee shop and hanging out at the beach by myself. I wouldn't have thought I would be so happy to get back to our 'routine' this morning, but it's oddly comforting.

"So what are you ladies doing on this beautiful Tuesday?" Heather asks, while filling up her thermos with coffee.

"I don't know, I hadn't really thought about it," I reply. "But it's a beautiful day, I'm sure we'll find something good to do," I say, looking outside at the glistening sun reflecting off the water.

"Can we go to Chatham again?" Brooke asks, involving herself in the conversation.

"Sure, it's fine with me, if it's okay with your mom," I reply, looking to Heather for permission.

"Really? You want to go to Chatham again? Maybe you should save that and do that later in the week," Heather replies awkwardly.

"We could go today and then later in the week. I don't mind the drive," I tell Heather, wondering if that is her concern and in the back of my mind thinking my chances of running into Brad are much greater if we go twice.

"It's not that, it's just that there's so much to do, that I want to make sure you get a chance to do everything," she says.

"But, Mom, I really want to go see my friends today. I even texted them and told them I was probably coming to the beach," Brooke whines, grasping her phone in her hand to make the point.

"Why don't you go to Hyannis?" Heather suggests. "Megan, you haven't been to Hyannis, have you?"

"I've only been to the airport," I reply.

"Okay, so that's perfect. You can all go to Hyannis today and then you can go to Chatham tomorrow or the next day," Heather says, seemingly relieved.

"Sure, that's fine with me," I reply, realizing that Heather is the boss and I should defer to her decision. "What should we do in Hyannis?" I ask.

"There's all the Kennedy things over there. You could take a tour, or go to the museum..." Heather trails off.

"Mom! We are definitely *not* doing that," Brooke asserts.

"Hmmm, okay, what if you went on a boat ride? Remember when we did that last summer? It was great. You should do that," Heather tells us.

"Okay, sounds good," I say, trying to be a team-player. "Brooke, let's give that a try," I say to her, willing her to agree and not start a fight.

"Fine." Brooke says, with her arms folded across her chest. "But we get to stay for dinner tomorrow night in Chatham, we get to go for the whole day and come home late," she challenges.

"Okay, it's a deal," Heather says, looking pleased she won this battle, although I'm not sure that she did.

"I'll leave you some cash for the boat ride and anything else you girls may want to do over there," Heather says, opening her Ostrich Prada wallet and placing a ton of bills on the counter.

"Where are *you* going today?" Brooke asks her mom, something I'm also wondering, but don't feel I can ask. Heather is dressed in navy shorts and a gray t-shirt, but I can see the tie of her bathing suit peeking out at the neck.

"I'm going to run a few errands," Heather says vaguely, "and then maybe I'll go to the beach for a little bit. I may try the public beach for a change of pace, but I'll probably just end up back here," she concludes.

"I'm going to head out now, to be at some of the shops right when they open, but I'm sure you will be gone by the time I get back, so I'll see you this afternoon," she says, gathering up a large orange tote bag with a beach towel, and many other less-visible items inside.

"Do you want me to pick something up for dinner?" I offer, feeling like it's the right thing to say, even though I don't know what I'll do if she says yes. We've been going out or getting take-out every night, but I feel like I should offer.

"Oh, you're so sweet," Heather says. "Maybe I'll grab something while I'm out today – it would be nice to have a home-cooked meal for a change," she says. I don't know if it will really happen, but I guess I'm off the hook.

"I'll see you all later, I don't want to be late," Heather says, walking over to plant kisses on Brooke's and Caitlin's heads.

"Have a great day," I call out. I'm a little disappointed that we aren't going to Chatham today, but I chastise myself for being ridiculous, and for thinking about Brad, when I'm sure I'll never see him again.

***

Twenty-four hours later, Brooke, Caitlin and I are heading down Route 28 on our way to Chatham. It is another spectacular, summer day, with crystal blue skies and a slight breeze (perfect beach weather). Yesterday in Hyannis was fine, but I'm much more excited about today. Unlike our last trip, we have packed up the car with chairs, towels, umbrellas and sand toys – and we even all have a change of clothes for this afternoon and evening since Brooke has made it clear that we are staying for dinner and to "hang out" on Main street with her friends outside Buffy's. I invited Heather to come along, since we will be gone for so long and I feel bad leaving her alone all day, but she assured me that she was happy to stay home, and Brooke looked equally relieved.

Getting settled at the beach proves to be more difficult than last time, since we have to park pretty far away, and then get all of our stuff from the car and down the steps to the beach; but now that we are here, it's worth it. Brooke instantly found her group of friends and abandoned us to lay out with them on the other side of the beach. Caitlin seems happy at the edge of the water, running in and out and letting the waves chase her back up the sand. I would love to take out my book, but I don't want to take my eyes off of Caitlin in the ocean, especially after what happened last time we were here.

I'm trying not to look around for Brad, but I admit I'm slightly disappointed that he isn't here. Even though nothing would happen, he was fun to talk to, and *so* good to look at. I shouldn't be worrying about him at all, especially after finally getting a text from Ryan this morning, but I can't stop myself from looking back at the stairs to see if anyone new has arrived.

It looks like Caitlin has made some friends; I can't tell if they are the same kids she played with last time, but in the last few minutes two girls who look about her age have joined her and they are all chasing each other at the edge of the water, but no one is going in past their knees – I wonder if that means it's really cold today? I know I still need to watch her, but with Brooke occupied by her friends and Caitlin entertaining herself, I find it hard to believe that I am at "work." Not for the first time, I wonder what I would be doing right now if I were in Manhattan.

Without Ryan and my friends in the City, I would probably be sitting in my room binge watching Netflix. I feel pretty lucky that Sabrina found this job for me. I can't imagine any other scenario where I make this much money sunbathing. It feels like fate played a hand here, just like two years ago when I lucked into the babysitting job with Danielle – forever changing my life. Maybe it's God's way of making up for giving me such horrible parents, but whatever it is, I'll take it.

***

"I can't get all the sand out," Caitlin complains as we try to rinse off and change under our towels.

I am having the same issue, but I'm trying to be upbeat for her sake. "Let me help you," I offer, quickly pulling my clean tank top over my head and tucking in my beach towel, so I can assist her.

"Aren't you guys ready yet?" Brooke asks. Since she never got near the water, she had a much easier time changing – she's practically sand-free.

"Give us a few minutes," I tell her. "You're not going to miss anything," I try to assure her, as she keeps glancing around at the near-empty beach and then at her phone.

"I think we're ready," I tell Brooke, looking down at my pink tank top and denim cutoffs. Brooke is wearing a black mini-skirt, blue sparkly halter top and platform sandals; which makes me wonder which of us isn't dressed appropriately.

"Let's just get this stuff back to the car and then we can go to dinner," I tell the girls. I'm not looking forward to carrying everything back to the car, but I don't see much of an option. I make a mental note; if we do this again, we have to pack sparingly.

"Want some help with that?" a familiar voice asks.

I try to hide my smile, but I can't help being happy that Brad turned up – especially since we really do need help carrying everything to the car.

"Yes, please," Brooke moans, happy to offload the beach chairs to Brad.

"Did you just get here?" I ask Brad, curious how I missed him all day.

"I was walking by," he points to the path at the very top of the beach, "and saw you down here, so I figured I would come say hi. And clearly it's a good thing that I did," he laughs, adjusting the chairs and umbrellas to his left side, so he can pick up the cooler.

"Can we just *go*?" Brooke says, impatiently.

"Where are you guys going?" Brad asks Brooke good-naturedly, seemingly amused at her exasperation.

"We're meeting my friends at the Wild Goose for dinner, but I was supposed to be there ten minutes ago," Brooke complains.

"That's where I was heading too. We can go together," Brad says confidently.

"Sure, whatever, let's just go," Brooke says, taking her bags and trying to hurry ahead of us, which is nearly impossible for her in those shoes.

"Are you really going there?" I ask Brad. I don't think my memory of him did him justice. He's even cuter than I remembered. His skin is almost the color of a Hershey bar, and so incredibly smooth that I have to refrain from reaching out and touching his arm. He's wearing khaki pants and a lime green polo shirt; although he's showing a lot less skin than last week in his bathing suit, he looks even sexier – maybe it's because I already saw him half naked, so now I can just imagine it.

"Yes, I'm going there," he laughs. "Did you think that I made it up so I could follow you?" he asks playfully.

My face burns with embarrassment, but I try to look straight ahead at the path in front of us, so he can't see the color of my cheeks. "No, of course not," I say, unconvincingly.

"But I *would* have changed my plans if that wasn't where I was going," he adds, making my cheeks burn again, but this time they are accompanied by a tiny stomach flip.

"Are you meeting friends there?" I ask him, trying to change the subject.

"I'm meeting my parents there, but I don't think they would mind if I ate with you instead," he tells me.

"I'm sure they would mind," I reply.

"Let's ask them when we get there," he says, stopping to put down the gear at the car, where Brooke and Caitlin are waiting.

"Um, okay," I say, unsure what else to say.

"Thanks for helping carry all of this stuff," I say to Brad after we've loaded it into the back of the car. "I guess I'll see you there?"

"Aren't you going to give me a ride?" Brad asks.

"Oh, I thought you drove," I say.

"Our house is pretty close to here, so I was going to walk to dinner and meet my parents. But if you're driving, I'll take a ride. Besides, it's hard to find parking in town, I can show you a secret spot that only locals know," he says, grinning.

"Sure, of course," I say, unlocking the doors.

"I guess that means I'm in back?" Brooke says, with an attitude I haven't missed hearing from her.

"I can sit in the back," Brad volunteers.

"No. *You* can sit in the front. Brooke is fine in the back," I say, giving her a dirty look, and then smiling to myself as I try to picture Brad folding up his long, muscular body to get into the backseat.

It's only a three minute ride to the restaurant, so I guess we could have just walked and left the car near the beach, but Brooke argued that we wouldn't want to have to walk back later in the dark. As promised, Brad helps me find a spot on a side street, and I get to avoid looking like one of the tourists aimlessly driving up and down Main Street hoping for someone to leave.

When we walk inside, there is an incredibly glamorous Black woman sitting at the bar, I notice her instantly because I swear she looks exactly like Michelle Obama. I know that probably sounds racist somehow, but she really does look like her – she even has the arms! As I'm trying not to stare at Michelle's look-alike, she looks right at me, and breaks into a huge grin, maybe it *is* the First Lady? Or maybe she gets mistaken for her a lot, so she is a good sport about it?

"Hi Sweetie! What took you so long?" Michelle's doppelganger asks.

I'm about to reply, when I hear Brad say, "Hey Mom, I ran into a friend on the way here. Would it be okay if I ate with her?"

Of course she's Brad's mom – why wouldn't she be? He couldn't just have a normal looking mom, like the rest of us.

"Who am *I* going to eat with?" Caitlin asks, looking up at me sadly. Brooke's friends seem to have secured a table, and she abandoned us the minute we walked inside. This leaves me, Caitlin and Brad standing awkwardly in the entryway of the Wild Goose chatting over the heads of a few families with Brad's mom.

"Of course you'll eat with me," I reassure her, smoothing her windswept hair and giving her a pat on the back.

"Bradley, at least come over here and say hello and introduce us to your friend," Brad's mom requests, taking a ladylike sip from a glass of white wine and motioning for us to come over to the bar.

"Hi Mom," Brad says, leaning down to kiss her flawless cheek. "This is my friend Megan. And this is Caitlin," Brad says. Caitlin is thrilled to be included and she sticks out her little hand to shake Brad's Mom's.

"It's lovely to meet you Caitlin - Megan, you as well. I'm Mrs. Montgomery, or Marilyn, whichever you prefer," Brad's mom tells us. She is perched on her bar stool like many of the other women at this local tavern, but something about her posture or her voice, or maybe her outfit makes her look almost regal. I really don't think I was very far off with my Michelle Obama reference, even now that I'm less than a foot away from her.

"Harvey, did you notice that your son is here?" Mrs. Montgomery says to the man next to her, who is engrossed in conversation with the man on his right.

"Hello Son," Brad's dad says, teasing him and his wife. "Is our table ready?" he asks, switching his focus.

"I think they said it would be ready in five minutes. But it looks like Brad is going to eat with his friends, so we can either give them our bar seats, or we can give them the table. There are three of them, and three of us, if we eat with Walt," she says, gesturing to the man next to Brad's dad.

"It sounds like you've done all the hard work. Just tell me where to go," he jokes.

"Where would you rather sit?" Mrs. Montgomery asks Brad.

I'm having trouble getting over how nice Brad's parents seem to be. I cannot imagine a scenario where I was supposed to meet my mom and dad for dinner and they decided it was fine for me to eat with a friend instead and then on top of that, they give me their table! Although, at this point, it's pretty hard to imagine having dinner with either of my parents, since I barely see or speak to them. But even when I did used to interact with them, nothing like this ever happened. Danielle would probably do something like this, but she's more like an older sister or a cool aunt.

"We'll take the table, if that's okay. I'm not sure if we are even allowed to sit at the bar without an adult," Brad adds, sounding a little embarrassed.

"Oh right, of course. Sorry! Just have your check sent over here. Enjoy your dinner," Mrs. Montgomery says, giving Brad another kiss on the cheek and sending us back toward the hostess stand to wait for our table.

We are seated almost immediately, and to Brooke's dismay, we are only one table away from her and her friends, but as far as I'm concerned, she should feel lucky to be here with as much freedom as she has.

Thankfully, Caitlin is busy coloring the kids' menu and occupying herself with the word search. I'm not sure how the dynamic will work with the three of us for the meal, but I find Caitlin's presence to be quite soothing, since otherwise this would feel like a date, and I definitely don't think that's a good idea.

***

An hour and a half later, we are emptying back onto Main Street, heading to the ice cream shop; although I'm so full of fish & chips, that I couldn't eat another bite. I'm not sure how ninety minutes passed at the restaurant, because it felt like it was over in an instant. Brad and I covered twenty different topics, from books and music to politics and Trump to what drugs we've tried (only pot for me, he tried shrooms last summer and hated them). I'm not going to win babysitter of the year for my work tonight, but I think everyone at our table was happy with the result - about ten minutes into dinner, Caitlin asked if she could borrow my phone and headphones, and I let her use them for the entire time – oh well.

Brooke and her friends are about twenty feet ahead of us, laughing and howling at pretty much everything anyone says. It's not a mystery why adults think kids are obnoxious, but I'm quite certain when I'm out with Georgia and Jessica, we look exactly the same – just with better accessories and bigger boobs.

Caitlin has run to catch up with them, and either Brooke hasn't noticed, or she is feeling generous after a day with her friends and she isn't yelling at Caitlin to leave her alone. Which leaves Brad and me walking together, just the two of us, down this picturesque street on a beautiful summer evening. A mixture of guilt and excitement rushes through me as Brad's hand nearly brushes my arm as he raises his hand to wave to a friend across the street. A nagging voice inside my head tells me that I should be sharing this kind of romantic moment with Ryan, not a hot stranger from Boston. But then I gain control of that voice and remind it that Ryan abandoned me to spend his summer three thousand miles away with bankers in London. We could have spent our summer evenings strolling around Manhattan getting ice cream and maybe even taking a weekend trip to Chatham; but instead, I'm alone, and he barely returns my texts and never has time to talk to me.

"So, do you have a girlfriend?" I ask Brad, feeling brazen and a little wild.

"Nope. I did, but we broke up a couple months ago. She is going to UCLA and we didn't want to do long distance. But we really hadn't been into each other for a while," Brad discloses with stark honesty.

"So, what about you?" Brad asks, turning to look at me.

"I definitely don't have a girlfriend," I say with a cheeky smile.

"That's a relief, at least I'm in the right ballpark," Brad laughs.

At that moment we reach the ice cream shop, and the line is out the door and weaves around the adjacent store. Brooke, Caitlin and the other girls are almost into the door of the shop – I can't remember if they have money, but I guess they'll come find me if they don't.

"I'll just wait out here," I tell Brad, making my way over to a pink bench.

"You don't want anything?" he asks.

"Nope, too full," I answer.

"I'm never too full for ice cream," Brad grins. "Save me a seat. Oh and you still didn't answer my question, don't think I forgot," Brad says, securing his spot in line, and giving me a smile that makes my stomach flip.

As I sit on the bench, surrounded by sun-tanned (and sun-burned) children and families and couples happily enjoying their ice cream, excitedly re-telling the days' events or planning their next day in the sun, I remember exactly why this feeling in my stomach is familiar. This is how I felt two summers ago when I first met Ryan and realized he might actually like me. Of course the circumstances were different, but the initial excitement and flirting and the thrill of what he might say or do next was all the same. I know I should feel terrible that I'm feeling this way with Brad, but I can't control it.

Brooke and her friends come out with their cones and head toward a bench at the back of the little garden; they are still talking a mile a minute, but now they are taking selfies with their ice cream. I try to get Brooke's attention, but it's no use. At least Caitlin is still with them, and it appears they did have money. It even seems that one of Brooke's friends is talking to Caitlin, so I'm going to chalk that up to a win and leave them alone.

"I got an extra spoon in case you change your mind," Brad says, easing himself onto the bench right next to me, his thigh about one millimeter away from mine.

"What flavor?" I ask, taking the spoon from his outstretched hand.

"Black Raspberry and Moose Tracks," he answers, taking a big bite of the purple scoop.

"Black Raspberry?" I question, in mock horror. "Seriously? I always wondered who got that."

"That's my favorite. You don't know what you're missing," he says confidently.

"Moose Tracks I can live with, but you need Milky Way, or cookie dough, or something with caramel. I've become an expert in the last few weeks," I say earnestly, taking a bite of the Moose Tracks. "I'm surprised my clothes still fit," I joke.

"I saw you on the beach today, I don't think you have anything to worry about," Brad says in a low tone, giving me a quick look that makes me feel naked and fluttery all at the same time.

I don't know how to reply, so I take another bite of ice cream instead.

"So, let's get back the previous topic," Brad declares. "Tell me about your boyfriend," Brad says.

"Who says I have a boyfriend?" I ask.

"I figured I would assume that you did, then I would be less disappointed," Brad reasons.

"So, I did have a boyfriend. But I'm not sure if I do anymore..." I tell Brad.

"Hmmm, intriguing, what does that mean?"

"I had a boyfriend, but he went to London for the summer, and he won't return my calls and he doesn't ever text me back. I'm not sure what's going on, but I'm starting to think I may *not* have a boyfriend," I tell Brad, realizing that I am exaggerating a tiny bit, but it doesn't seem pertinent to include a couple stray calls or texts from Ryan, when I barely hear from him.

"It sounds like it's his loss," Brad says. "He must be crazy."

"I think you're right!" I say, starting to see the summer in a whole new light.

Chapter 24 – Heather

It figures that after I finally give Jasper my cell phone number, I don't hear anything from him. We had a great time paddle boarding on Tuesday – I was terrible and he was clearly experienced, but it didn't matter, I laughed the whole time and loved every minute of it. I hesitated when he asked if I wanted to get lunch afterward, but it seemed harmless enough. Then we had one of the best bowls of clam chowder I've ever had at some little hole in the wall and I couldn't stop laughing there either. When we said goodbye after lunch, I suggested we exchange numbers instead of continuing to run into each other at the bike shop, and now it's Friday morning and I've heard nothing.

It's not like he owes me anything, and of course it isn't like we went on a date (that would be ludicrous – I tell myself); but we did have fun hanging out, and now I'm back to having nothing to do. Megan is keeping the girls busy all day long – they are back in Chatham *again* today. I tried to discourage them from going, but Brooke's friends are there and it seems silly to force her to stay here every day when her friends are only twenty minutes away. Megan is an absolute lifesaver; I don't know what I would do without her! She is happy staying in Brewster and going to the beach or the park or the Nature Center, but she is just as eager to take the girls to Chatham – and she doesn't even complain about staying there all day! I really need to talk to her about taking some time off. I know we are paying her well, but she probably deserves some time to herself.

The chime on my phone interrupts the swirl in my brain. I grab it off the coffee table, thinking it must be from Jasper, but then see that it's from Kevin, which makes sense because he's my husband, not the random guy I went for a few bike rides with – what is wrong with me?

Kevin: How are you feeling? I'm stuck at the office a little longer than I planned today, but should be there late tonight. Hope you're still taking it easy!

I wonder if paddle boarding fits into his definition of "taking it easy?"

Heather: All is well here. I feel great. See you when you get here

I look at my text after I send it and quickly add:

Heather: Travel safely

Kevin: I'll give the pilot your message ☺ Looking forward to seeing you and the girls

Heather: you too

When did our messages get so stiff? He's "looking forward to seeing us?" Isn't that what you say to distant relatives that you don't actually want to see? I know that many families on the Cape are operating under the same model that we are, with a dad (or mom) who only comes on the weekends, but it certainly doesn't feel like our previous years on the Cape. Although I don't know how much of it has to do with Kevin coming out on the weekends vs. the whole 'recovering from cancer thing'… I'm guessing most of the other families aren't dealing with that, and that may be the root of our problem.

Now that Kevin isn't going to be here until late tonight and Megan and the girls are in Chatham all day, I have the rest of the morning and the entire afternoon with nothing to do. I know most people would kill for this kind of free time, but I need to *do* something. I'm sure in a few months when I'm back at work and barely treading water, I'll look back at a day like today and kick myself; but unfortunately it just doesn't work like that.

***

As I wander the aisles of the Stop & Shop, I realize that my plan may have a few holes. I love the *idea* of surprising everyone with a fancy home-cooked dinner; but I'm more of a simple-recipe-type chef, not a wander-thru-the-store and throw-ingredients-together and make-something-fabulous chef. I should have thought about what I was going to make before coming here, or at least looked up a few recipes and made a list.

So far I have corn, lettuce, raspberries, tomatoes, bananas, basil, shrimp, M&M's, chocolate chip muffins and a baguette – I don't think this dinner is going to be making it onto the pages of Bon Appétit anytime soon.

The magic of the internet! Why didn't I think of this sooner? There must be a million recipe websites and apps that I can use to find the perfect plan for dinner. Just like everything else, it's like having an entire library of cookbooks in my purse. I reach into my bag to start searching for this phenomenal dinner, but my phone isn't in the side pocket where I always keep it. I pull my cart over next to the display of peaches and hoist my giant Gucci tote onto the front of the cart so I can rummage through it properly.

"Shit, shit, shit!" I mutter to myself, after five minutes of frantic searching reveals that my phone is definitely not in my bag. Now I can't find a recipe *and* I also don't know if Megan or Brooke are trying to get in touch with me.

"Everything okay?" says a familiar voice.

I turn around to find Jasper standing there, looking adorable in khaki shorts and a light blue t-shirt with an empty shopping basket over his arm.

"Hey there," I reply, feeling flustered. "I'm fine. I was looking for my phone, but it looks like I left it at home," I say, shrugging my shoulders like it's not a big deal.

"I hate when that happens! I feel so naked!" Jasper says sympathetically.

"It's ridiculous, but yes, that's pretty much it," I say with a smile. I have already forgiven him for not calling or texting me this week.

As if he can read my mind, Jasper says, "I'm sorry I didn't call you. I had to get pages to my editor by this morning. I've been working on them non-stop the past three days; this is the first time I've left the house since Tuesday!" he exclaims.

"No worries," I say, patting him lightly on the arm. "Congrats on getting your pages done!" I tell him, mentally congratulating myself for not saying anything snotty to him about his lack of communication.

"We should get drinks to celebrate!" Jasper suggests.

"That would be great!" I answer excitedly. "When are you thinking?"

"What are you doing right now?" he asks, his boyish grin in full effect.

"I'm attempting to buy groceries to make an amazing dinner for the girls tonight – can't you tell?" I ask, pointing to the random selection of groceries in my cart.

"Hmmm," Jasper says, eyeing the assortment. "What are you making?"

"I don't really have a plan. That was why I was looking for my phone, I was going to find a recipe, but now that isn't going to work," I say, with a hint of defeat.

"Do you have a grill?" Jasper asks.

"Yes."

"Do you all eat steak?" he asks.

"Yes." I answer again.

"Here's what you're going to do. Get four pieces of the marinated skirt steak from the butcher shop – it's surprisingly good here. You've already got your corn and tomatoes and bread. Oh and you have shrimp too – just get cocktail sauce when you're by the butcher and you have an app. Grab some baby spinach and some dressing for a salad and you're all set," he says triumphantly.

"That seems too easy," I say suspiciously.

"It's perfect, I promise. I have to get a few things as well. Let's finish our shopping and then you can run home and put your groceries away and we'll meet on the Terrace at the Ocean Edge Resort at two for a late lunch and drinks," he says definitively.

"Okay," I say, happy to have a plan for dinner *and* for the rest of my day.

***

I agonized over what to wear, but now that I'm sitting here, I think I made the right decision. I opted for a light-yellow, silk sleeveless top with a high neck and white linen pants. In the past my wardrobe consisted of many tops and dresses with deep v-necks and plunging necklines (cleavage being one of my best assets); but now I live in fear of my prosthesis popping out of my bra, so the higher the better.

I've never been to this resort before, even though I've driven past it too many times to count. The majority of the resort seems to consist of condos covering acres and acres of Brewster, but the main house, known as "The Mansion" is the original hotel, and there is a beautiful terrace off the back with a bar and restaurant, which is where I find myself now sitting and waiting for Jasper.

Dressed for the celebration, Jasper strolls in at two minutes past the hour wearing beige linen pants (something Kevin would never wear) and a navy polo shirt. His black hair is slightly damp from the shower, and I can smell some sort of lemony-citrus soap when he bends down to give me a kiss on the cheek before he takes a seat in his own chair across from me. It occurs to me that other than this morning when we saw each other in 'casual clothes' at the grocery store, we have only seen each other in sweaty workout clothes. Right now is the first time that Jasper has ever seen me right out of the shower with makeup and my hair done, etc. (due to the wig, my hair usually looks pretty good, but still...)

"You look lovely," Jasper says, as he takes his seat. Clearly, he is having the same realization that I just had.

"So do you," I say, repaying the compliment. "I mean, you look very nice," I say, stumbling to correct myself.

"So, what are we drinking?" Jasper asks.

"You choose, it's your celebration," I tell him.

"Champagne!" he says decidedly.

"I was hoping you'd say that," I tell him.

Shortly thereafter, the waiter brings two glasses of champagne and a basket of bread and I take a piece as soon as he puts it down.

"I know, I'm probably the last woman who still eats the bread, but I can't drink on an empty stomach," I tell Jasper.

"I hate women who don't eat," Jasper says. "Besides, what's the point of all the biking if you can't eat bread?" he jokes, reaching out and taking a roll.

"Here's to your next book!" I say, raising my glass to toast him.

"Cheers!" he says, clinking his glass against mine.

"So, I started reading one of your books," I tell him. "My daughter brought it with her and I found it in her room," I confess.

"Really?" Jasper asks, seeming genuinely excited. "Which one?"

"Oh crap. I can't remember the title. I'm so bad with book titles. Oh God, this is humiliating," I say, hiding my face in my hands. "It has a purple cover, and it starts with two girls sneaking out after a party," I say, trying to redeem myself.

"That's the third one in the series, you can't *start* with that one," he says, but his tone is playful.

"I'm only on chapter three. I can stop," I offer, taking a sip of champagne.

"No, don't stop. I like that you're reading it," he says, grinning at me and covering my hand with his.

A familiar warmth spreads through my chest, and I'm quite certain it has also crept up my neck as well. It must be from the champagne, but it seems oddly coincidental that it's happening just when Jasper touches me.

"I'm going to use the ladies' room, back in a minute," I say, standing up to excuse myself.

If I weren't worried about ruining my silk top, or worse, my wig, I would splash cold water on my face; but the downside seems pretty bad. One look in the mirror confirms my fear – I'm completely flushed and even a little sweaty; honestly, this isn't that different than how I look right after I have sex. Kevin always said I would never need to wear blush if we just had sex all the time. Not surprisingly, I haven't looked like this in a while since Kevin is afraid I'll break if he touches me – I guess it isn't a surprise that a warm smile and some hand-holding basically brought me to orgasm.

I wash my hands with some ice-cold water and try to figure out what I'm doing here. It was one thing when he was an excuse to get some exercise (or maybe the bike ride was an excuse to see him). But now we're meeting in the afternoon for champagne? What comes next? I'm fooling myself if I haven't thought about what could come next. I've told him about Brooke and Caitlin, but the way that I talk about them without ever mentioning Kevin, he must assume I'm single.

I have to tell him about Kevin. That's the only answer. If I tell him about Kevin, then it won't be like I'm leading him on, and we can just be friends. I glance again at my reflection and am relieved to see that my normal coloring has returned. There isn't a full-length mirror at the beach house, so I'm also happy to see that the linen pants flatter my long legs the way I hoped they would; and the light yellow and white set off my tan nicely. I know Kevin is worried that I'm getting too much color, but this is probably the only summer I'll ever spend out of the office, so I might as well take advantage of it.

Jasper appears to be on his second glass of champagne when I return to the table.

"Shall I order you another glass?" he asks gallantly.

"Oh no, thank you," I reply. "I'm not a great day-drinker. I can't really have more than one drink before six," I tell him.

"What happens if you do?" he asks, leaning forward in his seat, clearly hoping for something juicy.

"Oh, nothing very exciting, I just get a headache," I tell him. What I don't tell him is that I haven't had more than one drink since before I got sick, and I'm not really sure what my tolerance looks like anymore; but sometimes I do get a headache when I drink during the day, so it's not a total lie.

"So other than your gourmet dinner tonight, what are you doing this weekend?" Jasper asks.

This is the perfect opportunity for me to tell him about Kevin; I couldn't have asked for a better set-up if I tried. Which is why it's that much more troubling when I open my mouth to answer him, and this is what I say, "I'm not sure yet. The girls have been begging to go whale watching, so we may drive up to Provincetown to do that."

"So you aren't free for a bike ride?" Jasper questions, while draining his glass of champagne.

"Not this weekend. I'm going to give Megan most of the weekend off, because she's been working a lot. But I'm free on Monday afternoon or Tuesday," I tell him. It's like I can't control the words that are coming out of my mouth. I know I'm not making good choices, but I just can't make myself tell him about Kevin.

Chapter 25 – Sabrina

"Are you sure you're okay?" Peter asks, for the third time in as many minutes.

Thankfully we are in 'spoon' position, so I don't have to face him when answering his questions. "Yes, I promise, I'm fine," I say, hoping he will drop the subject.

"It's just that you've seemed really distracted recently, and even just now, it felt like you were really far away," Peter says.

I take a deep breath before I respond, because my initial instinct is to tell him that sometimes sex is just sex and he should stop being such a girl; but that is the old Sabrina talking and I know Peter won't respond well to that. Instead, I opt for a more physical response and turn my naked body around and press it against his and put my lips right next to his ear and whisper in my sexiest voice, "I promise, I'm right here."

That seems to do the trick, because I feel Peter start to grow hard. "Do we have time?" I whisper into his ear.

"You can be a few minutes late," Peter says, before rolling me over onto my back and positioning himself on top of me. "I'm the luckiest man in the world," Peter says, before leaning down to kiss my neck and gently pushing himself inside of me for the second time this morning.

***

I know sex isn't the way to solve a problem, or to end an uncomfortable conversation; but it seems to be the only way I can communicate with Peter right now. Parker has been true to his word and hasn't contacted me since we had drinks eight days ago (yes, I'm counting). I know that it shouldn't matter, but it feels like I lost him all over again, and it fucking sucks. He appears out of the blue, tells me that he never should have let me go and then disappears again. Am I just supposed to go back to normal and forget that it happened?

I've tried to forger. I've tried to focus on Peter. But I'm failing miserably. It's not so bad at work – I'm good enough at my job that I'm able to swing that with mild distractions; but with Peter it's nearly impossible! A few months ago everything was perfect. Peter and I were dating and living together and everything was great. Then the whole proposal thing happened and that definitely threw me off, but other than the actual wedding, I think I was getting on board with it; but then Parker happened, and now everything is a mess.

We're supposed to meet Peter's parents at the Pierre tonight for something (I don't remember what Peter said we were doing – probably just looking at the hotel, but maybe it was something else). Although, I'm not sure how I'm going to get through tonight, without it being a total disaster. Peter knows something's wrong, but I've been able to elude him with sex. But Peter's mom will be a different story. She's like a detective, and she won't give up until she is satisfied that she has all the answers (and I'm pretty sure I can't distract her with sex).

An alarm on my computer reminds me that I have a meeting in five minutes. Even in my personal tailspin, work has been busy enough that I can forget about Parker and what could have been, for hours at a time. If I am trying to get funding or find new mentees for the hundreds of girls that we sponsor, I seem to be able to focus.

Theresa pokes her head into my office, "your eleven o'clock is here. I put them in the conference room," she says.

"Thank you," I tell her.

I look at my calendar to remind myself which company I'm meeting with. Ugh, Theresa didn't even put the name of the firm on here, it just says "potential donor – tech company." Usually I go to the office of the firm where I am asking for a donation, but sometimes they like to come here to get a sense of what we do, so it isn't *that* unusual. But I would like to know who they are, so I don't look like a complete asshole.

When I walk into the conference room, I can't believe what I'm seeing. I'm sure there must be some sort of mistake, but I don't understand who's behind the joke, and it certainly isn't funny.

"Small world, right?" Parker says, standing up to shake my hand as I walk into the room and put my binders and laptop down on the table across from him.

"Sabrina and I went to college together," Parker tells the man standing next to him. "Sabrina, this is my colleague, Henry."

Henry offers me his hand, and I reach across the table to shake it, "it's a pleasure to meet you," I say, trying to regain my composure.

"We aren't usually fortunate enough to have Parker at meetings like these, but when I mentioned I was meeting with your foundation today, he insisted on joining me," Henry says. It's hard to tell if Henry is pleased or nervous to have Parker riding shotgun today.

I can give my standard speech about the foundation in my sleep, so that won't be an issue, and I have pretty much perfected my spiel about the importance of pairing smart, at-risk girls with successful women; but if I don't know where Henry and Parker work, I am going to fall flat on my face when it comes to asking for money. I thought I had just been distracted with Peter recently, but apparently I've also been letting things slide at the office. I've never gone into a meeting unprepared before – and now the cause of my dysfunction is the target in my meeting – what are the odds!?!

"Let me just give you my card, so we don't forget at the end," I tell them, slipping my card across the table and hoping that they will reciprocate.

Parker reaches into the inside pocket of his navy blazer and pulls out his card and slides it in my direction, Henry quickly follows his boss's actions, but his moves are not as graceful, because Parker makes everything look effortless.

I glance down at the cards before tucking them under my binder and let out a sigh of relief. I'll have to ask questions to fill in some holes, but I'm no longer completely in the dark. Parker is the Chief Product

Officer for Watson at IBM. Henry obviously also works for IBM, he is a development officer.

"I was reading about your foundation on your website," Parker says, leaning back in his chair and crossing his legs. Parker is clad in jeans and a light blue shirt, along with his blazer, the epitome of cool – only Parker could work at IBM and get away with wearing jeans. He continues, "I love the opportunities you're creating for the girls with your mentorships and your programs. We're happy to give you money, but I think we could also work closely together and create great educational experiences for them with Watson," Parker says.

Somehow, I manage to almost forget that Parker is sitting across from me and we spend over an hour discussing the amazing opportunities that IBM wants to make happen for my little foundation. Henry essentially becomes our note taker, and Parker and I talk non-stop about the products he is developing and the growth of the mentorship program.

"Thank you both so much for coming in today," I say to Parker and Henry, when we hit a natural stopping point in our discussion. It is almost 12:30, and we had only booked an hour for the meeting. I know that I have another call that I was supposed to make at noon, and I can't imagine that someone as important as Parker doesn't have someplace else to be.

"It was our pleasure," Henry says, seemingly anxious to say *something*, after being silent the entire meeting. Henry is actually a decent looking guy – average height and build, with brown hair and hazel eyes, but next to Parker, everyone pales in comparison.

"I'll send you a summary of the meeting from today, detailing the areas where we are most in need of funding," I tell them. I definitely hate this part of my job the most. In some ways it isn't that different than my old job in enterprise software sales, but then sometimes I just feel like I'm begging, and I never felt like that before.

"What's your number?" Parker says.

"Pardon?" I say.

"How much do you want? It's just so much easier this way. Tell us how much you want, and Henry will get you the money," Parker says confidently.

"Um, uh," I stutter. Shit, is he for real? Am I supposed to just throw out a number and he's going to write me a check, no matter what I say? There has to be a catch. There also has to be a number that's too high, but maybe this is my chance – my chance to do great things for the foundation and to make a name for myself with the board. It is still IBM (not the Gates foundation), and they are more about partnerships, so I do need to be somewhat realistic, but I also don't want to miss my chance...

"Two million dollars," I say, hoping that it sounds like a statement and not like a question.

"We should be able to do that, right Henry?" Parker says, turning to look at Henry.

"We should be able to make that work," Henry says. "I think we'll want to work out some additional terms, but IBM supports the work you're doing," Henry says, looking back and forth between Parker and me, like he wants to be included on our team.

"Henry, you can head back to the office without me. I've got a couple things to do before I leave," Parker says to Henry, without taking his eyes off of me.

We both wait silently for Henry to pack up his belongings and exit the conference room. I feel a little sorry for Henry – Parker hijacked his meeting and then sent him on his way, but I'm too preoccupied with my own situation to feel too bad for him.

As soon as Henry leaves the room, I blurt out, "I thought you didn't want to see me again?"

"I never said that," Parker says, reclining back in his chair and folding both his hands behind his head.

"Yes, you did. At the bar, you said you didn't want to see me again," I say, slightly annoyed that he doesn't remember. If he doesn't remember that, does that mean that he's also forgotten the other things he said?

"I said that I didn't want to be friends. I said that I couldn't just stand by and watch while you married some other guy," he says calmly. Parker is looking at me so intently with his bright blue eyes, that I swear he can see right through my green linen dress.

"Oh," I reply, momentarily unable to say anything else.

"Are you free for lunch?" Parker asks casually, packing up his laptop and the materials I gave him into his leather messenger bag.

"I'm still engaged," I tell him.

"I know," he says.

"So what's changed? Why are you okay being friends now?" I ask, genuinely curious, and maybe even a little disappointed.

"Oh, I'm still not okay just being friends; but we're not going to be friends. I'm going to show you that you're marrying the wrong man, and we should be together," Parker says assertively.

I know I should tell Parker to leave, or at least defend Peter. But Parker seems so confident, and I felt so awful the last time he left (not to mention the first time he left), and he did just give me all that money. So instead of doing what I know I should do or what I know Danielle would want me to do, I say this, "Where are we going to lunch?"

Chapter 26 – Molly

"What is *that*?" Derek says, with a combination of disdain and curiosity.

"It's a kale, spinach and apple smoothie," I reply, trying to sound upbeat.

"Is that what you're having for dinner?" he questions.

It is just after nine o'clock, and Derek and I are finally sitting down to dinner. Anna has been asleep for almost two hours, but Derek just got home from work ten minutes ago. Derek has a piece of baked cod in front of him, with a side of rice pilaf and asparagus. It actually looks like quite a nice dinner, and it only took me about fifteen minutes to make – I'm quite pleased with myself. It looks especially delicious considering the thick green sludge that is sitting in front of me.

"I'm doing a cleanse. I'm only having green juice for seven days," I tell him. "Today's my first day."

"Why would you do something like that?" Derek asks, taking a huge bite of his cod.

"I'm trying to get rid of the toxins in my body," I reply.

"Are you kidding me?" he asks, reaching for his glass of wine. "Where did you get this nonsense?"

"I'm also trying to lose some weight," I admit, taking a sip of my dinner and trying not to wince at the taste. I thought the drinks would get better as the day went on, but this is my fifth juice and they aren't improving.

"You're a size six! How could you possibly need to lose weight?" Derek questions, looking at me like I'm crazy.

"I was at a core fusion class, and I was definitely the fattest woman in the whole class," I tell him.

"You were at a what type of class? And you aren't remotely fat," Derek says.

I love that Derek is so supportive of me, and I know that he would love me if I weighed one hundred pounds or two hundred pounds; but he doesn't understand what I'm dealing with. I was so excited to go to the new class with Jeannie and Lisa yesterday and leave Anna with Hannah for the day. I felt great in my new Lululemon capri pants and yoga top with the built in bra (not surprisingly, the salesperson at Lulu also said I looked great). But then when I got to class, I felt enormous! All the other women were either size two or size zero, or maybe even smaller! I couldn't even focus on the exercise, because every time I looked in the mirror, I just saw my giant thighs or ass, next to the tiny, perfect, sculpted bodies of the rest of the class. On the way out, the instructor told me that I had a great first class, but then suggested I try a seven-day juice cleanse – I barely made it to the car before bursting into tears.

"The class is barre mixed with cardio. Jeannie says it's the new workout craze," I tell him, forcing myself to take another sip of the green muck and hoping it quiets my rumbling stomach.

"The whole thing sounds ridiculous to me. You don't need a crazy exercise class, and you certainly don't need to lose weight or do a juice cleanse," Derek says, shaking his head.

"Here, have some of my fish, it's delicious," he says, offering me a bite.

The fish does smell fantastic, but Jeannie and Lisa were so excited when I told them I was doing this stupid cleanse, I will be mortified if I have to tell them that I couldn't even make it through the first day.

"No, that's okay. I'm going to try and stick with this. At least for a few days," I say.

"So, where was Anna when you were at this crazy class?" Derek asks.

"Oh, she was with Jeannie's daughter and their au pair," I reply.

I don't *want* to lie to him, but I haven't figured out how to tell him about Hannah yet. I didn't imagine that he would think about that when I told him about the class, but I guess it makes sense.

"So, how was work?" I ask, changing the topic.

"It was okay," he says, but the look on his face says otherwise.

"Did something happen?" I ask, suddenly concerned.

"No, not really. I just had a meeting with my boss that didn't go exactly as I hoped it would. But really, it's not a big deal. I'm still trying to figure him out – he's different than anyone I've worked with before. I'm going to make some changes to my presentation tonight and then I'll go over it with him again tomorrow," Derek says.

"Is there anything I can do to help?" I ask, although I can't imagine what I could do to help him.

"No, thanks. Sorry to eat and run," Derek says, trying to make a joke. "I think I still have a few hours of work to do so I better get started," he says, pushing away from the table.

As Derek walks by me on his way out of the kitchen, I notice the dark circles under his eyes. I hope he doesn't have to stay up too late tonight, he definitely looks like he could use some sleep.

"What happened to the couch?" Derek calls out, as he walks into the living room.

"I had them put the old one down in the basement, because the new one is coming tomorrow," I tell him, walking into the bare room to join him.

"Do we need a new couch?" he asks, sounding puzzled.

"Our old couch didn't go with the color scheme," I say confidently, repeating what Rick told me.

"I didn't know we *had* a color scheme," Derek says, looking around the room. "Wait, when did you paint the walls?" he asks.

"They just finished yesterday, but you've been home so late and going straight to bed, you didn't even notice. Do you like it?" I ask.

Derek doesn't say anything, so I continue, "They used no-odor paint, so you can't even smell it, and it doesn't have all those chemicals that are bad for Anna."

"I guess it looks nice. I thought it looked good before. Let's not do that much more, okay? I think the house looks great as it is," Derek says, heading off toward his office.

"Okay sweetie," I tell him. I'm guessing he would think that the work I've approved qualifies as "much more" but I'm sure he's going to love it once he sees it.

***

"What are you doing for lunch today?" I ask Sabrina. I'm surprised Sabrina even picked up her phone, since I know she usually lets everything go to voicemail (unless it's Danielle), but for some reason I still try. I get that texting is super convenient, but when I'm trying to make Anna's breakfast, it's easier to be on the phone than to text.

"It's only 7:30, I have no idea what I'm doing for lunch. I'm probably eating a salad at my desk," Sabrina replies. "Why, what's up?" she asks.

"Do you want to have lunch with me?" I ask her.

"Sorry sweetie, I'm swamped today. There's no way I can make it up to Westchester," Sabrina replies.

"No, no, of course not. But I can come to you! Even if it's just a quick lunch, or maybe even coffee?" I ask hopefully.

"I might be able to do a late lunch or coffee, but what about Anna? Do you really want to drag her into the city?" Sabrina asks.

"I have a sitter," I reply proudly.

"Really? Do you want to waste your sitter time on having coffee with me?" Sabrina asks. I can't tell what she's doing, but she's clearly put me on speaker phone, maybe she's putting on makeup, or one of the other things she does at 7:30 that differentiates our days.

"More banana pwease," Anna says, holding up her bowl at that very moment, as if I needed further proof.

I slice more bananas into Anna's bowl and tuck my phone between my shoulder and my ear. "No. I got a full-time sitter! She's coming four days a week! Isn't that amazing," I squeal.

"Wow. Do you really need a full time sitter?" Sabrina asks.

"What do you mean?" I respond immediately.

"It's just that you're not working now, and Anna's only three, so why would you need someone there all day?" she asks bluntly, in very Sabrina-like fashion.

"You wouldn't understand because you don't have kids, but it's a lot of work, and there are a lot of things I can't get done during the day if I have to drag Anna with me," I retort.

"How does Derek feel about it?" Sabrina asks.

"What? What does that even mean?" I ask.

"Nothing. I just thought you said he didn't like the idea of an au pair, so I'm surprised that he's fine with a full-time sitter," Sabrina says.

"He didn't like the idea of someone living with us," I tell her, which is a fraction of the truth.

"Anna just dropped her cereal on the floor, I have to go," I say, "talk to you later."

"Bye," Sabrina says, but I've already hung up the phone.

I could text her to follow up about plans for lunch or coffee, but I'm not really in the mood anymore.

Chapter 27 - Sabrina

As soon as I hang up the phone I feel terrible. I don't know why I gave Molly such a hard time about getting a sitter. When Danielle had a baby, I pushed her to get a nanny and was genuinely supportive. Maybe it seems easier now that Anna is a littler older and Molly isn't working; but the last time I was there, I was exhausted trying to entertain Anna for just a couple of hours, and Molly has to do that all day long!

I should call her back and apologize. Or even better, I could see if Danielle can join us for lunch today. Maybe Molly is still having a hard time adjusting and Danielle could help her navigate Westchester and introduce her to some people (I meant to do that earlier).

I need to get going, since I'm already running a little late and I'm only halfway done with my hair and makeup, but I'll send Danielle a text and see if she can get away from the office this afternoon.

Just as I pick up my phone, I see a text that came in while I was on the phone with my sister.

Parker: morning sunshine

Parker: I can't stop thinking about you

My immediate reaction is to respond: "I can't stop thinking about you too," because he is all I have thought about since our three-hour lunch earlier this week, but I don't think I should write that.

Sabrina: hey there

Parker: do you have plans tonight?

Hmmm, I am supposed to have dinner with Peter and his sister and his mom to talk about wedding stuff – it would probably be easier for everyone if they did it without me, but I'm going to have trouble selling that.

Sabrina: I can't do tonight, maybe tomorrow?

Parker: I don't want to wait that long. Besides, we have urgent business to discuss ☺

Sabrina: I could probably meet for a late lunch or coffee…

Parker: I'll pick somewhere near your office

I think about it for a minute before texting back.

Sabrina: It doesn't need to be too close to my office

Parker: ☺

Parker: I'll text you in a bit

The smile is plastered on my face as I reassess what I am going to wear today – all thoughts of Molly and Danielle gone from my mind.

Chapter 28 – Megan

I was just about to turn off my light, when my phone chirps. It's only 10:30 on Friday night, but after dinner, and a game of monopoly, it seemed like there wasn't too much else to do. Then I heard Kevin's car pull up outside, so I decided that was the perfect time to head upstairs. I grab my phone off the table where it is plugged into the charger and wonder if it is Ryan texting, or maybe Brad.

Georgia: Hi!!!!!!

Megan: omg! Hi! How r u?

Georgia: Great!!!!! How's the cape? How's your summer?

Megan: It's good. How's DC?

Georgia: It's crazy!!!! It's one giant party. Tonight is the first night I've stayed in all summer - insane, right? But there's this outdoor festival that starts tomorrow morning at 9 and goes all day and all night, and I'm just so tired ☹

Megan: wow, that sounds great. How's your job? How's Ian?

Georgia: the job is a joke, but it will look great on my college apps – thanks Dad! Ian's amazing – we're practically living together. So, what's the party scene like there?

Before responding, I take a look down at my plaid pajama pants and think back to my wildest night so far this summer – getting ice cream with Brad and the girls.

Megan: it's more laid back, but I've met some awesome people

Georgia: Any hot guys? ☺ ☺

My face grows hot just reading her text. I know she doesn't mean anything by it, but I still feel guilty.

Megan: I've got Ryan

Georgia: Of course, I meant for Jess

Megan: Right! I'll keep looking

Georgia: Okay, gotta go, kisses

Megan: you too

I'm definitely not the party girl that Georgia is (and I can't even imagine the stories Jess is going to come back with from Costa Rica and Southampton), but hearing about Georgia's crazy summer makes me feel really lame. All I've done so far is hang out with two kids and explore the beaches and tourist attractions of Cape Cod. Also I've spent one evening with a really hot guy, but the girls were there for that too, so it doesn't even count. And to top it all off, Ryan is acting like I don't exist anymore!

In a wave of self-pity, I take out my phone and shoot Brad a text:

Megan: want to hang out tomorrow? I don't have to work the rest of the weekend

To my delight, Brad responds immediately.

Brad: Thought you'd never ask ☺ want to go to the vineyard?

Megan: for the day?

Brad: unless you want to stay over…

Megan: that's not what I meant ☺

Brad: we'll take the ferry in the morning and take the last ferry back tomorrow night

Brad: unless we miss the ferry and then we'll have to come back on Sunday

My heart is racing in anticipation of spending the whole day with Brad, and I know he is joking, but also at the crazy idea of getting trapped on an island and having to stay there together. I try to snap myself back to reality so I can write back.

Megan: where should I meet you?

Brad: I'll pick you up. What's your address?

Megan: 37 Swift Lane in Brewster

Brad: See you at 9

And just like that, it looks like my summer got a little more interesting.

***

Brad's car pulls up out front at 8:59. I desperately wish I could have asked for Danielle's advice on what to wear or what to pack, but I know she would not have approved of my day trip with Brad. Even though we're just friends, I know that Danielle would not have liked the idea of me going to the Vineyard with Brad. Unlike most moms (or stepmoms, or mom-types) who don't want their daughters to get too serious; Danielle loves Ryan and thinks he's 'one of the good ones.'

"That's a pretty sweet ride," Kevin says, looking out the window, and whistling.

I notice Brad getting out of a little convertible and walking toward the door, but I hadn't paid much attention to the car.

"What kind is it?" I ask Kevin, not wanting to look foolish in front of Brad. I've never really paid much attention to cars – probably because my dad cares so much about them, and that turned me off instantly.

"It's a Maserati Gran Turismo," Kevin says, once again admiring the car parked in the driveway. "Your boyfriend has good taste," Kevin comments, taking a sip of his coffee.

"Oh no, he's just a friend," I say, rushing to open the door.

"Hey there," I say as I open the door just as Brad was about to ring the doorbell.

"You ready to go?" he asks.

"Yup, let me just grab my bag," I tell him.

"Hi, I'm Brad," he says, making his way past the foyer into the living room to shake hands with Kevin.

"I'm Kevin. Nice to meet you," he says.

"Hi Brad," Caitlin squeals, running into the room in her Ariel nightgown with severe bed-head.

"Hey Caitlin," Brad says, giving her a fist bump.

"So what are you guys doing on your date today?" Caitlin asks, taking a bite of the muffin she is carrying around in her hand.

"It's not a date," I say to Caitlin quickly. I turn around to look at Brad and see his reaction to my statement, but he is no longer there.

"Where did he go?" I ask Caitlin.

"I don't know," she shrugs, and runs back to watch TV on her skinny little legs.

Then I hear Brad and Heather's voices and follow the sound into the kitchen. Heather is laughing at something Brad just said, but I was too late to hear what it was.

"You guys should get going, I don't want to keep you," Heather says, as soon as she sees me. Unlike the rest of the family, who is still in pajamas, Heather is fully dressed in mint-green twill shorts and a navy tank top. She looks particularly good today (maybe it's for Kevin's benefit). I think she's wearing the tiniest bit of make-up, but her skin is glowing and her golden hair looks fantastic, though her hair always looks great. If she wasn't more than twenty years older than me, I'd be a little bit jealous of Brad in here talking to her.

"Yup, we should probably leave soon, so we don't miss our ferry," I add.

"Right," Brad says. "We wouldn't want to miss the ferry."

"What will you guys do today?" I ask Heather, as I sling my tote bag over my shoulder. I'm sure I've over packed, but I threw in a bathing suit, a pair of jeans, a sweater if it gets cold later, and a few other things I probably won't need.

"Oh, don't worry about us, we'll figure it out," Heather replies. "Go have fun!"

"Okay, I'll be back tonight," I tell her.

Brad is already at the front door, so I hope he doesn't hear when Heather says, "we won't wait up!" and then gives me a conspiratorial wink. I guess I'm glad that I didn't tell her about Ryan, because then she'd probably think I was a slut. However, I'm having a harder and harder time convincing myself that this is totally platonic, since no one else seems to think it looks that way.

"You might want to tie your hair back," Brad suggests, when we get in the car. "It can get a little windy."

I could tell him that Ryan has a Jeep Wrangler, so I'm used to windy convertible hair, and was already grabbing a rubber band from my bag, but I decide that it isn't the right comment.

Although I may be used to a convertible, I'm definitely not used to a car like this. Brad must be going eighty-five miles an hour and I can barely feel a thing; I'm sure he would go faster, if there weren't other cars around. I can't believe we haven't been pulled over yet! It's too loud to talk, the only noises I can hear are the wind whipping past my ears and the purr of the engine as he occasionally shifts gears.

Sooner than expected, we arrive in Hyannis, and Ryan expertly navigates the city streets and uses a special card to open a gate and pull into a parking lot right near the harbor.

"Is this the ferry?" I ask him.

"Sort of," he replies, grinning at me. "Let's go."

For a second I get a sick feeling in my stomach; I don't actually know much about this guy, other than he's really hot, drives a super expensive car and his mom looks like Michelle Obama. Or maybe that wasn't even his mom? He targeted *me* on the beach – maybe this was all an elaborate set-up and he's going to sell me into a sex-trade! Danielle is always forwarding me those articles and I delete them immediately, but maybe I should have paid more attention!

"Are you coming?" Brad asks gently.

I realize I am still gripping the handle of the door, and I slowly close the solid Italian-made machine and follow Brad to what could be my doom.

"Aren't you going to close the top?" I ask, concerned for the fate of the buttery leather seats.

"It will be fine here," Brad responds, confidently.

I look around the lot and notice again that it definitely doesn't look like a public ferry parking lot. There are only six or seven cars in the lot and although Brad's may be the nicest, the other cars aren't too far behind.

"Where are we going?" I ask him, quickening my pace to catch up with his long strides.

"We're going to the Vineyard, remember?" he says, playfully.

"No, I mean, where are we going right *now*," I clarify.

"The timing of the ferries can be a little restrictive, so I thought it would be better if we went on our own," he explains, gesturing casually toward a gleaming red and white cigarette boat docked right in front of us. "Besides, it's more fun this way," he adds, with his trademark grin.

"Why did you say we were going to take the ferry?" I ask. I'm still trying to wrap my head around the change in plans, but I'm pretty sure he's not running an underground sex ring.

"I thought it would be fun to surprise you," he answers.

Moments later we are flying across the Vineyard Sound on our way to the Harbor at Oaks Bluffs, the seawater lightly spraying my face every time we hit a wake. For the second time today, I am less than a few feet away from Brad, but we can't say a word to each other – presumably when we finish travelling, we'll actually speak.

***

Brad is pointing out sights as soon as we are off the boat and on dry land. It seems he is just as comfortable here as he is in Chatham. I could tell him that I used to come here for a week in the summer with my family when I was little, when we were still a happy family of four. Maybe we were never a happy family, but until I was about ten or eleven, I certainly thought we were. I should also probably tell him that Ryan and I came here last summer for a weekend with a group of his friends from Columbia, but that seems weird to bring up – and it also feels like a lifetime ago.

I take my phone out of my bag to quickly check my messages. Last night after I made plans with Brad, I felt guilty, so I sent Ryan a text. It's now been over a week since I'd heard from him, but maybe he wrote back this time.

There's one new text from Danielle telling me about something funny Abby did, but nothing from Ryan.

I shove my phone back in my bag, and try to focus on what Brad is saying.

"We could head over to Edgarton, or Vineyard Haven? Or just get a late breakfast here? What would you rather do?" he asks.

"Let's walk to Jaws Bridge," I say with certainty.

"Are you sure?" he asks, looking at me skeptically.

"Why, are you scared?" I tease.

"No, it's just a bit of a hike," he responds.

"I'm up for it," I respond. "Did you bring your suit?" I question, noting that he doesn't seem to have anything with him.

"I'll just get one right now," he says, "back in a sec," and he disappears into the Vineyard Vines that we happen to be passing.

In addition to Brad's obvious good looks, he is also so confident and easy going. It's not that Ryan isn't *those things*, but there's something about Brad's assertiveness

236

that is incredibly sexy. And Ryan is over three thousand miles away and won't return my texts or calls and Brad is right here and actually wants to spend time with me.

"Ready to jump!" Brad says, exiting the store, carrying a pair of pink flamingo board shorts.

"Me too," I say, surprising both of us as I wrap my arms around his muscular shoulders and plant my lips on his. It takes him a second to realize what's happening; but then I feel one of his hands on the small of my back and the other gently hold the back of my head and our mouths open and he slips his tongue inside. Brad kisses exactly like I thought he would, and it's spectacular.

And just like that, on the corner of Narragansett and Circuit Ave, I become a cheater.

Chapter 29 – Heather

Another weekend is over. Kevin is on his way back to New York, and Megan and the girls are off at the beach. This was definitely the best weekend of the summer, but Kevin is still treating me like I'm made of glass. I convinced him that we could all go on a bike ride, but after two miles he made us turn around and come home. It was ridiculous, considering it took more time to rent the bikes then it did to ride them!

I wanted to tell him that I do three miles as my warm up, but that wouldn't solve anything. Either he would be so worried (and upset) that he would insist on staying here and watching my every movement, or he would make Megan do it, and that would be awful for both of us.

I know he thinks Megan is keeping an eye on me during the day; but Megan is far more useful to me keeping the girls happy. Caitlin adores her and even Brooke seems to like her most of the time (which is saying a lot for an almost twelve-year-old).

I was actually planning on spending the day with the girls, since they are lounging around at our private Brewster beach. But Megan asked if her friend Brad could come hang out with them later this morning and bring his brother, and Brooke and Caitlin finally made friends with a few kids on the adjoining beaches, so I think I will be an unwanted addition if I wander outside to join them.

I promised myself I wasn't going to contact Jasper today, but I feel like I'm about to break that promise.

I shoot him a text, wondering if he'll reply quickly or if it will be like last week and I'll never hear back.

Heather: I'm in the mood for chowder, you?

Within seconds, I'm rewarded with his reply.

Jasper: Yes!! I'm staring at my screen and nothing's happening – would love a break!

Heather: Where should we go?

Jasper: JT's? I'll meet you there in 20?

Heather: ok

I hadn't planned on it actually happening so fast, but of course that was what I wanted. I wonder if I should tell the girls where I'm going? Honestly, they won't even know I'm gone – I packed them lunch and they'll probably be out there all day. To be young, and have friends, and the beach and not a worry in the world – it must be nice. And Megan has that magnificent boy following her around – what I wouldn't give to be seventeen again…

I catch a glimpse of my reflection in the window and decide that I probably don't need to change my outfit for a bowl of chowder at JT's, or it will look like I am trying way too hard. Then I quickly remind myself that of course there is nothing to *try* for. I glance in the window again and decide that I could probably use a belt with my navy linen shorts and pink v-neck t-shirt, but other than that, I look casual and fresh. I grab my keys and purse, and slide a pair of flip flops on my feet from the pile of shoes by the front door, and head out for a spur-of-the-moment bowl of chowder.

***

Jasper is sitting on the back deck of JT's waiting for me when I arrive. Thankfully I didn't get any dressier, since he is wearing his black bike shorts and a grey dri-fit t-shirt with a Nike swoosh across the chest. Jasper stands to give me a kiss on the cheek as I approach the table, and I smell the mix of his woodsy aftershave and maybe a hint of sweat from his bike ride to the restaurant.

"You saved me!" Jasper declares, as we sit back down.

"I don't know about that," I say self-consciously.

"No, it's true. I've been re-writing the same two paragraphs all morning and then I got your text and it gave me the perfect excuse to take a break! I'm going to go for a ride after lunch as well, and maybe that will clear my head," he adds.

"Happy to help," I say. "Do we order here? Or should we go inside?" I ask. Looking around at the ultra casual nature of the restaurant, it seems unlikely that there is table service.

"I already ordered for us inside, it should be out in just a minute," Jasper adds, beaming at me.

As soon as the words are out of his mouth, a voice inside yells out, "order twenty-seven!" and Jasper jumps up from the table and hurries inside. He returns carrying a tray with two bowls of clam chowder, two iced teas, and a basket of fried oysters and French fries.

"Wow," I say, looking at the feast.

"You said you wanted chowder, but I didn't know if you wanted anything to go with it...and I didn't want you to be hungry," he adds, in a concerned tone.

"That's so nice of you," I tell him. The guilt is overwhelming as I take my first bite of soup. Kevin and I are definitely having a few issues, but I would never cheat on him. I have to stop leading Jasper on, it's just not fair that he's really starting to care about me, when nothing is going to happen.

"I'm going to need to bike for about five hours to have any chance of working this off," Jasper says, patting his absurdly rock-hard stomach. "Luckily, you don't have to worry about that," he says, winking at me.

I can't take it anymore. "I'm married, Jasper. I'm so sorry," I cry out. I'm relieved to have the secret out in the open, but terrified what will happen next.

"Oh, well, that's nothing to be *sorry* about," Jasper says, looking confused.

"I know I should have told you sooner, but I didn't know how to say it," I stumble on the words as they come out.

"Why wouldn't you want me to know you're married?" Jasper asks, leaning over to have a mouthful of chowder.

"Oh my God," I say, as the realization hits that Jasper never had any interest in me.

Unfortunately it gets a lot worse. "Oh Heather, oh honey. I'm gay. Didn't you know that?" Jasper asks, in a tone that can only be described as pity mixed with humor.

"No, I did *not* know that," I moan. My face is buried in my hands, so I'm not sure if Jasper can hear me or not.

I'm not sure if I will ever be able to face him again, but after a couple minutes of staring at the old French fries on the floor, it seems that it is more embarrassing to continue on this way. I slowly lift my head up and am faced with Jasper's worried gaze.

"Are you okay?" he asks.

"I'll be fine, a little humiliation never hurt anyone," I say, trying to be funny. "So, what is *this*?" I ask, motioning with my hand between the two of us.

"We're friends," Jasper says. "Don't you have any male friends?" he asks.

"Actually, no," I answer.

"Are you serious?" Jasper asks, looking at me intently and then grabbing a fried oyster from the basket.

"I used to have guy friends, but I don't think I've had any since I got married. I don't even know what happened to them. I had a ton of them in high school and in college, and when I first lived in the City – there was that blurry line with a lot of those friends between friends and boyfriends and friends-with-benefits, but then they all kind of disappeared. Now I have Kevin and some girlfriends," I tell Jasper, thinking it through for myself as well.

The silence hangs over us, as I poke my spoon into my white chunky soup and wait for him to say something.

"Maybe I shouldn't bring this up, but if you didn't know I was gay, and you are married, but you were pretending that you weren't, then what did *you* think this was?" he asks.

I can feel the heat spread across my face, and I know my cheeks match the shade of the lobster hanging on the wall. Last time I felt a bit of a blush with Jasper was when I mistook his friendliness for a come-on, but I know that this is pure shame.

I thought I was going to come to lunch and enjoy one more day pumping up my ego and then let Jasper down easily. I had honestly hoped that we could still be friends, because I enjoy spending time with him, but I had prepared myself that it might be too difficult if his feelings were too strong.

I couldn't be a bigger idiot! In the dictionary, next to the word idiot, there's a huge picture of me. How do I possibly explain this to him without sounding like a pathetic loser?

"It's kind of a long story," I say to Jasper.

"I love long stories," Jasper says, flashing me his beautiful smile, and giving me his full attention.

Jasper's grin makes me realize that maybe all along I needed a friend far more than a flirtation.

"So I guess it all started last November when we found out I had breast cancer…" I say, exhaling as I begin to let it all out.

Chapter 30 – Molly

"You look good," Jeannie says, giving me an air kiss on both cheeks as she enters the foyer and looks me up and down. "The cleanse is amazing, right?"

"I guess so. I definitely notice a difference," I tell her. While it's true that my clothes are looser after five days on this horrific green juice, I'm not sure I will ever be able to eat another piece of kale or spinach again – I practically gag when I open the bottle, each one is worse than the last.

"It's the best! I do it once every two months," she says, her chic blonde ponytail bobbing up and down. She must have just come from a class, or a session with her trainer. She is dressed head to toe in lilac spandex with x-shaped cutouts strategically placed on the legs, chest and back. There are few women who aren't strippers or hookers who could pull off this look – especially paired with over $75,000 worth of diamonds - but Jeannie manages to make it work.

"You could juice once a month if you want. You know, until you reach your goal," Jeannie says, giving me a knowing look.

Thankfully, Lisa interrupts before I can respond, because I'm already on edge from hunger and I'm pretty sure I will say something I'll regret.

"The living room looks nice," Lisa offers. "What are you doing next?" she asks, looking around like there's a bad smell but she can't quite place it.

"Rick is starting on the foyer tomorrow," I tell her. "But there really isn't much to do in here."

"Oh?" Jeannie and Lisa both say, doubting my response.

"I think Rick said he was going to paint and order a new hall table," I tell them, suddenly wondering if this is the truth.

"Rick's the best," Jeannie gushes. "He'll do whatever needs to be done. But I'd be surprised if he didn't do wainscoting in here and probably replace the crown molding, oh and definitely a new chandelier and some sconces, and the rug, but I'm sure it isn't much more than that," she assures me, placing her freshly manicured hand on my arm.

"Anyhow, we came over here today, because we wanted to ask you something," Lisa says, looking at Jeannie. Lisa is also sporting a fancy Lycra outfit that I would never attempt (even with weekly cleanses), but hers is a little more demure – black capri pants in a size zero or double zero, and a pale green open back top that reveals an elaborate looking black sports bra.

"I'll just come out and say it," Jeannie says, looking back at Lisa.

I have no idea what they are talking about and if I should be excited or nervous, but at this point, I'd just like to know.

"We wanted to ask if you would host the next mommy and me playgroup," Jeannie says excitedly, clapping her hands for emphasis.

I breathe a sigh of relief. I'm not sure what I thought she was going to say, but this is finally something easy. I hosted tons of playgroups in Boulder. We did one on Saturday mornings, since most of the moms in our group worked full-time. Thinking about the group gives me a twinge of homesickness as I remember the going-away party they threw for me last spring – I really should call and check in...

"Let's go take a quick look at the yard to see what we're dealing with, shall we?" Lisa says.

"What do you mean? Why do we need to look at the yard?" I ask foolishly.

Jeannie is already on her way to the kitchen and heading toward the sliding glass doors that lead to the blue slate patio. "We know the house isn't ready for you to host anything, but we wanted you to have a chance to meet more people," Jeannie says to me, while letting herself out the back door.

"Okay," I answer, following her outside. "But the living room is done, and surely the house is fine for me to have some people over for a playgroup," I say to her. I also wonder why they couldn't just invite Anna and me to someone else's house if they are anxious for me to meet people, but I keep that thought to myself.

"It's definitely coming along," Lisa says, in a sugary sweet voice, but if you're meeting these new moms for the first time, you probably want everything to be perfect."

"That's why we thought it would be easier to do the group outside," Jeannie says, surveying my backyard.

Unfortunately, Anna and Derek and I haven't taken as much advantage of our new yard as we should, but I guess she has a point. We have a half-acre of property with a flat lawn and a lovely patio; maybe it *would* be nice to have the playgroup outside.

"We don't have a lot of time, but my landscapers can do miracles," Jeannie assures me.

"What do you mean?" I ask her, looking around at the yard.

"You obviously need to fence in the whole backyard, and the grass isn't too bad, but I'll see what TJ says. You'll need to order new furniture, because clearly this is just temporary," she says, pointing to the table and chairs on the patio.

"Are you sure all of this is really necessary?" I ask. My head is starting to swim from her list of improvements.

"Definitely," Jeannie says.

"Yes, definitely," Lisa agrees.

"Hello, anybody home?" a man's voice calls. Shortly after I hear him, I see a short man, with biceps bigger than my thighs, lumbering into the backyard. He is wearing an olive polo shirt with 'TJ's landscaping' embroidered above his bulging left pectoral, so I'm guessing this must be Jeannie's landscaper.

"Hi TJ, we're over here!" Jeannie calls out, although by this point, TJ has already seen us, so I don't know if that's necessary.

"Hope I'm not too early," TJ says, as he walks up to our group.

"You're right on time," Jeannie says, smiling at him. "This is Molly," Jeannie says, introducing me to my new landscaper.

"Hi TJ, thanks for coming," I say, although I'm not sure that I *am* glad he's here.

"So, it's the fence, and the sod, and the shrubs?" TJ asks, addressing Jeannie.

"Exactly. And I know this is short notice, but is there any chance you could get it done this week? It *has* to be done by next Tuesday," Jeannie says, solemnly.

"It's going to be tough, but if I have my guys work overtime, I think we can get it done," TJ assures her.

I'm not sure what just happened, but it appears that Jeannie just arranged for her landscaper to re-do my lawn without even consulting me. Is that possible? Derek just told me not to do any more major projects, and although it's just some grass and a fence, I'm pretty sure he wouldn't be thrilled with this. I can't imagine it's going to be that expensive, but I wish I had some idea what it would cost.

"Thanks for making this work TJ," I say to him. "Um, by any chance do you know how much this will cost?" I ask him, trying to act like it isn't a big deal.

"I'll get you some numbers when I have a chance. But we'll be able to start this afternoon," TJ promises me.

Crap. "Okay, great," I say, trying to smile.

"Oh yay!" Jeannie squeals. "So glad this worked out! I'll send out the invites to the other mommies today," she tells me.

"Oh, Molly, one more thing. We always use Little Bakers catering company for our playgroups. They already know everyone's allergies and dietary restrictions, so it's sooo much easier. Just give them a call and they'll know what to do," she chimes. "I'll text you the info!"

"So glad this worked out!" Lisa says, "Can't wait!"

"Me neither," I reply, trying to sound excited.

Chapter 31 – Sabrina

"You're up early," Peter remarks as he walks into the kitchen in his scrub bottoms, and then presses his body up behind mine and starts to kiss the back of my neck.

"I'm out of the office for the next few days, so I want to get as much as I can done before I leave," I tell him. I try to grab the milk from the fridge to continue making my coffee, but it's somewhat difficult with Peter attached to me.

"Why are you out of the office?" he says with a yawn, releasing his grasp from my waist, and rubbing the sleep from his eyes.

"Don't you remember? I told you last night that I'm going to be in Armonk for meetings for a couple days," I tell him, slightly annoyed.

"Oh sorry," Peter says. "I guess you mentioned that when you came to bed last night, but it was really late. I was almost asleep when you came in," he adds.

"It's not a big deal. I'm going up there after lunch today and I'll be back on Thursday," I tell him. I grab an apple from the fruit bowl on the counter and take another huge gulp of my coffee as I run through the list in my head again to see if I've forgotten to pack anything.

"You're staying in Armonk for two nights?" Peter asks in a confused voice as he looks at the Tumi suitcase on the floor. "It's forty-five minutes away. Why would you stay there?" he asks.

"It just seems easier. I think the meetings are going to be all day and then I have dinners, and I'll have to get up and go back in the morning," I say.

"It's called commuting, people do it every day," he says, sounding a little annoyed.

"Sorry sweetie, I just thought it would be easier. Aren't you at the hospital anyway?" I say, trying to deflect back to him.

"I have a late shift tonight, but I'm off tomorrow," he says sadly.

"Oh, sorry, I didn't know that," I tell him. "Maybe I'll see if I can get home tomorrow night," I say.

"Have you had a chance to look at the hotel contract?" Peter asks me. He casually grabs a coffee mug from the cabinet and begins to pour himself a cup. I quickly glance at my watch (7:08), ugh, I wanted to leave here at 7, so I could be at my desk at 7:30! This is one of the worst parts of our opposite schedules – Peter doesn't have to be in until noon today, so he wants to have a leisurely discussion now and I need to run out of here.

"I took a glance at it," I lie. "I'll look it over today. But honestly, if you're fine with it, then I'm sure it's fine. Okay, I have to go. I'll see you on Thursday," I tell him, giving him a quick peck on the lips.

"Or hopefully tomorrow night," Peter reminds me.

"Right, hopefully Wednesday," I say, not holding my breath.

***

The afternoon is filled with discussions about the importance of integrating technology and education. I always considered myself to be an early adopter – I get the newest cell phone and the latest headphones, and I was the first of all my friends to have an iPad. But sitting here with the developers of these amazing products makes me realize that I have no idea what I'm doing.

It is fascinating to listen to them talk about technology that I thought only existed in movies, but apparently they are creating it right here! The idea of integrating these tools to help the mentors tailor their work for each of the girls is fascinating. And according to what I'm hearing, it's only the tip of the iceberg – there are so many more ways we can change the paths for these young girls.

I'm so absorbed in the presentation that I don't notice when Parker slides into the empty seat beside me.

"How am I supposed to focus, when you're sitting here?" he leans over and whispers in my ear.

"Shouldn't you be leading a discussion group or something?" I whisper back, but my smile is practically touching both my ears.

"I had a break," he says quietly. "How much longer is this going to last?" he whispers again.

253

"Shhh. I'm trying to listen. Besides, you're in charge, don't *you* decide when it's over," I whisper back, secretly loving the attention, while trying to ignore the dirty look from the woman next to me.

"Good point," he says very quietly into my ear and then disappears.

***

I feel a pang of guilt checking into the Ritz in White Plains, but I feel guilty for everything I do recently. I'm not spending enough time with Peter, I'm not doing enough for the wedding, I'm spending too much time with Parker, I'm not being a good sister to Molly, I don't have enough time for Danielle – the list goes on and on.

I know I should have gone back to the City tonight. It wouldn't have taken that much more time, but I miss spending the night in a hotel now that I don't travel for work – and if I'm being honest, I wanted a couple of nights totally by myself.

I strip out of my clothes the second I enter the room and toss them on the club chair in the corner. If it were a little warmer, I might sit around in just my black lace thong. But like all hotels, the air conditioning is cranked way too high, so I grab the fluffy white robe from the closet and wrap it tightly around my body. I pull the covers all the way down on the king-size bed before I sit down, because even at the Ritz, you can never be too careful.

The room service menu is comforting in its familiarity. There are obviously a few modifications from other Ritz Carltons, and more so from other brands, but the basic options are still the same. As I debate between the

Turkey BLT and the Caesar salad or Horseradish Crusted Salmon with a side of Truffle Fries, I am almost taken back to a time when I traveled four days a week and occasionally hooked up with random men in *foreign* cities (like Austin or Des Moines) and didn't think twice about it.

As if he can read my mind, Parker texts at that exact moment:

Parker: what are you doing?

Sabrina: I'm about to eat some dinner, watch something terrible on TV and then go to bed

Parker: Want company?

Why would he ask if I wanted company? Even for him, that's pretty bold to invite himself over –even if he knew Peter was working late, I would never have him over to our apartment. Unless…

Sabrina: Where are you?

My heart is racing as I wait for his response.

Parker: I'm in room 503

Holy crap!

Sabrina: How did you know I was staying here?

Parker: your assistant mentioned it. I thought it sounded like a good idea, so I got a room too…

Parker: so do you want company?

Oh my God. It's all finally real. I guess I shouldn't be so surprised considering all the recent flirtations, but until now, I could chalk it all up as harmless. I know that I don't 'owe him anything' and if I tell him to go away, he will respect my wishes and leave me alone. But the problem is that I don't want him to go away. From the second I saw him at the bar, I've wanted him. I love Peter, but I can't live the rest of my life knowing that I turned down the chance for one more time with Parker.

Sabrina: I'm in room 617

***

For a minute, I think about putting my clothes back on, but there's no reason for pretense. Besides, my entire body is burning just at the thought of touching Parker again, I don't think I could stand to put a suit back on and make small talk.

"This is quite the pleasant surprise," I say, when I open the door and welcome Parker into my room.

"Are you sure this isn't why you stayed here?" Parker says, challenging me.

"I promise, I didn't even think about it, it was just for the convenience," I tell him, although I can't help but smile.

"Okay, if you say so," he replies, holding his hands up in mock surrender.

"So, what are we going to order from room service? And what trashy TV will we be watching?" Parker asks, taking his shoes off and sitting down on the bed fully dressed in his dark jeans and pink button down.

Suddenly I'm worried that I've misread the situation - although that seems unlikely. I try to tighten my robe as I pick up the leather room service menu from the night-table and begin to study it like there will be a test.

"Or we could eat after..." Parker says brazenly.

"Thank God. For a second, I thought you really were here to watch TV," I joke.

"Are you kidding me? If that robe isn't on the ground in the next five seconds, I'm going to cut it off you," Parker says, reaching over and untying the belt and letting the robe slip off my shoulders and onto the floor.

"You're so beautiful," Parker says, surveying my almost naked body as I'm kneeling on the bed in front of him. "Is it possible you look better than you did when you were twenty-two?" he asks, reaching out and gently brushing his hand against my stomach.

"You don't look too bad yourself," is all I can manage in terms of a reply, since most of the oxygen seems to have left my brain.

"I'm only wearing a thong and you're still fully dressed, that doesn't seem quite fair," I comment.

"I think I can fix that," Parker says, and with that he sits up and takes off his button down in one quick move over his head and in another instant, he wriggles out of his jeans and his boxers.

"Is that better?" he asks, with a smirk.

It's an understatement to say that Parker looks better than he did in college, because then he was a boy, and now he is clearly a man. A man who takes very good care of himself and seems to know exactly what he wants, and it looks like right now, what he wants, is me.

The next half hour is a blur of sweaty bodies and orgasms and pure ecstasy. I'm shocked we don't get a call from the front desk with complaints from the noise level alone.

And then it's over.

"Oh my God, that was incredible," I say to Parker, trying to catch my breath.

"You've learned some new tricks," Parker says, twirling my hair around his finger.

"I'm starving," I exclaim. "I think we've earned our dinner!"

Parker gently moves my head off of his chest and swings his long legs over to his side of the bed, and starts searching for his clothes, which are strewn across the bed and the floor. "I've actually got some work to finish up, so I think I'll order something to my room and eat there. Is that okay?" he asks.

"Oh, um, yeah sure, I guess," I say, trying to recover from the shock of his announcement.

"I'll stay if you want me to," Parker offers.

"No, that's fine. You should go get some work done. I actually have work to do to," I tell him. I'm desperately searching for my robe, but it must be tangled up in the sheets on the floor; it seems to have vanished at a most inopportune time.

"I thought you were going to watch trashy TV?" Parker jokes.

"I can watch TV and work at the same time, I'm a multi-tasker," I tell him.

"I bet you are," he says, and winks at me.

"I'll see you tomorrow," Parker says, "sleep tight," and with that he's out the door.

My appetite has disappeared. Five minutes ago I was famished, and now I couldn't eat a thing. What the fuck just happened? I wish I could talk to Danielle about this, but she's the last person I could call (I guess Peter is the last person...)

That reminds me to check my phone. I vaguely remember hearing several messages come through while Parker was on top of me, but it wasn't really a good time to stop and see who was trying to reach me.

Ugh, of course they are all from Peter.

Peter: Hope you had a great day!

Peter: Thinking about you

Peter: Have a great time at dinner

Peter: Remember to look at the hotel contract if you get a chance

Peter: I love you xoxoxoxo

I'm the worst person ever.

Chapter 32 – Megan

"So what happens when you go back to New York after the summer?" Brooke asks.

Caitlin and Heather have gone to the Nature Center for a few hours this morning, so Brooke and I have the house to ourselves. We are sitting on the front porch reading in companionable silence, or at least we were until a moment ago.

"What do you mean? I just go back to New York and go back to school for my senior year," I tell her, a little confused by the question.

"I mean what happens with you and Brad?" she says, annoyed that I didn't understand her the first time.

"Oh, I don't know. I mean we're really just friends. I'm sure we'll still be friends when he goes to Dartmouth," I tell her.

"Oh come on! You are *so* not just friends," Brooke challenges me.

I want to object, but I know she is almost twelve, and not a little kid. Clearly Brad and I have not been doing a very good job of hiding what's been going on the last few weeks.

"I don't blame you. If I were your age, I would totally date him. He's so hot and really rich, and he has a really great body," Brooke adds assertively, taking a sip of her lemonade.

I'm about to tell her that she's too young to be looking at boys (and definitely not Brad!) but then I realize she'll just argue with me, so I decide to take another tactic.

"So what about you?" I ask.

"What do you mean?" she replies.

"Are you dating any of those boys that you hang out with?" I ask her.

"Ewww gross," she says, looking at me like I'm crazy. "I mean a couple of them are kind of cute, but mostly just gross. Besides, I'm only going to be twelve next month, I'm not even in seventh grade," she protests.

"Sorry!" I say, trying not to laugh. One minute she's judging the body of a college freshman and the next she's offended that I would think she liked another twelve-year old – I guess that's how it works.

"But seriously, are you guys going to stay together or break up when you leave here?" she asks, like I'm her guest on a daytime talk show.

"We're not together," I say, using my fingers to demonstrate air quotes around the word together, "so we can't break up." I don't know why I insist on arguing with Brooke about this, but I have to stand my ground.

"Oh, I get it. You're friends with benefits," she says, nodding her head knowingly and squinting her dark brown eyes ever so slightly.

"What? No! We're friends. It's complicated," I say, getting frustrated.

"Just admit that he's your boyfriend. If he were *my* boyfriend, I would want everyone to know," she tells me.

Although I'm happy Brooke is now so comfortable with me that we are arguing over the intimate nature of my relationship with Brad, I'm kind of wishing we could put the genie back in the bottle and go back to the beginning of the summer when she wanted nothing to do with me. It's been weeks since I've heard from Ryan, but I still feel weird calling Brad my boyfriend, or even admitting that we are dating, or whatever it is we are doing.

"Speaking of your boyfriend, I think he's calling you right now," Brooke says triumphantly, as my phone begins to ring.

I momentarily consider asking her to go inside so I can take the call, or getting up and walking out into the front yard to get some privacy, but then reconsider. Brooke has pretty much become a lovable, somewhat annoying little sister, and I know she'll just make it worse for me if I try to take the call by myself.

"Whatcha doin'?" Brad asks, when I pick up the phone.

"Brooke and I are just reading," I tell him. Brooke bends her blonde head down over her book, but I know she is listening to every word I say, and I'm pretty sure she can hear Brad's half of the conversation as well.

"What are you doing Friday night?" Brad asks.

"I don't know. I'm not sure if Heather needs me to work," I tell him.

"She doesn't," Brooke whispers loudly, and then begins to make kissing sounds before she breaks into a fit of laughter.

"What did you have in mind?" I ask him, trying to sound upbeat and casual and not at all sexy, since Brooke is two feet away.

"My parents wanted to know if you would come over for dinner," Brad says.

"Really?" I reply.

"Yeah, why is that so weird?" he asks. "They just want to get to know you better, since we're spending so much time together, and they know how much I like you." Brad says, proving to be the one eighteen-year old boy in the world who isn't afraid to share his feelings.

I hug my knees to my chest and try to think about my response. Obviously Brad and I are more than just friends, but we have been taking it slowly. We haven't talked about it, but I thought maybe he was even sleeping with someone else and that was why he was okay with this moving at such a glacial pace. Apparently he's taking it slow because he really likes me...

I'm still so messed up over Ryan that I don't know what to do or what to think, but I definitely didn't think I was going to be getting to know his parents anytime soon!

I think Brad can sense my anxiety from the length of silence, so he adds, "you've already met them, so really this isn't a big deal. Just come over for a quick dinner and then we'll go out and do something, okay?" he asks.

"Let me make sure Heather doesn't need me. I'll text you in a couple hours when she's back and let you know," I tell him.

"I *told* you he was your boyfriend," Brooke says, the second I hang up the phone.

Chapter 33 – Sabrina

The last few days have been torture.

When I saw Parker at the IBM office the next morning, he was friendly and a little playful, but if I weren't still a little sore from the night before, I would have sworn that I imagined the entire thing. I stayed in the hotel the second night just to give myself more time to regroup before facing Peter. I told Parker that I was staying a second night, but I overheard from his colleagues that he went back into the City for drinks, and I haven't heard a word from him.

Since I've been back, I've tried to focus on Peter and the wedding, but it's not an easy task. I told Peter that I wasn't feeling well, but it was a rookie mistake to tell a doctor and empathetic fiancé that I don't feel well, because now he wants to cure me of my imaginary illness.

"Are you sure you feel well enough to go out to dinner?" Peter asks, giving me a worried look with his green eyes.

"I promise, I feel better," I tell him. "We're both home and it's seven o'clock - that never happens. Let's take advantage of it!" I tell him.

"Where do you want to go?" he asks.

"I don't care. You can pick. Whatever sounds good to you," I tell him, my guilt pushing me along.

"Let's just do sushi, it's close and it will be quick," he says. "Then we can come back and watch the videos the bands emailed me," he says.

"Sounds good," I say, forcing a smile. "Let me just change quickly."

One white skirt, blue tank top and pair of flip-flops later and we are on our way out the door to our favorite sushi restaurant. It isn't listed in any Zagat's guide, but it's close and they know us and the tuna avocado hand-roll is to die for.

***

Somehow Peter and I manage to get through dinner and it almost feels normal. We don't even talk much about the wedding! I fill him in on the amazing new technology I learned about and how it could impact the girls in my program, as well as some of the new mentors who have applied recently. Peter tells me funny stories about patients (anonymously of course), and it *almost* feels like when we first got together.

"Hold on, let me just see who this is," I say to Peter, after I feel my phone vibrate multiple times from text messages and missed calls.

I look and see four missed calls from Parker and a string of text messages.

Parker: Thinking about the other night

Parker: It's all I can think about

266

Parker: What are you doing now?

Parker: I have to see you

Parker: Can you come over?

Parker: Or I can get us a room

Parker: Just name the place

Parker: I have to see you now

"Is everything okay?" Peter asks, looking concerned.

I quickly delete all of the messages on my phone before I look up at him. "Not really. I mean, it will be okay, but it looks like something's happened with this huge presentation I've been working on," I tell him, trying to think of something.

"Oh, I'm so sorry," Peter says, looking visibly upset that I've got a problem.

"I have to go into the office right after dinner," I tell him, "I'm so sorry."

"Really? You can't work on it at home?" he asks, deflated.

"No, all the materials I need are still at the office," I tell him. "But I don't think it should take too long. Only a couple hours," I say. "Maybe I'll just get going now, and then I'll be home sooner," I tell him.

"Do you want me to come with you to keep you company?" he asks.

"Oh no!" I say, a little too loudly. "I mean, you would just be bored. You should go home and relax," I tell him, pushing my chair back from the table and giving him a peck on the cheek as I grab my bag and make my way toward the door.

I raise my hand to hail the oncoming cab, as I reply to Parker.

Sabrina: what's your address – I'm on my way

Chapter 34 – Heather

Getting over the humiliation proved easier than I would have thought, mostly because Jasper wouldn't let me wallow. Especially once I told him about the cancer and the chemo and the struggles I'd been going through with Kevin. It's funny, because when I first met Jasper, I was desperate for him not to find out that I had been sick and now we talk about it all the time. He jokes that he should be charging me for all the free therapy, but he isn't completely off base. Once I realized he wasn't hitting on me, I started confiding in him and that's been better medicine than harmless flirtation, or whatever I thought I was doing.

It isn't one-sided either. Jasper broke up with his boyfriend over the winter, so we talk about that as well and I give him advice on the new men he's dating. I briefly mentioned him to Kevin, but I downplayed the amount of time we are spending together - primarily, because I don't want to share Jasper. I can't imagine them hitting it off, but I really don't want them to start talking to each other about me, and I like having Jasper all to myself.

"How was the weekend?" Jasper asks, taking a sip of his coffee.

We are sitting outside Eat Cake 4 Breakfast, which I now think of as our "usual place" and rehashing the weekend while we decide how to spend the day together. I'm dressed in gray gym shorts and a black tank top; my face is free from all make-up and my blonde wig is pulled back into a low ponytail (a far cry from the days when I thought coffee with Jasper was a date).

"It was okay," I admit. "We were pretty lazy on Saturday, mostly stayed at the beach by the house. But on Sunday we went to Marconi Beach," I tell him, while breaking off a giant piece of my almond croissant and watching the crumbs scatter on the deck.

"That sounds great, I should really get up there," Jasper comments.

"It was good until I suggested we go for a hike, and then Kevin got nervous and wanted me to relax on the beach while he took the girls, which left me annoyed at him the rest of the day," I tell Jasper.

"He really is overprotective, isn't he?" Jasper observes. "He should see you out here on your bike or on a paddle board; maybe then he would realize that you're back to your old self," Jasper suggests.

"He would go crazy!" I tell him, thinking about Kevin's reaction if he saw what I did during the week.

"But the worst part was on Sunday night," I say.

"What happened?" Jasper asks, looking at me intently.

"Actually, I probably shouldn't say anything. It's a little weird to talk about," I tell him.

"You can tell me. It can't be any weirder than the story I told you about the guy I met on Zoosk, right?" he asks.

"Okay, fine. That *was* pretty bad," I say, trying not to laugh as I remember the story.

"So last night, I told Kevin that I really thought I was ready to try again, and he said he didn't think it was a good idea, and we should talk to the doctor before we do anything," I tell him, feeling embarrassed with this revelation.

"Try again for what?" Kevin asks, running his hands through his jet-black hair, and squinting his eyes, like he's really stumped.

"Try to have sex," I whisper, even though there is no one around - I can't believe that he didn't get it.

"Why do you have to try? Oh my God? When is the last time you had sex?" Jasper asks, clearly horrified.

"Right before the surgery," I tell him, mortified to share this with someone I've known for such a short time, but relieved to finally have it out in the open.

"What an asshole!" Jasper says, suddenly angry.

"It's complicated," I tell him.

"How is it complicated?" he asks. "You are his wife. You are a beautiful, intelligent, sexy woman! Why doesn't he want to have sex with you?" Jasper asks me.

Although I wish he would keep his voice down, this is the same question I have been asking myself for months.

"I don't know. For a long time after the surgery it was impossible. I was in too much pain from the incisions and the drains, and I couldn't imagine being touched. And then I was so sick from the chemo, that there were only a few good days each month between treatments, and it just never felt right. But now I feel healthy and ready and Kevin is worried that he's going to break me if he touches me. Even when he kisses me, it's always so gentle. In the beginning, I loved being taken care of, but now it makes me feel like I'm still that sick cancer patient and I hate it," I vent to Jasper, saying things I've wanted to say for months.

"I'm really sorry," Jasper says, reaching over and patting my hand sympathetically.

"Thanks. I thought this summer would be good for both of us, but he doesn't seem to notice that I'm basically back to normal. Look, I even fit in my clothes again," I joke, pulling on the waistband of my shorts to emphasize that they're barely loose.

"I'm sure he'll come around. He better be careful, he doesn't realize that you almost had an affair with an incredibly handsome gay man," Jasper says, striking a pose and giving me his best model stare.

"It's a little too soon for that to be funny," I tell him, but I crack a smile in spite of myself.

"When do you have to be back today? Where are Megan and the girls?" Jasper asks, changing the topic.

"I'm free until dinner. You'll never guess where they are! Brad took Megan and the girls out on his yacht for the day," I tell him.

"Whoa! Wait, I thought you said he took her to the Vineyard on some speedboat – I'm trying to keep up," Jasper says.

"It seems there are multiple boats. This is his parents' yacht, so I guess there's a captain and staff, but Megan and the girls are out there on the water as we speak for a day at sea. Apparently he has WaveRunners on the boat, they were really excited about that," I tell him, repeating what Brooke told me last night.

"Not to overstep my boundaries, but how well do you know this boy?" Jasper asks.

"I really like him. He's been hanging around the house a lot because he is crazy about Megan, and I think he's a good kid. Even with all his money, he's mostly just a normal kid who's trying to impress a girl. And Brooke and Caitlin like him almost as much as they like Megan," I tell him.

"If you're okay with it, then I'm sure it's fine," Jasper says. From the way he is drumming his fingers on the table I can tell that he isn't convinced.

"Megan went to his house on Friday night to have dinner with his parents, and she said they seem great too, so that made me feel even better about it. I don't think she was quite as impressed with our little beach house in Brewster after she got home, but that's another story," I say.

"Where is all the money from? I'm going to assume that it doesn't come from writing YA novels," Jasper says, laughing at his own joke.

"Ha! I'm not sure exactly, but from what Megan told me, his dad developed something and patented it and then sold it and it's in every wireless device in the world - now he sits on about a dozen boards. And his mom is the founder of an elite all-girls school in Boston," I tell him.

"I can't offer you a ride on a yacht today, but what about a long hike to make up for the one you didn't get to do yesterday? We could head out to Wellfleet and do the Great Island Trail, it's only about five miles, so that shouldn't take us too long. Especially since you're in such great shape," Jasper says.

Chapter 35 – Molly

The incessant banging is getting difficult to take, but TJ swears they will be done with all the work today. I didn't realize that a fence would be such a big deal, but that was because I was picturing something simple and wooden. Although I guess they would have needed to pour the mini foundations, or footings, for that too. But the fence we've ended up with is wrought iron with brick pillars every six feet; there is no way that our backyard is deserving of this quality of fence. This wasn't lost on TJ, because he decided to pull up all the grass and put in new sod to compensate.

Luckily, Derek is on a crazy multi city business trip lasting twelve days and won't be back until early next week. He left the day TJ started doing the work and I told him I was doing a little landscaping with someone Jeannie recommended. Hopefully, he'll be so thrilled with how it looks, that he won't care how much it costs.

"Hannah's here! Hannah's here!" Anna shouts with glee, as Hannah's car pulls into the driveway.

Anna has been sitting in front of the dining room window for the last thirty minutes with her face pushed up against the glass, waiting for her new best friend to arrive. I definitely made a good call with Hannah. Anna loves her and she gives me time to actually get stuff done. I've even increased her hours, because she's such a

Godsend. It doesn't feel like she's here thirty hours a week, but even at $20 an hour (in the end I felt bad lowering her rate), it's totally worth it!

"Hi sweetie!" Hannah says, when she opens the door to let herself in.

Anna is waiting two steps from the door and she wraps her little arms around Hannah's legs and squeals in delight.

"Hi Mrs. Hansen," Hannah says, once she's done snuggling with Anna at the door.

"Please call me Molly, I've told you that," I tell her, feeling older and older each time she calls me by my mother-in-law's name.

"Sorry," Hannah says, looking slightly embarrassed, but still not using my name.

"Let's go play," Anna whines, grabbing onto the bottom of Hannah's jean shorts and trying to pull her toward the playroom.

"One second honey, let's just see if there's anything Mommy has planned for us," Hannah says in a soothing singsong voice.

"I hadn't really thought about it, but they'll be working in the yard all day, so maybe you can take her to the playground?" I suggest. "I also have a lot to do to get ready for this playgroup tomorrow, so maybe you could take her out to lunch as well?"

"Sure! That sounds great," Hannah replies.

"Okay, Anna, let's go play and then we can go to the playground and have lunch, how does that sound?" she asks Anna with great enthusiasm, making it sound like dinner and a Broadway show.

"Yay, yay, yay!" Anna says, doing a little dance and then running off toward the playroom, her strawberry blonde curls bobbing as she goes.

"This is for you, sorry, I almost forgot. It was in the door handle when I came in," Hannah says, handing me a thick cream letter-size envelope with my name written in script on the front.

"Thanks Hannah," I reply, curious as to what could be inside my hand delivered piece of mail.

I open the envelope and there are at least six pieces of thick cream paper inside and on the top right hand corner of each page is the logo from Rick Norson's Interior Design Company. There are so many numbers in the columns on the right hand side of each page that I can't quite understand what I'm seeing. I take the papers into the kitchen and sit down at the table so I can lay them all out in front of me and try and make sense of this.

Each page lists different items: furniture, accessories, paint, labor, etc. and then there are additional fees for "designer's hourly fee" which appear every third or fourth line.

Wait a minute. This can't be right. I know that I signed something with him that said $7,500 and then I gave him a check for that amount. I'll just go find the papers and confirm it and call his office – I'm sure there is just a misunderstanding. It might be a little awkward, but if we agreed on $7,500, then he can't charge me some absurd amount without telling me, so I have nothing to worry about.

I can already feel my heart rate returning to normal as I search through my pile of papers in my 'to be filed' folder. Even with all of the paperwork I've amassed recently with the new house, it only takes me a minute to find it, and I'm already preparing for what I'll say when I call his office to tell him about the issue.

Oh God! Oh No! That can't be possible. There's no way I signed that!

And there right in front of me is a piece of paper stating that there is a $7,500 deposit for Rick Norson's work, and that I am responsible for any and all fees incurred during the project.

Now I think back to the morning Rick gave me the paperwork and remember that Jeannie was here. I was nervous and I saw the dollar amount and signed it without really reading it.

How am I possibly going to explain to Derek that we owe $120,000 for redecorating the front hall and the living room?

Before I have a chance to think about the enormity of this, TJ raps his knuckles on the glass door to get my attention.

"What is it?" I ask curtly, upon opening the door. I don't even bother to try to hide my mood, because it's impossible.

"Um, just wanted to let you know that we're finishing up, if you want to come take a look," TJ says, trying to figure out what he did wrong.

"Sure, I'll come have a look," I tell him.

I take the two steps down onto the patio and survey the magazine worthy grass surrounding me, as well as the magnificent fence and well placed bushes and shrubs that dot the perimeter of the yard. To his credit, he certainly has transformed this space from a few days ago.

"It looks great," I admit, forgetting for a second that I'm miserable.

"So glad you like it," TJ says, smiling. "Now if you want to write the entire check to TJ's landscaping, I'm going to have to charge you tax on the whole thing. But, if you want to make a check out to cash for half of it, then that can save you a bit on the tax," TJ says, giving me a thoughtful look.

"Do you need the money now?" I ask, stunned.

"Yes, ma'am. The work is done, and I've already paid for the materials and I need to pay my guys," TJ says, gesturing to the half dozen men scattered across my emerald lawn.

"And how much is it?" I ask, terrified of the answer.

"Thirty-five," TJ says.

"Thirty-five hundred?" I ask, thinking that maybe it's not so bad.

"You're a funny lady, Mrs. Hansen. It's thirty-five thousand," he says, straight-faced.

"Let me go get me checkbook," I tell him, heading inside.

Thankfully, Derek's too busy to do anything but work this week, but I'm pretty sure he's going to notice soon that $35,000 is gone from our account. And as far as the amount I owe Rick, after buying this house, we don't even have that much money in our account – I have no idea how I'm possibly going to pay for that. It feels like a vice is squeezing my chest as I start to realize what I've done.

Just when I think it can't get any worse, the doorbell rings indicating that the patio furniture delivery is right on time. Somehow $20,000 worth of teak furniture no longer seems like as good of an idea as it did when Jeannie and Lisa talked me into it...

Chapter 36 – Megan

I'm pretty sure Brooke and Caitlin are never going to be satisfied with a day at the beach, some window shopping and an ice cream cone after today.

"I told you they would have a good time," Brad gloats, sitting down next to me on the lounge chair on the front deck of his family's gleaming white yacht. Brad drapes his arm around my bare shoulders and I smell the mixture of sunscreen, cologne, saltwater and sweat that is distinctly Brad.

"I didn't say they wouldn't have a good time. Who wouldn't have a good time doing this for the day?" I question. "I was just worried," I tell him.

"Worried about what?" Brad says, leaning forward and gently kissing me on the lips.

"I don't know," I tell him, honestly having trouble remembering what I possibly thought could go wrong.

"Can we sleep here?" Caitlin asks, appearing suddenly from the lower deck.

"No, we can't sleep here," I tell her, trying to pull away from Brad and straighten my bikini top. I know we aren't fooling Brooke, but I still don't think it's appropriate to show any level of PDA in front of either of the girls, even though Brad makes it quite difficult.

"Can we have dinner here?" Caitlin asks, trying again. She comes up onto the deck and lies down on the blue and white cushion on top of the bench and stretches out comfortably. "I could really get used to this," she says.

"Oh, really!" I say, trying not to laugh. "We already ate breakfast and lunch on the boat, I think we need to get back for dinner – your mom is expecting us," I tell Caitlin.

"Actually, we probably should start to get back," I say to Brad. "I haven't had any reception on my cell phone for a while and I want to tell Heather what time we'll be back."

"It's only four o'clock," Brad says, giving me his best attempt at puppy eyes.

"Okay, another half hour, and then we should get back," I tell him. Looking around at the sparkling blue waters of Nantucket Sound on this early August day, it's hard to make an argument to be anywhere else.

"Do you want to try one more time to catch something?" Brad asks Caitlin.

"Yes! Yes!" she replies, excitedly.

"I think Brooke is already back there, but go ask Mack if he'll help you try again," Brad suggests. Caitlin doesn't need any more prompting and practically runs along the deck to try her hand at fishing one more time. Having a crew of five or six on board seems to be quite useful.

"I think you need some more sunscreen," Brad says, turning toward me. "Let me help you," he says, giving me a sly smile. He grabs the lotion out of my bag and starts to rub it slowly onto my shoulders and back and ever-so-slowly around to my stomach where his fingers brush the underside and inside of my bikini top. I suck in my breath as he touches me and I feel the tone of the day change.

"We still have half an hour," Brad says softly. "And there are three bedrooms," he reminds me, in case I'd forgotten.

"But what about Brooke and Caitlin?" I ask, trying to keep my thoughts straight, while I feel Brad untie the back of my bikini top and his hand starts to roam.

"They're busy fishing. They won't notice we're gone," Brad says, kissing my neck with more urgency.

"I don't know," I tell him, responding to his wandering hands, but looking over his shoulder at the same time.

"I think I love you," Brad whispers into my ear.

I pull away from him as if I've been slapped. "What did you say?" I ask, unable to believe what I heard.

"I know it's fast, but I think I'm falling in love with you. I've never felt this way about anyone before," Brad says earnestly, reaching for me, trying to pick up where we left off.

I look at Brad's sculpted jaw and deep brown eyes and the way he is looking at me, like I am the only girl in the world. Unfortunately, all I can think about is how badly I miss Ryan and how devastated I am that he has completely forgotten about me this summer, like the last two years never happened.

Before I can reply to Brad, Mack's voice comes loudly from the stern of the boat, followed quickly by Mack. Somehow I am able to get my top tied and back in place before he appears.

"There's a storm coming in quickly. It wasn't supposed to hit until tonight, but it could be here any minute, we have to head back now," Mack says.

"Right, of course," Brad answers, glancing up at the sky. I look up and we both notice the ominous clouds rolling in, turning the water an eerie shade of navy from the brilliant blue it was only moments before.

"Why don't you take the girls down to the cabin, I'll help them get everything secured up here and make sure we have all of our stuff," Brad says, suddenly all business – obviously aware of the dangers of a storm at sea.

"It should only take twenty or thirty minutes to get back," Mack assures me.

"Okay great," I say, realizing it's the only thing I've said since Brad's confession.

"I'll go get Brooke and Caitlin, so we can get changed and ready to go," I say to no one in particular.

***

The rain is coming down hard as we pull into the Chatham Yacht Basin, but luckily we are getting in before the storm gets really bad. It also helps that we are on an 80-foot yacht and not a tiny sailboat.

My phone finally has service after going in and out for most of the day, so I decide to text Heather to let her know that we are back and will be home shortly; but when I grab my phone I know that something is terribly wrong.

I have seventeen missed calls, twelve voicemails, and thirty-one text messages. My heart drops as I wonder what happened to Danielle or Abby or Kyle?! I don't know where to start with all of these messages, but I'm thrown off when I see that all of the voicemails are from Kevin. I don't know why he would be calling me, but I can't imagine it's for something good.

I listen to the most recent message from Kevin to see if that will help me figure it out. He sounds exasperated as he says, "I still can't imagine where on earth you could be, but my flight is getting in at seven, it's the earliest one I could get on. I will meet you at the hospital, assuming you *ever* get this. Hopefully you and the girls are safe, I can't handle anything else today."

The hospital? What does that mean? What's going on?

And then I scroll through my text messages and start to piece it all together. Heather is in the hospital. She's been there since early this afternoon. Jasper and Kevin have been trying to get in touch with me for the last three hours.

"Is everything okay?" Brad asks, walking across the spacious living area to check on me.

"No. Heather is in the hospital," I say quietly, hoping the girls don't overhear.
"Oh my God! What happened?" he asks.

"I'm not sure. I have all these texts and calls from Jasper and Kevin trying to find me, but I can't figure out what happened to her. We need to get to the hospital as soon as we get off the boat," I tell him.

"Okay, I can drive you," Brad offers.

"We don't even fit in your car," I remind him. "And I can't leave my car here," I tell him. I appreciate chivalry, but not when it supersedes practicality.

"Okay, then I'll follow you," Brad says.

"That would be nice," I tell him.

I know that I need to say something about what happened earlier today, and I'm sure Brad hasn't forgotten either, but it looks like I've been given a small reprieve to figure out how to deal with it, even if I don't deserve it.

Chapter 37 – Sabrina

Parker: Are you sure you can't come over this morning?

Sabrina: I can't – wish I could

Parker: I need you. I'm lonely without you ☹

If he's so lonely without me, then why haven't I heard from him in four days? Why didn't he return my texts asking if he could meet up on Wednesday night? Why did he rush me out of his apartment on Monday thirty minutes after we had sex, when I assured him Peter would be at the hospital all night? I wish I could figure out how to put that succinctly into a text, but all I come up with is:

Sabrina: Sorry

Parker: it's Saturday morning – what are you doing?

I just can't figure him out. He said he wishes he never let me go, but now he's giving me mixed signals – and I'm running out of time.

Sabrina: Just some errands. I might be done around 1 -maybe I could come by then?

Parker: text me when you're done

***

The bridal salon at Monique Lhuillier looks exactly the same as it did four years ago when I was here with Danielle. Surprisingly, she didn't have any issue coming back here today. Perhaps it's because her wedding to Jim doesn't mean anything to her anymore; she got Abby out of her marriage and now she has Ted. She's also about to have another baby; she doesn't even have time to think about Jim, much less dwell on a 12-month long bad marriage.

"Can I get you anything? Maybe a glass of champagne?" the saleslady asks.

"Sure, I'll have one, thanks so much," I reply. "My sister and best friend should be here shortly," I add.

"Okay, we'll start as soon as they get here," she says, handing me a crystal glass filled with golden, sparkling, liquid. It may only be 10:30 in the morning, but wedding dress shopping definitely calls for champagne.

"I think your friend is here," the saleslady says. And when I look up, I see Danielle walking into the serene white and gray room.

"Can you believe it's your turn?" Danielle squeaks, giving me a huge hug. It's harder to get close to her with her expanding baby bump, but the rest of her hasn't changed at all, so she still looks amazing.

"It's a little weird to be back here?" I say, looking at the white dresses hanging all around us.

"I told you not to worry about it!" Danielle says.

"Are we ready to start?" the saleslady asks, reappearing as if from nowhere.

"My sister isn't here yet, let me check and see if she's close," I tell her.

Sabrina: you ok? When will you be here?

Molly: so sorry! Running late. 20 minutes?

Sabrina: okay

"She's going to be late, let's just get started with some dresses," I tell the lady, aware that there must be an end-time to our appointment so another bride can come find the dress of her dreams.

"Do you know what style you are looking for? Do you want white? Or ivory? Sleeves or sleeveless or strapless? We just got in some beautiful dresses with ballgown skirts," she says excitedly.

"I haven't really thought about it," I answer truthfully.

The saleslady looks at me in awe, like I'm the first woman to come in here and have no idea what I'm looking for.

"C'mon Breen, you must have thought about it a little bit," Danielle says. "What did you picture when you thought about yourself getting married when you were little?" she probes.

"I keep telling you, I didn't spend my life dreaming about it. I'm not like everyone else; I don't go all mushy when it comes to this bride crap. If Peter's mom hadn't made this appointment, I wouldn't even be here, I would have just ordered a white sundress from J. Crew and called it a day," I say defensively.

After an awkward moment of silence, the saleslady says in a chipper voice, "you have a beautiful figure, and arms I would die for. Why don't we start with a beautiful mermaid style and then a few strapless and backless dresses so you can see the different options?"

"Sounds perfect," I say, trying to make up for my outburst.

"Just take everything off except your panties and I'll bring you the first gown," the saleslady says, pointing toward the dressing area.

"It's like going to the doctor," I joke, but nobody laughs.

Although it may not be my favorite, I have to admit the mermaid dress with the plunging neckline is quite dramatic and flattering. After I'm zipped in, I step out to show Danielle.

"Wow," she says. "Just wow."

"Is it too much?" I ask, twirling around and viewing myself in the three-way mirror.

"You look amazing, but that is not even the right size and already I think Peter's parents might have a heart attack. When they actually tailor it to fit you, I can't imagine what they would think," Danielle laughs.

"It's probably a bit sexy for their crowd," I admit, "but Peter would like it," I say. And then before I can stop myself I think how much Parker would like it as well.

"Molly just texted you, she just got out of the subway at 68ᵗʰ Street, she should be here soon," Danielle tells me.

"Should I leave this one on until she gets here or try on something else?" I ask Danielle.

"I think you can probably try on something else. We're in trouble if that's your best option," she laughs, taking a sip of what I assume is sparkling cider.

"Why don't you try this one?" the saleslady suggests. "This strapless column dress will still be very flattering, but perhaps a little more conservative, and it has a little lace on the bodice, for an extra feminine touch," she adds.

"Sure," I shrug, taking the dress from her, as if it were a tank dress from Club Monaco and not a $5,000 gown.

I initially tell the saleslady that I don't need her help, but I have trouble with the tiny buttons and after a couple attempts, I have to call her back to ask for assistance.

"You okay in there?" Danielle calls out.

"I'm fine," I yell back. "I'll be out in a second."

I stare at my reflection and although I don't think this is the moment that other brides describe, I can almost feel what they might be talking about. Looking at myself in this dress, I can *almost* picture myself getting married. Although what I can picture is the wedding. I can see myself in this dress and a beautiful up-do and then Peter beaming beside me in his custom-made tux. I can envision the party with all of our friends and the band and the food and the flowers and all the other things that

Peter and his mom have been working on so diligently. But then when I try to picture what happens *after* the wedding, being married to Peter and never being with Parker, that's where I start to have problems.

"What do you think?" I ask, opening the curtain to show the dress to Danielle.

"I can't believe my baby sister is getting married," Molly wails, bursting into tears.

Molly must have walked in right as I walked out of my little room, because it doesn't look like Danielle has even seen her yet.

"Don't cry," I say, giving Molly a hug and trying to comfort her. I always hate it when she cries, even when they're happy tears.

"So what do you think?" I ask taking a step back.

"It's stunning!" Molly says, drying her eyes. "I'm insanely jealous at how good you look, but I'll try to get past that," she says.

"Danielle, what about you?" I ask.

"What is this?" she asks me, holding up my phone.

I can't see what she's talking about, but I start to get a sick feeling in my stomach.

"Is Parker that guy from college?" she asks accusingly.

"Were you looking through my text messages?" I ask angrily, although I know that's not the issue.

"Your phone was sitting on the chair and the text popped up from Molly saying she was late. I looked at it again when another text came through because I thought it was from Molly again; clearly it wasn't. Sabrina, what the fuck is going on?" she asks, glaring at me.

For a minute I think about denying it. Depending on what he wrote, I can probably talk my way out of it. But I've wanted to talk to someone about this since the second I saw Parker again, let alone since we started sleeping together.

"Wait, Parker, like Parker Avery!" Molly practically shouts.

I sink down onto the gray velvet couch, in my couture gown, and face my sister and my best friend.

"I don't know if I can marry Peter," I tell both of them, feeling instant relief at having the words out in the open.

"This is just cold feet," Danielle says. "You've been through this before. But you love Peter, and he is the best. He is so good for you," she adds.

"I don't understand. How is Parker involved? You haven't talked to him in years. I thought he lived in California. And I thought we hated him," Molly says.

"I met up with him at an alumni thing at the beginning of the summer and then we got back in touch," I tell her.

"Is everything okay in here?" the saleslady asks, poking her head into the room.

"We're fine. I really like this one," I tell her, noting the dress I'm still wearing.

There's no way that she hasn't heard every word of our conversation, but maybe this isn't the strangest thing to have ever happened at a bridal appointment. Perhaps she sees this all the time and she knows if she keeps her mouth shut that the bride always ends up buying the dress, no matter what secrets are revealed and she still gets her commission.

"Should we go talk about this somewhere else?" I suggest to Molly and Danielle. "This doesn't really seem appropriate," I say, looking around at the tulle, lace and duchess satin.

"We can talk about this right now," Molly says. "I can't believe you didn't tell me you saw Parker! He broke your heart before, but that doesn't mean anything anymore. You have Peter now and he's wonderful. Why are you even texting with Parker?" she asks.

It looks like Danielle and Molly may not get the full extent of what's going on with Parker. I was hoping that I wouldn't have to do this, but it doesn't seem like I have a choice.

"It's not just cold feet. I'm sleeping with Parker. I think he wants to get back together. I don't know what to do," I admit, hanging my head so I don't have to look at either of them.

"Oh no," Molly gasps.

"How could you do that to Peter!" Danielle says, anger and disappointment dripping from each word.

"I didn't plan on it. It just happened," I say.

"You should never have said yes," Danielle says.

"I know! I know I shouldn't. I told you I was scared and you told me it would be fine. Look at me now! It's not fine," I tell her.

"So, it's my fault?" Danielle asks.

"No. I didn't mean that. I just don't know what to do," I say, repeating my new mantra.

"Maybe you just need more time?" Molly suggests.

"More time for what?" I ask.

"A longer engagement? Take more time before you get married? There's really no reason to rush off and get married and have kids and move to the suburbs," she says wistfully.

"Are you okay?" I ask Molly, suddenly concerned, and realizing again how little I've talked to her since she's moved here.

"Sure, sure, I'll be fine," Molly says, but it's not very convincing. "Let's worry about you right now," she says, like the dutiful big sister.

"I think I need to figure out if I have a future with Parker," I tell them. "He was always who I thought I would end up with, and now that he's back in my life I need to give that a chance," I say.

"He's just going to break your heart again," Molly says.

"You don't know that. He told me that leaving me was the biggest mistake he ever made," I say.

"What are you going to do about Peter?" Danielle challenges. "Are you just going to keep cheating on him?" she says angrily.

"I'm going to figure it all out very soon," I promise her.

"Have you ladies made any decisions?" the saleslady says, popping back in.

"Can you put this dress on hold?" I ask her.

"Seriously, Sabrina?" Danielle says to me.

"I told you, I'm going to figure it out, but I did like this one, and if I do need it, I don't want to have to go dress shopping all over again."

Chapter 38 – Heather

"Mommy, can you come to the beach *today*?" Caitlin pleads with me. She is curled up in a ball at my feet like a cat.

Before I have a chance to answer, Kevin responds, "Maybe Mommy can come sit outside this afternoon, but I don't think she can do the steps all the way down to the beach sweetheart."

I wish that I could protest, but I know that he's right.

"I can come to the beach with you?" Megan offers, poking her head out from the kitchen where she's cleaning up from breakfast.

Kevin takes a deep breath before responding and then looks up from his computer and says, "that would be great Megan, you can take them to the beach and I'll stay here with Heather."

I look over and try to catch Megan's eye and smile. The poor girl is terrified to be around Kevin now after the way he yelled at her at the hospital. I keep trying to reassure her that it wasn't her fault and she has nothing to worry about. Kevin still has the crazy idea that Megan was supposed to watch my every move this summer and that she could have prevented this from happening. I've explained to him over and over that Megan was babysitting the girls, which was her only job, and I'm the only one responsible for my bad choices, but he's a little slow to come around.

"I'll finish up in the kitchen and then let's go get ready," Megan says to Caitlin.

"Okay," Caitlin says, somewhat disappointed in the outcome, but I know she'll have more fun with Megan than she would with me anyway.

"You can bury me in sand," Megan offers.

"Yay!" Caitlin screams, jumping up from the couch and heading up to her room to get dressed.

A knock on the door interrupts the silence.

"Who would be here?" Kevin asks.

"Please don't tell me you forgot that Jasper is coming over this morning," I say to him.

"Oh right," he grumbles, getting up to get the door.

I haven't seen Jasper since the hike. He stayed at the hospital until Kevin arrived, but Kevin was pretty quick to kick him out the second he got there. Kevin is also mad at Jasper, even though Jasper had no way to know, but he would rather direct his anger at Megan and Jasper than at me.

"Please come in," Kevin says through a forced smile, as he opens the door.

"Thanks so much, it's so good to see you." Jasper says, embracing Kevin in a one-armed hug with a back pat. It's bizarre to see the two of them together. Looking at them side-by-side, I can't believe that I was attracted to Jasper. Kevin is clearly more my type (which is a good thing) – the classic boy-next-door preppy guy grown up, compared to Jasper with his jet-black hair and tight clothes and rock-hard everything. Also, now that I know Jasper is gay, I can't *not* see it when I look at him.

"I'll take this upstairs and leave you two alone," Kevin says, grabbing his laptop and heading up to our bedroom.

"Thanks sweetie," I say, thankful for the gesture.

"How are you?" Jasper gushes, leaning over to give me a gentle hug, and then pulling over a chair to sit down next to me.

"I've been better, but I guess I'm doing okay," I reply.

"I'm so sorry," Jasper begins, but I cut him off.

"You have nothing to be sorry about," I assure him.

"But I suggested we go on that hike," he says.

"I'm the only one to blame," I tell him. "I've been pushing myself all summer because I didn't want to think anything could happen," I tell him.

"So what did happen? Is it the cancer?" Jasper asks cautiously.

"No, it's not the cancer," I sigh. "During one of my many doctor appointments over the last year they found that I have Hypertrophic Cardiomyopathy," I tell him.

"What is that?" he asks, giving me the same look I first gave the doctor when they told me the fancy diagnosis.

"It's not as glamorous as it sounds," I say, trying to make a joke. "It basically means the walls of my heart are thicker than they are supposed to be and the blood doesn't flow as well as it should. But I never had any symptoms, and they just found it by chance," I tell him.

"So you *don't* have a heart problem?" he asks.

"I didn't really believe them," I say, wrapping the blue chenille throw blanket around myself for comfort. "I had never had any chest pains or any of the other problems they talked about, and I was so sick of the cancer and being sick, that I just didn't want to deal with it," I say, realizing how ridiculous it sounds.

"Oh," Jasper says, taking a minute to think about it.

"And then I finally felt better after the chemo and I still didn't notice anything with my heart, so I figured they must have been wrong," I tell him. "They said there was a chance I could collapse or have heart failure, especially from over-exerting myself, but I felt so good that I didn't think it could happen."

"Is that why Kevin was always so worried about you?" Jasper asks, putting it together.

"Yes," I admit sadly. "Kevin was terrified after the diagnosis, especially since he had barely gotten over the fear of losing me from cancer. He was sure I was going to die of some terrible heart problem, hence his desire to protect me from everything," I say.

"I guess I should have listened to him," I say sheepishly.

"Wow," Jasper says.

"Right?" I reply.

"No, I mean, poor guy. I can't believe what he's had to go through," Jasper says.

"I know," I say, feeling guilty all over again.

"So what happens now?" he asks.

"I'm going to rest here for another two weeks and then we'll go back home as planned. Kevin was supposed to be here now, so that's good timing. And then when I go home I'll see the cardiologist and probably listen to her this time when she tells me to take Beta Blockers or whatever it is she wants me to take," I tell him.

"I know you don't see it this way right now, but you're pretty lucky," Jasper says.

"How do you figure?" I ask him.

"Most of us are out there just trying to find *someone*, and maybe the lucky ones find love; but your husband loves you so much he would do anything to protect you and keep you safe – most people go their whole lives without finding that kind of love," Jasper says.

"I know," I say quietly.

"And now you have me, so it can't get much better than that," he jokes.

"Will you still hang out with me if I can't bike, or paddleboard or hike?" I ask him.

"Of course I will," he says, placing his hand on his heart.

"What will we do?" I ask.

"It's obvious," he says, "we'll eat cake for breakfast." Jasper reaches out to squeeze my hand and I know that it's going to be okay.

Chapter 39 – Molly

Last week's mommy and me playgroup was a success, or at least Jeannie and Lisa seemed happy. The whole event was a bit of a blur for me. It was a flurry of perfectly dressed, very thin women telling me how pleased they were to meet me and how happy they were to welcome me to town. Back in Boulder, the moms and kids actually interacted at the Saturday morning playgroups, but at this one, everyone brought their au pair or nanny, so the moms just stood around with mimosas (or sparkling water for those on dry weeks) and either raved or bitched about their child-minders.

I attempted to make polite conversation, but I couldn't concentrate on anything except for the envelope from Rick, which sat burning a hole on my kitchen counter. It seemed like everyone at the playgroup was about to design or renovate something and that was all they wanted to talk about. I tried to force a smile and engage, but I wanted to throw up every time I thought about the six-figures I owed, and these women were casually throwing around projects that would cost two and three times that amount.

Unfortunately, I did overhear someone at the party mention "Jeannie's latest project." At first, I assumed they were referring to her plans for the pool house, but after hearing the rest of the conversation, it became clear that the women were referring to *me* as her project. Apparently Jeannie gets bored if she isn't "fixing people."

But it all got worse the day after the party when I got this text from Derek:

Derek: coming home a couple days early. Will be home late Saturday night. We need to talk

I just wrote back with a simple "okay," because I couldn't imagine getting into it with him over text. He must have seen the $35,000 withdrawal from our checking account. But if that was making him freak out, I couldn't imagine what he would do when he found what was really going on.

And now I've been on autopilot the last few days, just going through the motions until I finally have to confront Derek and tell him the truth. I couldn't even focus properly today at Sabrina's bridal dress fitting. If there was ever a time when she needed my full attention, today was it, but I'm still too buried in my own problems.

I've been so busy with the house and Anna and trying to fit in, that I didn't see what was happening between her and Peter. And more importantly, I didn't even realize she had gotten involved with Parker again! As soon as I fix this disaster with Derek, and figure out where I'm going to find $140,000, my first priority will be making sure Sabrina stays away from Parker and works things out with Peter – that's my job as her big sister.

***

I'm almost relieved that it will all be out on the table, because the waiting is killing me. With only a couple minutes until Derek is due to be home, I'm starting to re-think that logic.

I take a deep breath as I hear Derek's key in the door and try to remind myself that he is my husband and he loves me. Derek opens the door and he walks in very slowly, dragging his suitcase behind him. He looks terrible. There are dark circles under his eyes, his hair is shaggy and looks like he's spent the entire flight raking his hand through it, and his suit is hanging off his body (is it possible he lost ten pounds in less than two weeks?)

"I didn't realize you'd still be up," Derek says, upon seeing me sitting on the bottom stair, clad in my pink and white striped PJ's.

"I thought we should talk now," I tell him, trying to keep up my courage.

"Oh," he says. "I thought it could wait until the morning," Derek says, sounding a little uneasy.

"I don't think I can go to sleep like this," I say to him, wringing the bottom of my pajama top in my hands.

"Let me get a drink first," he says, abandoning his suitcase in the middle of the hall and walking over to the bar in the living room.

"Is this new?" he asks, referring to the bar, as he pours himself a gigantic glass of scotch, and takes a large swallow.

"Yes, it is," I say, and wince as the words come out.

Derek takes a seat on our ludicrously expensive sofa, and I follow behind and take a seat opposite him on the equally absurd ottoman.

"I'm not sure exactly what to say," Derek begins.

I hadn't expected him to go first, but maybe it's easier if he says his piece and then I try to explain.

"Okay, if you think that's best," I reply.

"I'm not really sure how else we would do it," Derek says, giving me a confused look.

"I got fired," Derek says quietly, staring down into his tumbler of scotch.

"What?!" I blurt out, not thinking before I speak. Of all the things I was expecting him to say, this was nowhere on the list! I try to recover, but the look on Derek's face tells me I'm a little late. "I mean, I'm so sorry. What happened?"

"I'm just not the right guy for the job. I've been miserable since I started, and my boss knew it," Derek says.

"I'm so sorry," I say again, looking at Derek for the first time properly in the last two months. Just like with Sabrina, I've been so wrapped up in my own life, that I haven't even noticed what's been going on with Derek.

"So what happens now?" I ask. I know I have to tell him about the money, and I have to do it now, but it's going to be excruciating to pile it on top of this.

"There's some bad news and some good news," he says, smiling at me for the first time since he walked in the door. "Which do you want first?" he asks.

"The good news," I tell him, desperate to hear something positive.

"So, it was actually a very agreeable discussion with my boss and we did end on good terms. It turns out there is a pretty good separation agreement in my contract, so even though I've only been there a few months, I get a full year of salary as severance," Derek says.

"Oh my God!" I screech, unable to contain my relief at this sudden turn in events.

"It even gets a little better, but here's where the bad news comes in. I ran into my old boss at the conference in Phoenix on Wednesday, before I got fired, and he offered me a job. He said he wouldn't be able to match my salary, but he said they really miss me and he would do whatever they could afford to do to get me back."

"Derek, that's amazing. I'm so happy for you!" I say, reaching over and squeezing his hand.

"But Molly, this means we would have to move back to Colorado. We would have to leave this house and all of your new friends and go back to Boulder. I don't think it's fair to do that to you," Derek says sadly.

"I'm not happy here either," I tell him. "I don't fit in and I don't love the house. I don't belong here," I divulge.

"Are you serious?" he asks, shocked at my revelation.

"I am. But before we go any further I have to tell you what I've done. Because it may mean that we can't do any of this," I confess.

"What did you do?" he asks, looking worried.

"You know how I've been doing some decorating work on the house?" I say cautiously.

"Yeah, it looks great," he says looking around at our magazine worthy living room and foyer.

"I also did some landscaping - a lot of landscaping," I admit.

"And?" he asks.

"It cost a lot of money. I mean a lot more money than I thought it would cost. And now we owe a lot of money, and I don't know if we can pay it," I say, holding my head in my heads, because I can't bear to look him in the eyes.

"How much money?" Derek asks cautiously.

"A lot," I say, unable to get the words out.

"Molly, it can't be that bad," Derek says.

I take a deep breath and just say it, "$120 for the living room and foyer, $35 for the landscaping and $20 for the patio furniture."

"Are those all in thousands," Derek asks, his face a look of complete shock.

"Yes," I say quietly.

"So $175,000?" he asks, still dumbstruck.

"Holy fuck!" he says with exasperation, but his lips are curving up into a smirk.

"Are you laughing?" I ask, with disbelief.

"No, definitely not. This definitely isn't funny. But my other option might be crying. It's just that I was so nervous to come home tonight and tell you what happened, and it looks like we both have some problems," Derek says, shooting me a sympathetic smile.

"I've been thinking that our only way out is to sell the house. And maybe with the improvements we've made, we'll be able to make back some money?" I offer. "When we bought it, the realtor said that we got it for a good price, so maybe we could list it for $175,000 more than we paid?" I suggest hopefully. "But when I thought about selling the house, I was worried we wouldn't find anywhere else here to live, and even more worried that you wouldn't want to move," I tell him, revealing the fears I've been carrying around.

"I guess it's a good thing for both of us that we're moving back to Boulder," Derek says, leaning over and wrapping me in a hug, both of us letting the tension release from our bodies for the first time in months.

Chapter 40 – Megan

"I can't believe I only have one week left until I go back to the City," I say to Brad, gazing out at Brewster Bay. We are sitting on matching red and white striped beach towels on the hard packed sand watching Caitlin look for Hermit Crabs at low tide. One of the things I like about Brad is that he is just as comfortable sitting here drinking Snapple iced tea on the sand as he is driving his own boat, or managing a crew on a yacht – he is quite the chameleon.

"Yeah, but you're going back for senior year, that's the best year," he says longingly. "In two weeks I'll be moving into a dorm room with some guy named Brandon from Kansas City." It's the first time I've heard him sound anything other than confident and it's rather cute.

"At least you don't have to spend the year taking SATs and AP exams and filling out college applications and then waiting to see if you get in. You're already done with all that," I remind him.

"You're right," he says, "that does suck," he jokes. "I'm sure I can put in a good word for you at Dartmouth," he says playfully. But even the idea of thinking about what happens with us after this summer makes me unsettled.

This is the first time we've been alone since Brad told me how he felt on the yacht, and we're not even really alone now. I've tried to be on call for the girls and Heather and Kevin all week to help out, especially the days she was in the hospital, but also since she's been home. Heather has tried to assure me countless times that none of this was my fault and I had no way to know she was going to collapse from heart failure. However, Kevin seems to think differently, and after his initial tirade at the hospital he has been less than friendly. I know deep down that I could not have known, but at the same time, Kevin did ask me to watch out for her again and again at the beginning of the summer and I just assumed he was being overprotective.

Part of me wants to bring it up so that we can discuss it and I can tell Brad that I'm not ready for that kind of relationship and that it wouldn't be fair to him. But the rest of me wants to pretend that it never happened and just enjoy the last week I have on the Cape. I want to go back to the way it was before, when we were flirting and hanging out. Then I can go back to New York and face reality and figure out why Ryan abandoned me.

"I know we're both thinking about it, so I'm just going to come out and say it. I really like you a lot Megan, but I know I freaked you out with what I said the other day, and I'm sorry about that," Brad says, looking at me intently with his dark brown eyes. He is definitely the most mature eighteen-year old boy around; I've heard Danielle and Sabrina talk about men their age and they don't seem to be as open and direct with their feelings.

"I do like you. I'm just not over Ryan," I tell him honestly. "I thought I was ready, but I don't think that I am, and that's not fair to you. Anyway, do you really want to go off to college with a long distance relationship? I'm pretty sure you and Brandon want to be free to meet as

311

many single freshman as you can," I say, trying to make a joke and lighten the mood.

Continuing in his role as nicest-guy-ever, Brad tries to put me at ease and plays along, "Oh, you know Brandon and I won't have any trouble with the ladies," he laughs. But then he changes he tone and gets more serious, "but if you change your mind, you know where to find me." He gives me a kiss on the cheek and gets up and walks back toward the stairs and his waiting Maserati. And just like that, my summer romance, with one of the hottest, wealthiest, nicest guys, is all over – way to go, Megan.

***

"Everything okay?" Heather asks, "You seem kind of down."

"I'm fine," I reply, not wanting to bother her with my problems. "Do you need anything else? If not, I'm going to go upstairs and start packing," I tell her.

"I can't believe you leave tomorrow," she says, repositioning herself amongst the multiple pillows and blankets on the couch.

"I know. It's crazy how quickly it went," I say.

"It was a great summer. The girls love you and I loved having you here. You know that right?" she asks.

"I guess so," I say, unsure how to respond.

"This had nothing to do with you," she says, gesturing to her chest. "I honestly would do it over again the same way if I had to do it again," she says.

"Really?" I ask, surprised that she would make that statement.

"I know it sounds crazy, but it made me feel alive again. I need to be careful, I get that know. But I don't think I would take back that time I had with Jasper – I really think it's part of the healing process," she says.

"Okay," I say, somewhat skeptical, but happy to hear yet again that she doesn't blame me – maybe Kevin will come around soon too.

Unfortunately the disaster that greets me in my room has not improved since I was last here earlier today. I don't feel like I did much shopping this summer, but I can't believe that everything that is strewn across this space is going to fit in two suitcases and a carry-on.

Luckily my phone rings before I can even begin to pack, providing at least another few minutes of distraction. I'm guessing it is Danielle, since I don't think Brad is going to call anymore, and everyone else only texts. It takes a couple rings to locate the phone under some shirts and bathing suits on the bed, but when I finally do, I am paralyzed by what I see on the caller ID – Ryan is calling me. I've been dying for this moment all summer and now I don't know what to do. Why is he calling now? After ignoring me for almost six weeks, what could he possibly want?

"Hello?" I say, my voice shaking.

"Megan? Is that really you? I just got back! My plane just landed at JFK!" he says excitedly.

"You're back?" I ask, because that is all I can think to say.

"Yes! I'm still on the plane, but we just landed and I had to hear your voice. I don't even know what time it is for me, so I think I'm going to go home and shower and maybe sleep a little, but then I'm going to come straight over, okay?" he says eagerly.

"I'm in Cape Cod," I tell him, baffled by this exchange.

"Oh crap, you're still there. When are you back? I can't wait to see you baby!" he says.

This feels like the twilight zone. I haven't heard from him almost all summer and it's like he doesn't think that's an issue.

"I actually fly back tomorrow morning. But Ryan, I don't know what's going on. Why didn't you answer any of my texts? I haven't heard from you all summer?" I ask.

"What do you mean? Of course you have. I've been emailing you. I told you that we couldn't get texts because our phones didn't work well in Kenya, and we only had occasional email access. You're the one who never wrote back to me," he says, but just in a matter-of-fact tone, not judgmental. "Hey Meg, it looks like we're starting to move off the plane. I'll give you a call back in a bit. I love you!" he says, and hangs up before I can reply.

I scan through my gmail account and don't see a single message from Ryan. What on earth is he talking about? And then I log into my Dalton account, one that I haven't checked since June, and there are a few emails about back to school events and class registration and a reminder that SAT prep classes start in September, but far more important than all of that are the twelve unread emails from Ryan. The first one from early in July – right around the time he stopped texting me, and the email is titled, "on my way to Kenya!!"

I spend the next half hour reading through the emails and I feel worse as I read each of them. It seems that they moved Ryan off of the glamorous project in London to a project in Kenya where the firm was investing in the infrastructure to improve drinking water and irrigation in Kenya and partnering with the government and a few other agencies. Ryan spent the last six weeks working with two associates in remote villages of Kenya counting wells and farms. Once or twice a week, they would travel back to Nairobi and then he would have internet access and he would send me an email to check in. I have no idea why he used my Dalton account instead of my gmail account, but that's really not the issue. While Ryan was working to improve the life of millions of Kenyans, I was hooking up with Brad because I thought Ryan deserted me.

I know it's lame, but I need a little more time to figure out what to do, so I send Ryan a quick text now that his phone is working.

Megan: welcome back! go get some sleep, I'll let you know when I'm back in NYC tomorrow xoxo

***

"What are you going to do?" Jess asks. She has been hanging off my every word, and now I've finally finished telling her about Brad and Ryan and the emails. I got back from Cape Cod about an hour ago, but Danielle is still at work. I texted Jess from the airport this morning and told her it was an emergency, so she was waiting at my apartment when I got here.

"I don't know!" I wail. "That's why I'm asking you!"

"Brad sounds amazing. It's totally unfair that you get him *and* Ryan and I still have no one," she says.

"That's really unhelpful," I tell her.

"I know, I'm just saying it would have been nice if I could have met Brad," she says. "Hey, maybe you could still set me up?" she asks hopefully.

"Seriously?" I ask, giving her a look.

"Sorry," she says, but I know she isn't *that* sorry. "Why do you even have to tell Ryan?" she asks. "He'll never find out," she says.

"I know, but I'll feel terrible about it," I say.

"Maybe you should wait to see how you feel when you see him," she suggests. "Maybe you won't even like him that much anymore," Jess suggests, while filing her nail with the file she found on my nightstand.

"Jess, I love Ryan, I'm not going to feel differently after not seeing him for the summer," I tell her.

"You say that, but when you thought he dumped you, you had no problem hooking up with Brad all summer, so maybe you don't love him as much as you think," she says brutally. "You're too young to be so serious. Look at Georgia and Ian, you don't want to be like that, do you? They're seventeen and practically married. Maybe you should be single with me this year, it's really not so bad – especially if we're doing it together," she says hopefully.

Although the prospect of going on double dates with Jessica is not remotely appealing, something she said does make me think. Maybe being on my own for a little while wouldn't be the worst thing, especially for the last year of high school. Ryan has been one of the best things that has ever happened to me, and maybe we are meant to be together, but I'd be lying if I said I didn't have fun with Brad this summer too. Ryan was there for me when my dad was at his worst and has been by my side through my move to the City. I would never want to hurt him, but I'm thinking about the advice I gave Brad, and maybe it applies to me as well. What if I do want to explore on my own for a little bit and go off to college without a long distance relationship?

"You might be right," I say to Jess.

"About what?" she says, looking up at me from her nail filing, like she's already forgotten what she's said.

"I know that I'll always love Ryan, and maybe we will end up together eventually, but I think after this summer I do see him differently. I can't do anything to hurt him, but I think when I see him this afternoon I'm going to figure out what I need to do that makes both of us happy," I tell her.

"See, I told you so," Jess says, looking up at me, this time from her phone, barely listening to me, but it doesn't matter, because amazingly she's helped me figure it all out.

Chapter 41 – Sabrina

This is Molly's third phone call of the morning. I don't really want to hear what she has to say, but after what happened yesterday I probably owe it to her to at least pick up the phone.

"Hello," I say, flinching slightly, like I think she may slap me through the phone.

"I've been trying to reach you all morning. I'm so sorry I didn't call you last night," Molly says.

"Don't worry about it," I tell her, thinking that I expected both her and Danielle to call, but thought it would be to lecture me, not apologize.

"I know you rushed out after the whole wedding dress thing, but I should have followed you, or at least called to check on you," she apologizes.

"Really, it's fine," I tell her. "I actually wanted to ask you the same thing. You seemed pretty preoccupied yesterday, are you okay?" I ask, trying to change the subject.

"There was a little thing, but it's mostly taken care of now. I'll fill you in soon, but for now I really want to talk about Parker and Peter," she says.

"Oh," I sigh, wishing we could just avoid the topic.

"Parker is an asshole. You know he's going to break your heart again," she says, not wasting any time.

Suddenly, I wish we had the ingredients for Bloody Marys or Mimosas, because I think I'm going to need a drink for this conversation. We have plenty of beer, wine and liquor, but at 9:30 on a Sunday morning, that seems a little extreme.

"Parker is not an asshole. He was young last time. And he *knows* me," I tell her, trying to defend him.

"And Peter doesn't *know* you?" she counters. "Peter loves you no matter what. He would never run off to California and leave you miserable. He will be your best friend in the good times and the bad times, and will always be there for you," she rambles.

"You sound like a greeting card. What's with you?" I ask her.

"Sorry. I'm just saying that Peter is a great guy and I think you should marry him," she says.

"And what do I do about Parker?" I ask her.

"The same thing that he did to you. You leave him," she says definitively.

"I can't do it. I know you don't understand, because you have Derek and he's perfect and you've been in love forever. But Parker is like that for me. He was my first love, and I thought we were going to be together forever. But then he left me and I had to start all over. It's been a series of guys for the last ten years and Peter is obviously the best of them all, but I just have to know about Parker," I tell her.

"Okay," she says sadly.

"I'm going over to Parker's now," I say. "I'll let you know what happens."

***

Parker's apartment door is open slightly when I get there, so I let myself in and close the door behind me.

"I'm in here," Parker calls out from his bedroom. I slip off my sandals and follow his voice.

"I've been waiting right here for you since yesterday," jokes Parker. He is lying on the bed on his side wearing navy and white boxers, and nothing else.

"Sorry, yesterday morning didn't work out," I apologize. "You must be getting hungry," I tease.

"I'm sure it will be worth the wait," he says, reaching for me and pulling me over to his side of the bed.

Parker starts to kiss my neck and it's almost impossible to resist, but I have to have this conversation before anything else happens. "Can we talk for a minute first?" I ask.

"What is it?" Parker asks, rolling over and propping himself up on his elbow.

"I need to tell Peter if I'm going to go through with this," I say to him.

"Go through with what?" he asks, looking confused.

"The wedding!" I say, raising my voice. "I can't go on planning the wedding like this and lying to him if it's not going to happen."

"Sabrina, what we have right now is fantastic," he begins. "I know I said that I wanted more, and at the time I said it, I really *did* think that was what I wanted, but I just don't think I can make that kind of commitment. But we've found out that we are still great at *this*," he says, grabbing for my ass.

I am so shocked I don't know what to say or how to react.

Taking advantage of my silence, Parker continues, "I don't see why this has to change anything - at least not until the wedding. I'll just help you get over your cold feet," Parker laughs, reaching out to try and unzip my skirt.

I can't believe this is happening again. It's not exactly like last time, but it certainly feels familiar. I have to get out of here. I need to get home and see Peter and figure out if there's any way to salvage my relationship. Molly was right – Peter is the good guy and Parker is the asshole – why can't I ever figure these things out?

"I've got to go. I should have known better. Please do us both a favor and have Henry take over everything for the project – I don't think it would be fair for the girls to suffer because of this, but I also don't think we can work together," I tell him.

"Breen, I'm really sorry," he says, giving me his killer smile, and looking so sexy that I *almost* believe him.

"No Parker, it's my fault," I say, "I was stupid enough to think you had changed."

***

I'm nervous to see Peter in a way I haven't been before. I've decided that I'm not going to tell him about Parker, but I *am* going to throw myself back into the relationship headfirst. Technically I have nothing to be nervous about, since he doesn't know anything about Parker. However, I feel like when I see him now, it's a new start and that has me on pins and needles.

"Hi sweetheart," I say when I open the door.

"Hey gorgeous," Peter calls out. "Where have you been? I got back from my shift and you were gone."

I hadn't thought this part through. It would make sense if I was at the gym or at a class on a Sunday morning, but I'm definitely not dressed for that.

"I went out to get coffee and then decided to stay at the coffee shop and read my book. It's been such a long time since I've done that," I tell him. I feel bad for lying (again), but this will be the end of it – from now on, I will be the perfect fiancé.

"That's great. You've been so busy with work, I'm glad you took some time for yourself and just relaxed. You deserve it," Peter says lovingly.

"Do you want to go get brunch?" I offer, desperately trying to change the subject from how much I deserve nice things.

"I'd love to. I was going to take a quick nap, but I can do that later," Peter says.

"If you want to nap first, that's fine with me," I say, "whatever you want to do."

"I'm not that tired. I'm actually pretty hungry now that you mention it," Peter says as he walks toward our bathroom and starts stripping off his scrubs.

"By the way, my mom emailed me her list for the invitations. Did you get a list from your parents? Maybe we can go over it at brunch?" Peter suggests.

"Sure," I say, trying to force enthusiasm into my voice.

***

An hour later we are seated at an outdoor table at Balthazar, perusing the menu and blending in with the other upscale New Yorkers and tourists who are happy to overpay for delicious Sunday brunch and fantastic people watching.

"What are you thinking?" Peter asks, smiling at me.

"Nothing," I say quickly, jostling the table with my arm as I move to sit up straight in my chair.

"I meant, what are you thinking of ordering," Peter clarifies. "Is everything okay?" he asks.

"Oh right," I laugh. "Of course. I'm totally fine. I'm deciding between the avocado and poached eggs on toast and the apple cinnamon pancakes," I reply.

"Perfect. We'll get those and we can split them. Then you can have them both," Peter says happily.

"Are you sure?" I ask. "What were you going to get?"

"I couldn't decide. Everything looks good. And I'm still pretty tired, so it's good to have this decision taken care of for me," he says.

"As long as you're sure," I say.

"Sabrina, it's fine - especially if it makes you happy. And I know you want the cinnamon bun on the side, even if you're only going to take one bite," he says, picking up my hand and kissing it lightly.

"Ugh," I groan. "I'm never going to fit in my dress. I should just get a small salad," I complain.

"You could eat everything on this menu and you would still fit into the most beautiful wedding dress they make," Peter says, looking at me adoringly.

"You wanted to look at invitation lists for the wedding?" I remind him. In the spirit of turning over a new leaf, I remember to bring up something about the wedding before Peter has to remind me.

"Yes, I have the list from my mom," Peter says, pulling his phone out of his pocket. "Do you have names from your parents?" Peter asks.

"Not yet," I confess, but I'll send my mom a reminder right now. I quickly compose an email to my mom as Peter places our order with the waiter. The email to my mom is less of a reminder and more of a first request, but at least I'm doing it. I still have a knot in my stomach as I hit send, but it's not like I'm *mailing* the invitations, I'm merely requesting addresses from my parents.

"We've got some work to do on our list if we don't want my parents to dominate the wedding," Peter says.

"What do you mean?" I ask.

"My mom has one hundred and eighty people on her list," Peter admits, shrugging his shoulders.

"Are you kidding?" I cry out. I don't know why I'm surprised, since I knew about his sister's wedding, but somehow I'm still appalled by the number.

"Between our family and all of their friends, she can't really make it any smaller," Peter says.

I try to remind myself that I don't care about the actual wedding anyway, and it doesn't matter if there are one hundred people or five hundred people. It will just be a fancy party (that Peter's parents are sponsoring) and I'll be wearing a white dress.

"Do you want to start writing down names of people we would have on our joint list?" Peter suggests.

"Perfect," I reply, trying to get back in the game.

Less than five minutes later we have finished our joint list and we can't come up with more nine people, and that includes our doormen.

"There have to be more than that," I insist.

"I think everyone else is either on your side or my side," Peter says. "But I think that's normal. Once we've been together longer, we'll have more friends that are *ours*."

Bless the waiter for choosing that moment to bring out our food. I'm sure Peter is right about not having many joint friends, but I have a nagging feeling that it's not a good sign; and for an instant I actually got the feeling that Peter sensed it too.

***

Amazingly, we fill the rest of the day with errands and typical Manhattan Sunday "chores" like a pedicure for me, a haircut for Peter and a stop at the local wine store. Eventually, Peter's fatigue catches up with him and he takes a much-needed nap. I take back-to-back barre and cardio box classes to try and work off my breakfast, but mostly to keep busy so I don't think about Parker and what happened this morning.

Dripping with sweat, and feeling slightly better, I enter the apartment, yet again vowing to focus on Peter and move forward. Maybe if I remind myself of this several times a day (like a mantra), then eventually it will just become natural.

"How was the gym?" Peter asks.

"It was good," I reply. "Violet was teaching the cardio box class – she's the best," I tell him.

"I'm so glad," Peter says, grinning at me.

"How was your nap?" I ask.

"It was great. I feel *so* much better," Peter says. "Only a few months left of this terrible schedule and then I'll start to have more normal hours. Won't it be great when we can actually see each other more than a few hours a week?" Peter asks.

"Of course. That will be wonderful," I tell him, wondering what it will be like when that happens. "I don't know how residents put up with these crazy schedules – I feel so bad for you," I say, and I really do mean it. Even though I'm not sure what Peter and I will do with our time together, the hours he works are practically torture!

"You've been so great about it too," Peter says.

"What do you mean?" I ask, confused.

"I don't think I say it enough, but you're so patient with me about my schedule. I hear from a lot of the residents I work with that their girlfriends or boyfriends or spouses complain all the time, but you've never, ever complained or made me feel bad about the commitment I have to make to the hospital," Peter says.

"It's really not a big deal," I say, trying to brush it off, since I know I don't deserve the praise.

"No, Sabrina, it is a big deal. I can't wait until I can make it up to you, but until then, I got you a little something.

Just to show you how much it means to me that you understand how important surgery is to me. You're so understanding," Peter gushes.

Before I can respond, Peter pulls out a red Cartier box and hands it to me.

"It's just a little token," Peter says, a smile spreading across his face.

Although Peter is a very down-to-earth rich guy, he also doesn't know the meaning of "little token." I open the box and am proven correct when I find three diamond LOVE bracelets.

"The lady at the store said that you'd want to wear more than one, so I bought three," he says, grinning at me.

The guilt in my stomach is gnawing a hole so large that I'm pretty sure it is going to be visible on the outside very soon. "Peter, this is too much," I say.

"Don't be silly. It's just a little something to show you how much I love and appreciate you. Here, let me get the little screwdriver out. Kind of crazy that they have to get locked on, right?" he says, as he is fishing around in the box for the tool.

And then it happens. It's almost like I'm watching myself and not really the one speaking... Peter is kneeling on the ground in front of me, locking the first of three $10,000 bracelets on my arm and I just can't take it anymore.

"Peter, I can't do this," I blurt out.

"You don't like the bracelets?" he questions, looking up at me, with his beautiful green eyes.

"No, it's not the bracelets. It's everything. I can't get married," I say, balling my hands into fists, so I can feel my nails dig into my hands.

"What are you talking about?" Peter asks, looking stunned.

"It's just too much. I should have never said yes. You should be with someone better. Someone who deserves you – someone who wants a big wedding and wants all of the same things that you do," I say, stumbling over my words.

"Sabrina, we can have a small wedding if that's what you really want. I know my mom can be overbearing, and I should have pushed back more, but it's not too late to fix it. I'll call her tonight and tell her that we're going to do something small," Peter says, trying to reach for my hand, although I've made that impossible.

"It's not the size of the wedding. It's not your mom. It's me! I'm the problem. Can't you see that? I shouldn't be getting married," I plead, jumping to my feet and beginning to pace around the living room.

"Sabrina, there's nothing wrong with you. Of course you're not the problem. Planning a wedding is stressful. And then you add my crazy hours on top of that and of course it's going to feel a little nerve-racking, but it's nothing to worry about," Peter says.

I look at Peter's sincere face and I want to believe him. I want to trust that it's just normal cold feet and there's nothing wrong with me; but then I remember that I was in Parker's apartment less than twelve hours ago and I was ready to throw this all away. I don't want Peter to get hurt, but it isn't fair to him if I stay, because eventually he'll get hurt, and it will be a lot worse.

I take a deep breath before I speak, "Peter, I don't deserve you." He begins to interrupt me, but I stop him. "Let me finish. I am the problem. You are kind and generous and wonderful, and someone will be so lucky to have you," I say.

"Sabrina, why are you saying this?" He says. And then, as if a light bulb goes off, he asks, "is there someone else?" The mask of pain washing over his face is almost impossible to watch.

"No," I reply. "There's no one else. But, I don't trust myself. I don't think I can make this kind of commitment, because I know myself and someday there will be someone else," I tell him. I know it's a lie, but no good will come from the truth in this situation.

"Sabrina, I don't know why you insist on sabotaging this. I've worked so hard to give you everything I thought you wanted, but if this still isn't enough for you, then there's nothing else I can do," Peter says sadly.

"I know," I say, looking down at the floor because I'm too ashamed to look him in the eye.

"Maybe eventually you'll figure out what you really want and find someone who can actually give it to you," Peter says, with a mix of pity and sorrow.

"I hope so," I say, "I really do."

Epilogue – The Following June

"Can you believe she graduated from high school?" Sabrina asks.

"No. I really can't," Danielle says. "I remember the first time Jim introduced us and I thought she was this stubborn, awful thirteen-year old who would come between me and her dad. It's hard to believe that she is now practically my daughter, or little sister depending on the day. Now neither of us even speaks to Jim!"

"Is he even here today?" Sabrina asks.

"Nope. He was going to come, and then something came up, so he sent her a diamond Van Cleef & Arpels bracelet instead," Danielle says.

"He always did have a way with jewelry," Sabrina jokes.

"You know I can hear everything you're saying," I say, leaning over and sticking my head between theirs. We are all gathered at a small restaurant near our apartment to celebrate my graduation from Dalton. Danielle insisted on this little party, but because all of my friends are having their own little dinners at the same time, tonight is really only for my family and a few non-school friends. It's been thirty minutes and we are still at the bar waiting for our table, because only Sabrina, Danielle and I are here so far.

"Yes, I know," Danielle says. "Did I say anything that you wouldn't have told her yourself?" she asks.

"No, I guess not," I admit.

"Congratulations!" Heather says, as she and Kevin and the girls burst through the door of the restaurant. "So sorry we're late," she says.

"Megan," Caitlin screams, running across the room to give me a hug. "Where's your cap and gown?" she asks, looking at my flowered sundress.

"I wore those this morning, but I had to give them back," I tell her.

"Of course she did, everyone knows that," Brooke says to Caitlin, showing that she hasn't changed too much from last summer. "Hey Megan, congratulations," she says to me, trying to act mature.

"Thanks Brooke. Thanks so much for coming, all of you," I say gushing at the whole family. I saw them briefly in December, but I didn't realize how much I missed seeing all of them.

"It's really nice to see you," Kevin says kindly. Thankfully, Kevin is a lot warmer since the end of last summer and with Heather's renewed health, and some time, all seems to be forgiven. "And a huge congratulations on Stanford," he says. That's quite an accomplishment."

"Thanks," I say, trying to be humble, but proud and excited at the same time.

"We're so happy you decided to come back this summer," Heather says.

"I know, me too," I reply.

"Even though it's only three weeks, it will be enough time for me to finish preparing for the launch. And the girls are so excited for you to be there," Heather says.

"Even Brooke?" I joke.

"Yes, even Brooke. How else is she going to get to Chatham every day? She knows I won't drive her," Heather laughs.

"We really are glad you're coming back, Megan," Kevin says, brushing an imaginary speck of lint off the sleeve of his sport coat. "As you know, this has been a long year for us, but Heather has been amazing; managing her condition and figuring out how to go back to work at the same time. You being there will allow her to work and get time to rest," he says, gently nudging her, but with a sly smile.

"Yes, I will take a nap every day, and launch my new PR site. I promise," Heather says, smiling, but she looks healthy and happy and Kevin doesn't even look too worried.

Heather pulls me aside while Kevin takes the girls to the bar to get a drink. "So, what's going on with Brad? Ryan? Are you going to see Brad this summer?" she asks, intrigued. After Heather got out of the hospital last summer, I told her everything about Brad and then about Ryan, and now she wants the updates. She calls it her little soap opera and says she has to live vicariously through me.

"I'll probably see Brad when I'm in Brewster," I tell her. "But just as a friend."

Heather gives me a look that conveys a significant amount of skepticism.

"No, it's true. Brad and I have been texting since the fall and we really are just friends now," I tell her. I almost believe this is true, but I'm still not sure what will happen when I see him in July.

"And Ryan?" she asks.

"Not much going on there. I did get a text from him this morning that said "Congratulations" but other than that we haven't talked much this year," I tell her.

"Oh that's too bad," Heather says. "It would have been nice if you could have stayed friends with him too."

"I think that would have been asking too much. I'm still glad that I never told him about Brad, but he knew something was off when I broke up with him last August. We saw each other a few times after that, but it was just too weird," I tell Heather.

"My mom used to say that everything happens for a reason," Heather says.

"I'd be an interesting case study for that," I say with a laugh. "I wouldn't want a long distance relationship at Stanford anyway. And it's actually been pretty good to be single this year. My friend Georgia broke up with her boyfriend too, so Jess, Georgia and I had a really fun year," I say.

"To be young again," Heather says wistfully, but with a smile.

"I want to be young again," Sabrina says, throwing her arm around Heather's shoulder and joining the conversation.

"You'll always be young," Heather says to Sabrina.

"That's just not true, but thank you for saying so," Sabrina says.

"How are you doing?" Heather asks Sabrina. "I hear you moved to the Upper West Side?" Heather questions.

Danielle filled me in on a lot of what's gone on with Sabrina over the year, but I don't know everything, so I'm always curious to hear what Sabrina says, her life makes mine seem quite G-rated.

"I needed a change," Sabrina says. "You know Peter stayed in the apartment, since it's his, but then I rented that furnished, temporary apartment in Murray Hill right after I moved out and it felt so sterile. So I decided to buy something. I figured I should be close to Danielle, since I spend all my time with her anyway," Sabrina jokes.

"What about your sister? Doesn't she live near here?" Heather asks.

"Oh my God, how don't you know this? It hasn't been that long since I've talked to you," Sabrina says, taking a sip of her white wine.

"We talk about us and about the site launch, but I didn't hear about your sister, what happened?" Heather asks.

"She moved back to Boulder last September. She was only here for four months and then they moved back. Her husband took a job with the same company. She went back to teaching at the same school, and they even bought a house on the same street where they used to live! It's like their whole time here never happened," Sabrina says.

"That's so funny," Heather remarks.

"It is, right? But what's funnier is that she's so happy now. It's like nothing has changed, but she's happier than she's ever been," Danielle says.

"Good for her," Heather says.

"It is. I'm happy that she's so happy," Sabrina says.

"And you?" Heather asks Sabrina, probing gently. I feel like perhaps I shouldn't be listening to this part of the conversation, but it seems weird if I excuse myself now, so I just stand there with my virgin daiquiri and listen.

"Work is going really well. The board is happy and we're growing like crazy," Sabrina tells Heather.

"That's fantastic," Heather says. "And everything else?"

"Eh. It's getting there. I heard Peter has a girlfriend, so my guilt is finally going away," Sabrina says.

"How do you feel about that?" Heather asks.

"It felt weird at first, but it's not like I have any claim to him. Honestly, I think it's good. He deserves to be happy, and I don't think that we were right for each other," Sabrina admits. "I've finally come to terms to this on my own, so it's good to say it out loud."

"But you should be happy too," Heather implores.

"You know what? I am happy. I've forgiven myself and I'm finally over Parker and I'm over Peter. I'm ready to find somebody, but I'm not in a hurry. I'm definitely not in a rush for something serious *or* to get married. I'm finally getting to know myself and like myself, so this time around when I find the right person, I'll be ready."

THE END

Acknowledgments

I am grateful to my readers. Thank you for buying and reading *Only Summer*. Your support means the world to me.

A huge thank you to my sister, Sarah Nelson, who read *Only Summer* as I was writing it and provided encouragement along the way – if only I could write as fast as you can read.

I have to thank three very special friends and editors for their feedback and help reviewing this book. Erin Ginsburg, Kathy Soderberg and Aimee Linn Kaplan – thank you from the bottom of my heart for your help making this book so much better!

Thank you to my friends near and far – for reading my books, for supporting me, and for embracing my second career with open arms. I am so fortunate to have collected such wonderful friends over my lifetime – camp friends, high school friends, college friends, business school friends, NYC friends, London friends and of course Pelham friends. It's hard to believe that I have only known some of you a few years, because I couldn't imagine my life without you.

More than anything, I need to thank my family. My entire family has been incredibly supportive of my dream – even when they didn't know the right questions to ask, they smiled and told me to keep going. But my daily encouragement comes from my 3 girls and my husband, and without them, none of this would be possible. So thank you Doug, Emily, Samantha and Lexi for believing in me and supporting me – I love you more than you will ever know.

Finally, if you are still reading this, I would like to ask you a favor. Reviews are an important element in book sales (I'm sure you factor reviews into your purchasing decisions) - if you would consider writing a review of this book on Amazon or Goodreads, I would be eternally grateful. Thank you!

Rachel Cullen is a graduate of Northwestern University and NYU Stern School of Business. She worked in consulting and marketing in San Francisco, London and New York and currently lives in Westchester, NY with her husband, three children and her two dogs. *Only Summer* is her third novel; she is also the author of *The Way I've Heard It Should Be* and *Second Chances*.

www.rachelcullenwriter.com

www.facebook.com/RachelCullenAuthor